Since You're Leaving Anyway . . .

Before Debbie Sue could respond, all six feet and two inches of James Russell Overstreet, Jr., the most beautiful man in Texas, walked through the doorway. The powerful legs of the horseman he was filled his starched, knife-creased Wranglers. A silver badge hung on the pocket of his white-on-white striped shirt. His skin was as tanned as his alligator boots, he had a thick black mustache Tom Selleck would envy, and his lean jaws shone from a fresh shave.

Her heart thumped. Every female cell in her body squealed and fainted. She resisted the urge to look down, certain the soles of her boots had melted. Still, she forced an act of cool detachment. She had to. If the dike damming up her emotions ever sprang a leak, anything could happen.

Buddy's finger touched the brim of his gray Resistol. "Ladies." He turned to Debbie Sue. "My secretary said a crazy woman called and insulted her. I figured it had to be you."

Dixie Cash

Since You're Leaving Anyway, Take Out the Trash

AVON BOOKS
An Imprint of HarperCollinsPublishers

This is a work of fiction. Names, characters, places, and incidents are products of the author's imagination or are used fictitiously and are not to be construed as real. Any resemblance to actual events, locales, organizations, or persons, living or dead, is entirely coincidental.

AVON BOOKS
An Imprint of HarperCollins*Publishers*
10 East 53rd Street
New York, New York 10022-5299

First Avon Books paperback printing: September 2004

Avon Trademark Reg. U.S. Pat. Off. and in Other Countries, Marca Registrada, Hecho en U.S.A.
HarperCollins® is a registered trademark of HarperCollins Publishers Inc.

Printed in the U.S.A.

10 9 8 7 6 5 4

I dedicate this book to everyone who has ever told me I'm funny and to my sister and writing partner, Jeff, who kept telling me, "You can do this." Without her, I'd still be funny, but thanks to her, now I'm a funny author.

—Pam

I dedicate this book to my sister Pam, who loves to laugh and whose very dreams must be comedies.

—Jeffery

One

Debbie Sue Overstreet sat at the payout desk of the Styling Station, staring at the balance column in her big black checkbook. From the bottom line of check stub #938, a fat goose egg glared back at her. She groaned. The payment on her pickup truck was past due again.

Okay, so opening a beauty shop—that is, a salon—in Salt Lick, Texas, hadn't been the most profitable decision she had ever made. But couldn't anything go right? She was twenty-eight years old and had been a failure at everything she had tried. Marrying, mothering, rodeoing, and now, beauty shopping. Maybe she should have finished college.

Her mental calculator churned into action. If she could do a dozen perms and/or coloring jobs between now and the end of the week, she could get the pickup payment in the mail on Saturday and at least avoid the tacky phone calls from those collection people. Add a few drop-in haircuts, and she might even be able to buy a pizza and a six-pack Saturday night. Or maybe she would get *really* lucky, and Pearl Ann Carruthers would come in for the works, head-to-toe. If that happened, she might make *two* pickup payments.

A disc jockey blathered from a radio in the background. "Sun's up, folks. Eight-thirty, temperature's ninety-two degrees, no rain in sight. Here's a blast from the past by Joe Diffie, all about the devil dancing in empty pockets. How many out there in our K-Country audience can relate to that one?"

Debbie Sue stared at the radio. Was that DJ psychic?

Eight-thirty. Ninety-two degrees. Another hour and the salon's air-conditioning system would be taxed to the max by the relentless September heat of West Texas. The little dial adding up kilowatts on the electric meter would be spinning out of control, kicking the power bill into the stratosphere.

Thank God for the blue-hairs who came in once a week, rain or shine, hell or high water. Their big hair, dyed and teased to the extreme, paid the utility bills.

She slapped the revolting checkbook closed and walked over to the four-foot-square mirror in front of her station. Her chestnut hair with its carefully placed sun-in highlights hung to the middle of her back and felt like a horse blanket. Hot. One of these days she intended to cut the mane on her head within an inch of her scalp.

She grabbed up a giant plastic clip and pinned most of the thick mop into a twisted roll. Instantly a few sheaves escaped, giving her the bed-head look. Oh well. Some of her best customers strove for the popular style.

She had left the house without makeup this morning, so she dug in a drawer for cosmetics. The owner of one of the only two beauty salons in Salt Lick couldn't appear before her customers looking like something the dog dragged in. She applied a few flicks of black mascara and a swipe of Coral Reef lipstick. She gave up on herself then, snatched a bottle of Windex off the shelf under the counter, and turned her attention to the smudges on the mirror.

As she fogged the mirror with cleaner, a car door slammed outside. That would be Edwina, Debbie Sue's only employee and one of her two best friends in the whole wide world. Edwina Perkins manned the Styling Station's second chair and was as much a fixture in the salon as the row of four dryers with teal padded seats or the two maroon shampoo bowls in the back room.

Edwina had been a hairdresser in Salt Lick for over twenty years. Debbie Sue hired her hoping she had a following, and indeed she did, but putting the Styling Station's books in the black would take a heck of a lot more customers than either she or Edwina could pull in. Maybe she could set off a bomb under the competition down the street.

The front door flew open. The Christmas bells

tied to the knob whacked the door and clattered as if in pain. Edwina charged in, super-sized plastic cup in hand, cigarette clamped between her teeth. In addition to a following of loyal salon patrons, Edwina had an addiction to Marlboro Lights and Dr. Pepper.

The five-foot-ten brunette's wooden platform heels clomped like horse hooves across the vinyl-covered floor. Panting for breath, she placed her cigarette on the edge of her station's counter in front of her mirror, then set down her drink and purse. "She finally done it. She's gone."

"I don't believe it." Debbie Sue rose on her tiptoes and swiped Windex off the top of her mirror.

"Well, believe it, girl. I heard Harley's brother at the Kwik-Stop tell Marsha while she rung up his coffee. She didn't come home last night."

The fact that she and Edwina could read each other's thoughts and carry on gossip without using names came from living a lifetime in the same town, knowing the same people and places and recycling the same rumors year after year. "Humph. Just because she didn't come home doesn't mean she's gone. She could be shacked up somewhere."

Edwina gave her a flat look. "With Harley in town? I don't *think* so."

Edwina's smoldering cigarette was searing a brand onto the teal Formica counter. Debbie Sue glowered at it and doused it with a squirt of

Windex. "Cri-ma-nee, Ed, you're gonna set this place on fire."

"Hey, I might've won the bet." Edwina ignored both the reprimand and her extinguished smoke and rummaged in her tray of permanent wave rods and brightly colored curlers. She came up with a folded paper on which a wagering grid had been drawn. The Styling Station's faithful customers had maintained a pool, betting exactly when Pearl Ann Carruthers would finally leave her husband.

For ten years the richest, unhappiest woman in Salt Lick had told the town's citizens that "someday" she would leave Harley Carruthers and move to Cowtown. Fort Worth, where skintight Wranglers and good boots were the only real necessities of life. Moving to Fort Worth was better than going to heaven, according to Pearl Ann. In heaven you might be promised eternal peace, but in Fort Worth, you were *guaranteed* fun and sin.

If anybody could appreciate the latter, it was Pearl Ann.

The Christmas bells jangled again, and Debbie Sue's other best friend dashed in, frantic and as out of breath as Edwina. "Did y'all hear, did y'all hear?"

"We're ahead of you, C. J. We already know about Pearl Ann. She's probably gonna be at happy hour in Fort Worth this very afternoon, guzzling margaritas with some tight-assed cowboy."

Carol Jean Anderson's blue eyes flared wide. "Fort Worth! Where she went is the great happy hour in the sky."

"The Petroleum Club?" The posh private club on the top floor of the Frost Bank Building in downtown Fort Worth was the only elevated bar Debbie Sue could think of.

"She's *dead*, Debbie Sue. She killed herself. She blew her brains all over the front seat of her new Cadillac."

Silence hung in the room for several heartbeats. Edwina broke into a coughing spasm.

"It's true," C. J. said, beginning to sniffle.

Edwina's upper lip skewed up under her nose. "Eee-yew! Ain't that Cadillac a pale yellow?" At the stunned look C. J. aimed in her direction, Edwina added, "Okay, excuse me. I think it's awful, but I also have a vivid imagination. That's all I meant."

Tears gathered in Debbie Sue's eyes. She had known Pearl Ann her entire life, and unlike most of the women in Salt Lick, had liked her. Oh sure, Pearl Ann was obnoxious at times. Well, to be honest, she was obnoxious damn near *all* the time. Lord, she never missed a chance to let everybody know her clothes came from Neiman-Marcus or that her husband bought her a new Cadillac every year. Her jewelry was equal to the economy of a Third World country. Even more intimidating was her Victoria's Secret face and body that were the fantasy of every red-blooded man and nightmare of every woman in Salt Lick.

But she had been a loyal, generously tipping customer since the day of the Styling Station's opening. Debbie Sue and Edwina had cut miles of her hair, dyed it a rainbow of colors, and applied a thousand protein packs. "But—but that's just not possible. She just got a new perm and had her lips and—"

"We need details." Edwina pried out a Marlboro and lit up. "I'm fixin' to call Buddy." She clomped to the payout desk and picked up the phone.

"Wait a minute," Debbie Sue set down her Windex bottle with a thud. "If anybody's calling my ex-husband, it's gonna be me."

C. J.'s brow arched into a knowing look. Edwina made no attempt to hide an exaggerated eye roll as she handed over the receiver. It was just pure hell having people know you so well. "What?" Debbie Sue growled to throw them off track.

"She just happens to know the number by heart," Ed said to C. J.

"Will y'all stop it?" Debbie Sue keyed in the sheriff's office number. "I'm a businesswoman. I'm supposed to know how to call the law. In case I get robbed or something."

"Yeah," Edwina said. "I was just thinking that very thing. Beauty shop robbery is a real threat in Salt Lick."

An exaggerated Texas drawl came on the line. "Good morning. Sheriff Overstreet's office. How may I assist you?"

Oh puh-leeze! Since being promoted from "the woman who would recognize the ceiling tiles in motels across West Texas" to sheriff's office dispatcher, Tanya had taken on a condescending attitude. Unsavory rumors about her and the sheriff had swirled through Salt Lick like an Easter Sunday sandstorm, but Debbie Sue was unaffected. Tanya herself had probably started the tall tales. If Debbie Sue knew anything about her ex-husband, it was how seriously he took his job as county sheriff. He would never take a chance of smearing his reputation by having a fling with an employee.

Debbie Sue put on a professional, no-nonsense voice. "Sheriff Overstreet, please."

"Buddy, er, uh, Sheriff Overstreet is, uh, uh . . . in-dis-posed. Is there anything *I* can do for you?"

"Only if I had a hard-on and a ten-dollar bill. Just tell him to call me." Debbie Sue slammed down the receiver. "Slut," she muttered.

Edwina blew out a stream of smoke. "Tact is one thing I've always admired about you, Debbie Sue. Tell me again how you no longer care a thing about that man."

C.J.'s brow crinkled into a bewildered look. "What does a hard-on and a ten-dollar bill have to do with anything?"

"Well . . . She said he was *in-dis-posed*. You tell

me. Where'd Tanya Metcalf learn a three-syllable word?"

Her blond friend's eyes bugged. "He was into what?"

"C. J., one of these days you're gonna drive me to drink."

"But you already drink."

Debbie huffed an exaggerated gasp. "Holy cow, C. J. Look, I don't want you to take this the wrong way, but shouldn't you be at work?"

"I called in sick. When I heard about Pearl Ann, I just couldn't make myself go."

Before Debbie Sue could respond, the door opened again, and all six feet and two inches of James Russell Overstreet, Jr., the most beautiful man in Texas, walked through the doorway. The powerful legs of the horseman he was filled his starched, knife-creased Wranglers. A silver badge hung on the pocket of his white-on-white striped shirt. His skin was as tanned as his alligator boots, he had a thick black mustache Tom Selleck would envy, and his lean jaws shone from a fresh shave.

Her heart thumped. Every female cell in her body squealed and fainted. She resisted the urge to look down, certain the soles of her boots had melted. Still, she forced an act of cool detachment. She had to. If the dike damming up her emotions ever sprang a leak, anything could happen.

Her thoughts flew to that schoolteacher in Odessa she had been told he was dating. Debbie

Sue had never met her, never seen her, but she was sure the woman was too short, too tall, too fat, and too thin, and wouldn't know a good saddle horse from a hobby horse. What could Buddy possibly have in common with her?

Buddy's finger touched the brim of his gray Resistol. "Ladies." He turned to Debbie Sue. "The office radioed that you called me?"

Debbie Sue willed her tongue to untie as chocolate-colored eyes bored into hers. "I did?"

Buddy opened his palms and gave her a questioning look. "Tanya said a bitchy woman called and insulted her. I figured it had to be you."

The nerve! Debbie Sue gathered her composure and hoisted her chin. "We heard about Pearl Ann."

"And what?" he snapped. "You want the gory details to yak about in the beauty shop all day?"

Debbie Sue extended her air of wounded pride. "We were friends of Pearl Ann's. We saw her at least once a week, sometimes more. We're entitled to know what happened."

"Entitled?" He glared down at her for a few seconds, then started for the door. "If you don't need anything, I gotta go. People are waitin' on me."

She marched behind him, all the way to the driver's door of the county's white Tahoe parked in front of the Styling Station. "Well, 'scuse the hell out of me, Wyatt Earp. I have some information you might like to hear, but now I'm not even gonna tell you."

"Oh, I don't believe that or you wouldn't've followed me out here."

"Well . . . well . . . Ed just tattooed Pearl Ann's lips and eyelids a few days ago."

Buddy's eyes squinted into a pained expression. "What the hell does *that* mean?"

"Well, dammit, Buddy, it hurts to get tattooed. Would somebody do it if she was planning on blowing her head off?"

Buddy sighed. "Give me a break, Flash. I'm up to my ass in alligators on this. By noon the press will be filling up the motel and I'm still trying to figure out what happened." He yanked open the Tahoe's door.

Debbie Sue could see the man to whom she had been married for five years, who wasn't easily shaken, was just that. Shaken. Why wouldn't he be? The oil-rich Carruthers family were icons in West Texas. Harley Carruthers and Buddy had been in school together, had played on the same sports teams. And Pearl Ann was . . . well, what *had* Pearl Ann been? Besides being high school homecoming queen once, her claim to fame was marrying Harley. "You mean you don't think she killed herself?"

"Hell, I don't know. I called in the forensic boys from Midland. We'll hear in a day or two." He cranked the engine. "By the time this spreads around, the whole town will be in an uproar. I don't need any more headaches, so you girls just cool it." He backed in an arc, stopped and looked back at her, his hat brim set just above his eyes, his elbow cocked on the windowsill. "Please?"

The county rig roared out of the parking lot, spraying sand and caliche.

Debbie fanned away a cloud of white dust and stamped her foot. "Dammit, I just hate him."

She hesitated before going back into the salon. *Flash.* The pet name her dad had given her when she was a little kid winning barrel-racing competitions in Little Britches rodeo. Buddy was the only one who still called her Flash. From him, as from her dad, it had been an expression of affection. The memory made her heart hurt.

The county SUV's taillights disappeared from sight, and she couldn't keep from thinking about another day three years ago when she had stood in this same spot and watched his taillights. The day he had said if she didn't calm down and give up rodeoing, it was over between them. She told him to go to hell, get out of her life, and take his badge with him.

And he did.

The painful irony was that the divorce did force her to give up rodeoing, and she hadn't even missed it. The only thing she missed was Buddy.

Two

 As Buddy pulled away from the Styling Station, his eyes kept stealing to his side mirror and the woman who had cost him damn near everything, starting with his heart and ending with most of his material possessions. He couldn't keep from remembering three years ago, the day he drove out of this same parking lot and left her standing in that same place.

He wished she didn't get better looking every time he saw her. This morning she wasn't wearing so much black gunk on her eyes, and he liked her without it. Green eyes as pretty as hers didn't need that beauty shop crap. Her body had never had an ounce of flab anywhere and still didn't. Her tight Wranglers and those little T-shirts she had always worn never failed to set off an urgency in his groin.

As burdened as he was by all that was going on around him, he still smiled at her calling him Wyatt Earp. She had never let him get away with being too full of himself.

He guessed she still hated him as much as she had that day he handed her an ultimatum and she told him to go to hell. Little did she know that after he left her, hell was exactly where he went. He had lost himself in a harem of women, some of whose names he couldn't even recall. If he hadn't been sheriff, forcing Debbie Sue out of his heart and mind might have driven him into some even more perverse activities. Moving on had taken a long while, but he *had* moved on, and now life was a lot less complicated.

Until this morning, that is, when he walked up to a new yellow Cadillac and saw a pretty woman with a quarter-sized hole in her head, a woman he had known as long as he could remember.

How had Debbie Sue and her goofy friends found out about Pearl Ann so fast? It wasn't even ten o'clock.

A crackle on his two-way broke him out of his mental meandering. "Sheriff Overstreet, some people from Midland are here waiting on you."

The message snapped his mind back to his job. "I'm on my way, Tanya. Be there in three minutes."

At his office, three crime scene investigators introduced themselves, and he led them out to the landfill a couple of miles out of town. There he had left Salt Lick's one deputy, Billy Don Roberts, with instructions to surround the area with crime scene tape, then stand guard over the corpse and the Cadillac.

As he brought the Tahoe to a stop, he saw the deputy had strung enough yellow tape to stretch from Dallas to El Paso. It draped from sage bush to sage bush, the perimeter bigger than a football field. Billy Don wasn't the sharpest knife in the drawer, but at least he had followed directions—if to the extreme.

Buddy had already made his own limited investigation of the death scene and taken pictures, so he turned it over to the CSI team. They started work at once, attempting to beat the deterioration caused by the scorching heat. He helped as much as he could, but mostly he stayed out of their way. Hours later, one of them approached him. "We'll take the body and the samples we collected back to Midland. I'll call you later today with our progress. We'll have a formal report after the autopsy."

"Any preliminary thoughts?"

"I'd say you were right, Sheriff. I don't think we can call this suicide. We've done a gunshot residue test. As you probably know, that may or may not help you discover who did this. It's not a contact wound. Quite a bit of tattooing around the entrance. Shot probably fired from the passenger seat."

Buddy had made the same observations and reached the same conclusion. His heart pumped hard as he recalled walking up on the death scene and the 9mm automatic pistol lying on the pas-

senger seat. His very first thought had been that
the pistol lay in an odd location for a self-inflicted
wound. "I saw," he said. "You get the pistol?"

The expert squinted up at him, blinded by the
brilliant sunlight reflecting off the white caliche
landfill. "Know who it belongs to?"

"I'm checking on it. I'm guessing it belonged to
her or her husband. They both had permits to
carry."

"Doesn't do as much damage as some guns, but
the result is the same."

"Yep. Dead is dead."

Whoever had shot the wife of Harley J. Carruthers obviously had more bullets than brains.
While Harley and Pearl Ann might not have had a
perfect marriage, the powerful Carruthers family
was close-knit. None of them would appreciate
somebody putting a bullet into Harley's wife's
head.

Buddy's mind sorted what he knew about the
victim, whose appearance and personality reminded him of old Marilyn Monroe movies. She
was twenty-eight, the same age as Debbie Sue.
When his ex-wife and Pearl Ann had been girls, to
say Pearl Ann's family was poor was a compli-
ment to their standard of living. For Pearl Ann
and her siblings, there had never been enough of
anything—food, clothing, or reasons to hold up
their heads.

Still, she'd had a way about her that could make
a man feel he was more than he was. With little re-

gard for boundaries, tangible or intangible, and while still a teenager, she had managed to lasso one of the richest men in Texas.

Every Salt Lick citizen whispered about her liaisons outside the marriage, but Buddy had personal knowledge of just how predatory she could be. An invitation had been extended to him personally on more than one occasion, and he had been tempted a time or two. Thank God, good sense and respect for her husband, a man he had called friend most of his life, had prevailed.

No telling how many men Pearl Ann might have slept with or which ones could be suspects. Besides men, plenty of wives or girlfriends would be happy to see her gone.

Then there was her husband, and two questions Buddy was duty-bound to consider. Did Harley know she cheated? And if so, did he hate her enough or love her enough to shoot her?

Earlier Buddy had instructed the owner of the only tow truck in Salt Lick to stand by and wait for his call. He flipped open his cell phone and called him to come for the Cadillac and take it to the impound yard. Then he headed for the Carruthers ranch.

It was late afternoon by the time he passed over the cattle guard that was the doorway to the Flying C's sprawling fifty sections. The thirty thousand acres-plus wasn't the biggest spread in West Texas by a long shot, and it wouldn't run many cows, but it was big enough, especially when oil wells were scattered all over it. Multiple pump jacks sawed up and down on the horizon pumping precious black gold from deep in the ground. Buddy thought back to childhood when he and his friends climbed astraddle and rode them like bucking broncs.

Located more or less in the middle of the ranch, the main house was a ways from the cattle guard. Buddy wended up a wide caliche road that took him through a pasture dotted with Hereford, Black Angus, and Brahma steers. Any day now, they would be hauled to market. For a brief moment he wondered what price these premium animals would bring this year. Back when he had owned a few acres and a few head, he kept up with the daily price of prime beef-on-the-hoof. He no longer bothered. After his small herd had been sold during his divorce from Debbie Sue, he no longer had the heart.

Some five hundred feet before reaching the house, he passed the large party barn Harley built soon after marrying Pearl Ann. Its interior was patterned after the old Stage Coach Inn in Stamford, which had been a bowling alley before it became a dancehall. Harley's barn had seen countless revelers. Food and liquor had always been abundant, and dancers logged a thousand miles on its concrete floor. Some of the biggest names in country music, personal friends of Harley's, had entertained from an elevated stage inside.

As a kid, Buddy hadn't had a concept of how rich Harley was, but the party barn and the shindigs that occurred there put into perspective just how much money a man could piss away when he had more than he knew what to do with.

Lord, how many evenings had he and Debbie Sue danced away in Harley's barn, then gone home and made love 'til daylight or lay in each other's arms laughing about the events of the evening? Bittersweet memories better left stored in the far reaches of his mind.

At the rambling Spanish-style ranch house, he was surprised to find the owner absent, particularly after he had told Harley he would come to the ranch as soon as the CSI team left. The Mexican housekeeper said, in a mix of broken English and fluent Spanish, Harley had gone to the pueblo to take care of business. The gist of it, Harley had gone to the funeral home.

Taking a look around outside, Buddy drove along the two-track driveway that took him to the corrals and pens surrounding a series of barns. In the distance he could see three small houses, homes to the Flying C's manager and the ranch hands, and he pondered what kind of relationship Pearl Ann might have had with the ranch's employees.

By five o'clock Debbie Sue had a headache the size of Houston. The day had been a virtual tornado of women coming and going, leaving bits and pieces of gossip, sucking up something new and blowing on.

She couldn't find it in herself to participate in the talk. Her mind was preoccupied with a nagging question. Why would a woman who loved two things beyond all else—money and her own good looks—commit suicide when she had a bounty of both? And why would she choose to mar those good looks by putting a gun to her head? The scenario just didn't fit.

Off and on all day, her thoughts drifted back to the evening when, a few months ago, she had stayed late to give Pearl Ann a last-minute trim and perm. The voluptuous blond kept lifting a flask from her purse and doctoring her Diet Coke. The more Diet Coke she drank, she looser her tongue became.

She told a bizarre story. Having signed a prenuptial agreement as an ignorant child, she feared a divorce from Harley would leave her as poor as she had been when they married. Years of collusion with one of the Carruthers accountants in Midland, plus a cash kickback, had resulted in her squirreling away a sizable sum from her monthly allowance and any other place where cash could be removed unnoticed, not excluding the kitchen and housekeeping budgets. Her "getaway fund," she called it.

And if what she had hidden wasn't enough to pay for her freedom, she would resort to other means. She had lived with Harley long enough to know where the bodies were buried. If the IRS knew the methods by which Carruthers money was relocated, reinvested, and reinvented, they could be busy for years.

With Pearl Ann having sworn her to secrecy, Debbie Sue had never told anyone of the late-night revelations, but the conversation gave credibility to the notion that the restless wife *would* someday leave Harley. Where had Pearl Ann's plan gone awry?

After the last customer left, Debbie Sue went to the payout desk and began to sort the day's receipts. She took payment from customers by cash, check, and credit card, even laughed and told a few of them she would take pigs and goats if they didn't have cash. Unfortunately the joke was frighteningly close to being on her, because if someone wanted to hand over livestock, she did have a place to house it out at her mom's.

Edwina finished up a cursory cleaning effort, then stuffed a partial pack of cigarettes into her purse and picked up her Dr. Pepper cup. "I'm outta here," she said. "Why don't you come by the trailer this evening. Vic's cooking up something good, and he gives the best neck and shoulder massages this side of Dallas. If that doesn't unwind you, there's always the other man in my life, Jose Cuervo."

Debbie Sue hadn't eaten since she downed a strawberry Pop-Tart for breakfast. Edwina's significant other could impress anyone with his home cooking. While in the navy, he had been all over the world and knew how to use exotic spices and seasonings. Debbie Sue's mouth watered, thinking what he might be cooking compared to what she had in her own refrigerator. "Guess I'd better pass. I really need to drive out to Mom's. I'm sure she's heard about Pearl Ann, and she might want to talk."

"Your mom hasn't been in to have her hair done in nearly two weeks."

"I know. That's why I have to go see her. And Rocket Man."

Edwina tsked and shook her head. "Most people would have sold that horse a long time ago, Debbie Sue."

"Bite your tongue, Ed. Rocket Man's my pal. He's won me a roomful of trophies and belt buckles and even a little money. He's earned the right to roam the pasture and get fat and lazy."

Besides her mother, the brown and white paint horse had been the most constant living being in her life since she was fifteen. He had seen her through the loss of her dream of a pro-circuit barrel-racing career, the loss of her precious baby boy and her husband. Hell, he had even been there the night of her seventeenth birthday, when she lost her virginity to Quint Matthews behind the horse trailers at a rodeo in Lubbock.

But most important of all, the horse had been a gift from Buddy. She would keep him until he died. Or *she* died. Whichever came first.

"Okay, hon, but don't work too much longer. You look tired. Tell Virginia *and* Rocket Man hello for me. You know I love them both."

Debbie Sue locked the door behind Edwina. One good thing had come from the day's exceptional number of customers. She had more than enough money to make her pickup payment. She plopped down in the chair at the payout desk and pulled her checkbook out of the bottom drawer.

Edwina threw her purse in the back of her car and removed the bath towel that covered the driver's seat and steering wheel. Leather upholstery exposed to the Texas sun all day could burn a blister on your butt before you knew what happened. And turning the steering wheel using only your fingertips was frowned on by the law.

She had left all the windows down to allow ventilation, but the Mustang still felt like a sauna. God, how much longer would this heat hang on? As a native, she knew how to deal with the West Texas weather, but there came a time when enough was enough.

Pulling out of the parking lot, she made one last glance at the silhouette of Debbie Sue bent over her bookkeeping. *Bless her heart*. The news of Pearl Ann's death had been a double whammy for her. Debbie Sue was nice enough to have really cared for Pearl Ann, and the self-centered blond's death meant a financial blow to the salon.

Sometimes being the older, more experienced

friend wasn't easy, Edwina thought. She had been in Debbie Sue's shoes and knew how uncomfortable they could get. Broke, but independent and hardheaded, was a combination that could depress the pope.

Then there was Buddy. Debbie Sue still loved that good-looking sucker. Edwina had always thought Buddy felt the same, really, but now that he was seeing a schoolteacher from Odessa, she feared his feelings might have taken a turn. She had known about the woman in Buddy's life for a while now—hell, everybody in town probably knew—but she wouldn't mention it unless Debbie Sue brought it up first.

Maybe something or someone would come along and change things for Debbie Sue, someone like Vic Martin. After three worthless husbands, Edwina had sworn off men forever until she met Vic.

Thinking of her live-in partner reminded her of the message left on voice mail last night by his ex-wife, Brenda. Vic and Brenda had been divorced ten years, but their history went back twenty. She appeared to be two-stepping her way through another twelve-step program, which always prompted a phone call in which she begged Vic to meet her and take her back.

Vic always returned her calls, talked to her sometimes for over an hour. No way was Edwina not going to eavesdrop, especially when she heard him speaking in soft, soothing tones. He always sounded like a parent talking to a small child, but that didn't keep Edwina from chewing on her skillfully sculpted acrylic nails.

Edwina was puzzled by Vic's attitude toward his ex-wife. From what she knew of Vic, he had little tolerance for weak people, was a firm believer you didn't let destructive circumstances determine your fate.

Even with that philosophy, he had sympathy and mind-numbing patience with Brenda and her alcohol addiction. He had never said why, but Edwina rationalized he blamed himself for leaving her alone on naval bases while he played war games.

Edwina worked at not letting the periodic phone calls rock her world, but she had been to a rodeo or two and stayed for the dance. She knew a woman who became overconfident and thought her man wouldn't leave her was a fool.

She closed her eyes and thought about the day she and Vic had met and the happy years between then and now. He had brought more stability to her life than she had ever known. She turned the key in the ignition, anxious to get home and show him how much he meant to her.

Three

Debbie Sue closed the checkbook and left the shop for another day. On the way out of town, she dropped the day's receipts in the bank's night deposit and slid her pickup payment into the mailbox in front of Salt Lick's tiny post office.

Afterward she stopped off at City Grocery & Market, the town's only grocery store, and picked up some apples and carrots, then added Twinkies and a six-pack of Coors. The carrots and apples were for her, the beer and junk food for the horse. Rocket Man had always been an unconventional animal.

Debbie Sue's mom lived on twenty-five acres ten miles out of town in a vintage clapboard house where Debbie Sue had grown up. As a grade school kid she had hated covering that ten miles in a school bus that had no air conditioning, hated arriving at school covered with dust. As a teenager the drive had been a pain in the ass, and she usually had been in such a hurry to get from home to town or vice versa, she never noticed her surroundings.

Now, driving through the stark, treeless landscape, she thought of something she had heard a rodeo announcer say once: In West Texas you could look farther and see less than anywhere else on earth. More truth than not to the words.

In recent years she had come to realize she loved the miles of unfettered visibility and the big sky and the sense of boundless freedom the landscape gave her. She loved the endlessly shifting sand, wasn't put off when it dusted her dishes inside the cupboards. She even loved the tumbleweeds plastered against the barbed-wire fences. Why would *anybody* want to move to Fort Worth?

Nearing the turnoff to her mother's driveway, she spotted the first fence post where her eighteen-year-old horse grazed. She eased the Silverado to the shoulder of the road and began tapping the horn in staccato beeps. Ears at half mast, Rocket Man ambled to the fence and blew through his nostrils. Uh-oh, he was unhappy.

She climbed down from her seat and met him at the fence. When his gentle brown eyes with their spidery long lashes met hers, she scratched his neck, then placed her cheek against his, whispered her apologies for letting two weeks lapse since she had seen him, and reminded him of his beauty and stature. The horse soon warmed up, rubbed his head against her outstretched hand, and nibbled at her hair.

The bond between them was simple. Debbie Sue provided all his needs, or at least the ones she knew about. He, in turn, gave her unwavering loyalty and affection. In their barrel-racing days, he had performed to the utmost of his ability and never disappointed her. Her relationships with people—well, with men—had been less successful.

She carefully climbed through the barbed wire fence. Rocket Man nickered when the Twinkies and beer surfaced from the grocery sacks. She fed him the spongy cakes one by one and watched in amusement when he clasped a can between his teeth, tossed his head back, and guzzled the sudsy stream of cold beer. "One more for you, ol' sot," she said, laughing, "and that's it."

She placed a hand on the paint's side, and together they walked the quarter mile to her mother's modest house, which sat in the shade of huge pecan trees planted decades ago. A warm breeze touched her cheeks, and she glanced toward the sinking sun. "Red sky at night, old friend," she said, patting her horse's side.

Soon flowering plants in beds at the edge of the front porch came into view, adding to the welcoming appearance of her childhood home.

A laughing Virginia Pratt stepped out onto the wooden veranda. "Are you with the posse or are you the bank robber?"

Mom had greeted her with a laugh and that

same question since Debbie Sue was a little girl. "That depends on whose side you're on" was the standard comeback.

The woman who looked closer to forty-two than fifty-two walked toward the fence, wisps of blond hair stirring in a gentle wind. Debbie Sue met her and offered her the remaining four cans of Coors. "Want a cold one?"

"Sounds good. Hot today." She reached for the cans. With her other hand, she rubbed Rocket Man's face, then gave him a kiss on his nose. "I hope you weren't feeding this horse Twinkies and beer."

Debbie Sue squeezed through the fence wires. "Does he need more hay?"

"We're okay for now." Her mother started for the house, popping the top on a beer as she walked. "All day I've been hearing about poor little Pearl Ann."

Debbie Sue fell in step beside her. "Yeah. Me, too."

Her mom passed her a beer. "Just goes to show you, money doesn't buy happiness."

"Maybe not, but it sure buys a heap of other stuff." Debbie Sue took a swig of the cold liquid, letting it cool her from the inside out.

Entering her mother's dimly lit, air-conditioned house felt like stepping into a time warp. Pictures lined the walls and sat on tabletops chronicling Debbie Sue in every stage of growing up.

Above the sofa, in the mix of life captured by

camera, was a faded rectangular outline on the ageg green wallpaper, evidence that something had hung there at one time. Virginia Pratt had left the empty spot on purpose, her way of saying something was there and now it was gone. The picture that had filled the space, the *only* picture of Debbie Sue and her dad, was tucked between quilts in the linen closet.

Tom Pratt had walked off when Debbie Sue was eight years old, taking nothing and leaving everything, including a note that said, "Sorry. You both deserve better." Well, he had been right about that.

Next to the empty rectangle hung Debbie Sue and Buddy's wedding picture. Smiling back from the frame were two young people in love, with a baby on the way and happy times ahead of them.

She wished the wedding picture was hidden away, too. She couldn't look at it without remembering the day she made a special trip home from her sophomore year at Tech and told Buddy she was pregnant. She had been so nervous, dreading his reaction.

His plans to become a Texas Ranger had already been sidetracked by his dad's unexpected death. But he had erased her fears when he knelt in front of her, wrapped his arms around her waist and placed a tender kiss on her stomach. "We'll call him Luke," he said. She laughed and asked, "What if it's a girl?" He assured her it would be a boy because a big brother would be needed to defend the honor of the beautiful sister who would follow.

They had made love that evening. He had been afraid of hurting her and the baby, but she urged him on. Buddy was a man's man and strong as a plow horse, but no lover could ever be more tender than he had been that night.

Then the baby came premature and lost his struggle for life en route to the neonatal unit in Midland. The scar left by losing Buddy was a scratch compared to the bleeding slash left by losing their baby boy. That period of her life was too unbearable to ever dwell on. Suffice to say, she no longer fussed over babies of friends or otherwise. Even now the sight of a little boy waddling alongside his mother, dressed in tiny Wranglers and a too-big hat, could, in an instant, plunge her into a pit of sadness.

She didn't need any more pain today, so she halted her detour through the halls of her memory and glanced toward the den at the Post-it notes plastered all over a bulletin board and an upright piano. Her mother supported herself as a part-time surgical assistant at the vet's office, but the other part of her life she spent writing country-western songs. She'd had small success. A few Texas bands played her music in honky-tonks. "What're you working on, Mom?"

"I've got one in my head I'm still fiddling with."

Her mother walked to the bright yellow and white kitchen and placed the remaining two cans of Coors into the refrigerator. "I'm calling it, 'Since You're Leaving Anyway, Take Out the Trash.'"

Debbie Sue laughed for the first time all day. Her mother composed tongue-in-cheek lyrics because she found most country songs too sad and depressing. "Here's one for you, Mom. 'I Miss My Ex, but My Aim's Getting Better.'"

"Awww, you must have seen Buddy today." Her mom slid an arm around her waist. "I guess he's got his hands full, doesn't he?"

Debbie Sue sighed inwardly. Her mother adored Buddy. She mentioned him at every opportunity. He must still think a lot of her, too, because he stopped by from time to time to visit her. A moment of silence followed. "What Buddy's got his hands full of is a schoolteacher from Odessa."

"Maybe you just *think* that. He's never said anything to *me* about her."

"Now why would he say anything to you about his girlfriend? You're my mother."

"You might be surprised at some of the talks Buddy and I have had over the past three years. I think he gets lonesome for someone to be open and honest with. You were his sounding board before. You should talk to him. I know he's strong, but with Harley being his friend and all, I'll bet he could use some moral support right now."

"Buddy and I haven't had a real conversation since before he left me."

"Then maybe it's time you did." Her mother released her and moved to the refrigerator. "Had supper?"

Behind her mother's back, Debbie Sue wiped away a tear. "No, but that's okay. I'll find something at home. I'm exhausted. I'm gonna collapse in front of the boob tube with my feet up. I just came out to check on you and Rocket Man. You haven't been into the shop. You're due a cut and color, you know. Want me to bring the stuff out here this weekend and do it for you?"

"Heavens, no. The last thing you should be doing on your day off is my hair. You work too hard. Always have." She smiled and patted Debbie Sue's shoulder. "Okay, so much for the sermon." She went to the refrigerator door and began taking out food. "I fixed myself some chicken-fried steak and fresh black-eyed peas for supper. I'll just send the leftovers home with you."

Without allowing Debbie Sue time to protest, her mother pulled a brown paper bag from a crevice between the refrigerator and the end of the cabinet and began adding to it emptied plastic margarine containers of leftovers. Black-eyed peas, mashed potatoes and gravy, and a foil-wrapped package of meat. Also a hunk of fresh cornbread. A banquet. Debbie Sue's stomach rumbled and growled.

She said good-bye, promised to come back when she could stay longer, and walked with Rocket Man back to the Silverado. And a flat tire.

"Shit. This day just gets better and better," she told her horse.

Rocket Man snorted and ambled off.

She couldn't remember if the spare had been repaired after her last flat. With night rapidly approaching, there wasn't much time to debate her options. She lay down on her back and scooted under the rear end where the spare was bolted to the chassis. A vehicle crunched to a stop on the gravel shoulder. A door slammed.

"Debbie Sue?"

She recognized the voice and thought a word too bad to say. "What?"

"You got a flat?"

She twisted around to look at the boots. Yep, tan alligator. "Is a snake's ass close to the ground?"

Buddy chuckled. "God, I needed that. Come out from under there."

She inched out and clambered to her feet, brushing off dirt and debris. "Well, I didn't need this."

Her bed-head hair-do and clip sagged halfway to her shoulder. She loosened the clip and ran splayed fingers through the thick tresses.

He plucked a dried grass stalk from near her temple. "Your hair looks pretty."

"It does not.

"Okay, it looks like shit. I'm too tired to change this tire. I'll take you back to town and we'll get Leroy to tow it into the station."

"I can't afford for Leroy to tow it."

"Don't worry about it."

"Well . . ." She hesitated, but the idea of some-body else changing her flat tire and Buddy paying for it was too tempting to resist.

From behind the fence, Rocket Man whinnied. Buddy walked over to the fence, and Debbie Sue followed. "How's the ol' boy doing?"

Rocket Man's head sawed up and down and he nuzzled Buddy's shirt pocket. As Buddy rubbed the long neck and apologized for having no pep-permints in his shirt pocket, Debbie Sue hid a smile. Horses fell in love with Buddy as often as women did. "He's in better shape than I am."

Buddy's eyes locked on hers. "I wouldn't go *that* far." He turned back to the horse. "Gotta go, sport. You behave yourself." He gripped Debbie Sue's arm and herded her toward the county rig. "Let's go. I've had a long day."

She freed her arm. "Wait, I've got to get a sack out of the cab."

"I'll get it."

She settled an admiring gaze on his butt in his tight Wranglers as he walked toward her pickup and reached into the cab. As he sauntered back to-ward her, his wide shoulders blocked out the set-ting sun's neon orange, shoulders that hadn't been built in a gym, but sculpted by years working on ranches and in the oil fields. Buddy had never shirked hard work.

A memory crashed down on her—his naked, near-perfect body crossing their bedroom. She used to lie in bed and take pleasure from just watching him and knowing that only she had the right to trace the whorl of black hair that traveled down his stomach to the thick curly thatch of his groin or touch the little brown mole hidden just at the edge of it.

As he came nearer, strands of jet black hair curled from beneath the sweatband of his hat. He inhaled deeply and grinned. "Lemme guess. Your mom's chicken-fried steak. I'd walk ten miles in worn-out boots for Virginia's cooking."

I'm not sharing it. Debbie Sue gave him a squint-eyed evil grin and grabbed the sack. Served him right for planting erotic memories in her head.

She hadn't been alone with Buddy in years. If her feet didn't ache, she wouldn't accept his offer for a ride. Uneasiness intact, she approached the sheriff department's Tahoe and threw a glance at the heavy steel mesh separating the driver from the backseat. "I'll ride in back."

"No, you won't. That's for prisoners. Get up front."

She eyed the shotgun braced between the dash and the front seat. *Okay, he's protected, but what about me?*

Except for the radio hissing and sputtering, they rode in uncomfortable silence for a mile. Finally she could no longer stand it. "Been out to Harley's, huh?"

"Yeah."

"I expect they're all real torn up."

"Yeah."

"Everybody's wondering about the funeral."

"Probably."

"Humph. I had a better conversation with Rocket Man."

"Don't be horsey, Debbie Sue. I got a lot on my mind."

She shrugged. "Fine. Whatever."

The last sliver of sun sank below the horizon, leaving them in semidarkness. She stared at his movie-star profile, marred only by his mustache. "Are you worried, Buddy? Aren't you scared?"

"Scared? Of what?"

"What happened with Pearl Ann is awful. I know you. I can tell when you're uptight and scared."

She could see a faint sag of his shoulders as he braked at the intersection with the highway. "If I tell you this, you have to promise me you won't blab it in that *damn* beauty shop."

"You know I won't blab."

"It's not official, but it looks like Pearl Ann didn't kill herself."

Fuck! Debbie Sue drew a sharp breath. It was hell to always be right. "Is that what *you* think?"

"I'm not thinking. I'm waiting for science to tell me." His thin smile was almost, but not quite, hidden by his mustache. "I should have known that head of yours was busy when you made that tattooed hip remark. Pretty sharp of you to catch that."

"Tattooed *lip*, Buddy. *Lip*."

He reached across and brushed her bottom lip with his finger. "Lip. Yeah, I got it."

She jerked her head backward as if his finger delivered an electrical shock. "Don't do that." Her own fingers flew up and covered her mouth.

His cell phone warbled and she jumped again.

"You're sure spooky. What are *you* scared of, Debbie Sue?" Pulling onto the highway, he unclipped the phone from his belt, flipped it open, and stuck it against his ear "This is Overstreet. . . . Hey, there . . ." He turned his head left and spoke toward the side window, the tenor of his voice softening. "No, uh, I'm not finished yet . . ."

Rat!

He gave a soft laugh. "Yeah, uh, so did I. . . . Sure, that'd be great. . . . Okay, see ya then." He snapped the cell shut and replaced it on his belt without another word.

Rat bastard!

Within seconds he turned off the highway onto her street, but Debbie Sue scarcely noticed. She was now focused on how his phone voice changed from curt and professional to warm and engaging. The Tahoe rolled to a stop in front of her small tan brick house, the home her driver and she had shared for the duration of their five-year marriage. Every part of her wanted to ask who called on the goddamn phone. What *woman* had his *private* cell number?

Damn his overtanned hide. Damn his ever-loving cowboy charm. Damn his intense eyes that could undress you and make you love it. She couldn't get out of this SUV fast enough. When she jerked the door handle, it didn't respond. Realizing control of the doors and windows was under the direction of the driver made her even angrier. She glared at him. "Well?"

Buddy released her locked door. She shoved it open and all but sprawled onto her sparse lawn. She caught herself and climbed out. "Thanks for the ride, Don Juan. And just for the record, that *damn* beauty shop is my livelihood."

She slammed the door and stomped toward her front door, heard the squeal of tires as he dug out and roared away.

Inside the kitchen she stopped. She was empty-handed. *Well, fuck.* She had left her sack of food with Buddy.

Dirty rotten double-rat bastard.

Four

 Debbie Sue stood in front of her open, vintage refrigerator, which did *not* have an ice and water dispenser on its door, and stared at the sparse contents inside. *Where the hell is that TV chef when you need him?*

The thought of Buddy sitting down to enjoy her mother's chicken-fried steak and fresh black-eyed peas was galling.

"I could call his cell phone and demand that he bring my food back," she grumbled, bobbing her head to the empty refrigerator, "but *I* don't have the number."

She didn't dare let herself think about the lacerations inflicted on her heart from hearing Buddy talk on the phone to another female in that tender voice once reserved for her.

She pulled out a jar of dill pickles and a bottle of Corona. She had read a magazine article that told her beer was full of vitamin B. She found a half sack of Fritos in the cupboard and placed all three items on the lamp table beside the distressed leather reclining chair that had cost a month's wage from the salon.

By now it was debatable if her stomach or her feet protested the louder. She returned to the kitchen and dragged out a plastic dishpan, filled it with hot water and dumped in some Epsom salts, then carried it, too, to the living room and placed it on the floor in front of her chair. Last she grabbed her portable phone, found the TV remote between the sofa cushions, and settled in front of the screen. With a groan, she tugged off her boots and socks, then immersed her feet in the warm water. They nearly sighed.

Surfing channels, she found a mariachi band, high school football scores, a lot of preaching, and a *whole* lot of news. Her feet hurt too badly to dance, she couldn't care less about the football scores, and preaching would only worsen her headache. And God knew she'd had enough news for one day. A hundred damn channels and nothing to watch.

She had just chomped down on a pickle when the phone rang. Buddy, calling about her food. She didn't need caller ID to tell her. She keyed the *on* button. "Just leave it on the front porch and hurry up, while it's still hot."

After a pause a male voice replied, "Well, okay, but aren't there laws against that kind of thing?"

Fuck. Quint Matthews. She hadn't talked to him

since last December at the National Finals in Las Vegas. He had shared his box seats with her, Edwina, and C. J. After the show he took her to dinner in one of the most obscenely opulent restaurants she had ever seen in her life, then took her to his room, which was the most luxurious hotel room she ever *hoped* to see.

Oh, he'd called since then and left messages on her voice mail, but she hadn't returned the calls. It wasn't that she didn't find him interesting or attractive. *Au contraire.* After seven or eight margaritas one night, she had declared to Edwina that "Clint made her wees neak." And he was available. *Texas Monthly* had named him one of the Lone Star State's most eligible bachelors.

Only one thing was wrong with Quint. When she had opened her eyes in that king-sized bed in Las Vegas and looked into the face above hers, there was no black mustache and no chocolate brown eyes.

"Well, my Lord, Quint. I've been wondering how you are."

"I'm just fine, darlin'. Can I use my imagination about what's still hot or are you fixin' to tell me?"

Debbie Sue couldn't help but grin. She had a propensity for bad boys, the badder the better, and Quint was the baddest. "It's too long a story and I'm too tired to go into it. Just talk nice to me because I've had a really rotten day."

"I can do better than that. I'm gonna be in your

part of the country Saturday. How 'bout I take you out for dinner and some boot scootin'?"

Danger. Danger. World champion bull rider. Moving in perfect rhythm, thigh to thigh, breast to chest. Hard muscles against soft flesh. "That sounds terrific. Call me when you get to town."

"Call you? I've been leaving you messages for over six months. I know when a woman's playing hard to get." He laughed. "I'm not accustomed to it but I recognize it."

She laughed, too. Quint was nothing if not cocky and ornery.

"I'll get there early enough to come by your shop. I've been wanting to see your operation, and I'd like to say hello to Ed and that pretty little C. J."

My operation? Yikes. "Great. Ed will be thrilled to see you, too. I nearly broke my leg tripping over her dropped jaw when she met you in Vegas."

Debbie Sue and her two friends had been buying programs at the rodeo when somebody yelled, "Hey, Debbie Sue Pratt!"

It had been years since anyone called her by her maiden name, and she almost hadn't responded. When she did, she saw her old boyfriend from her teen years. In the eleven years that had passed since their last face-to-face, he had transformed from seventeen-year-old heartthrob to full-grown hunk who made other places throb. Edwina had gone into a complete twitter when he winked at her and kissed the back of her hand.

Debbie Sue's life had been full since she and Quint parted. She had fallen in love and married. Had buried a baby and divorced. His life had probably been more entertaining, but she didn't see how it could have been more real.

"Okay, darlin'," he said on a laugh. "Saturday. Where'd you tell me your shop is? On the main drag?"

"You can't miss it. It's on the corner. It used to be a gas station. You know those old-fashioned round gas pumps? There's two of them out front, dressed up in women's clothes."

"Say that again?"

Debbie Sue felt her cheeks flush. The explanation for the gas pumps in costumes was too long and too difficult. "Never mind. Just take my word. You can't miss it."

A guffaw came across the line.

Well, what was so damn funny?

After she disconnected, her thoughts lingered on Quint. Most people wouldn't describe him as handsome, but he had a presence so potent and undeniably male, no woman's hormones could resist a sudden upsurge—especially if said woman hadn't been touched in all the right places since she saw him nine months ago.

She had a sexual history with Quint all right, starting at the beginning of her seventeenth year. She and Rocket Man had been racing barrels, and he had been riding bulls. It had taken only a few hours for his twinkling blue eyes and easy laugh to charm her right out of her underwear.

Since then he had parlayed his ability as a first-rate bull rider into a pro rodeo career and three world champion bull-riding titles. He had snagged multiple endorsements and the hand of 1998's Miss Rodeo America. Fourteen months later, they divorced. At the time his quote to the press had been, "Guess she was ready to cut me from the herd." *Poor Quint*. He deserved better.

Feeling upbeat for the first time since morning, she transferred from her chair to the bathroom, mouthing a song. "If you got the money, honey . . ."

She ran a bath and sank into a tub of imaginary bubbles. Just because West Texas water was so hard that bubble bath refused to bubble didn't mean she couldn't use it. If she ever got rich, one of the things she would buy was a water softener.

Her thoughts drifted back over the three years since Buddy had told her he wanted a divorce. She had been a different person each year. She spent the first year of freedom cursing the day she laid eyes on Buddy Overstreet. The second year she partied and enjoyed the singles scene.

The third year had brought a reality check in the form of the chance encounter with Quint in Vegas. That night he made several references to "we" and "us," speaking of the future and including her in it. It was then she realized that while in Quint's company it seemed easy to dismiss Buddy from her here and now, she could *never* imagine him absent from her future.

She told C. J. and Edwina that her uncustomary silence on the flight back from Vegas to Texas was exhaustion, but in fact she was fully alert and had a plan. She could hardly wait to tell Buddy she had changed. She knew her own destructive behavior had destroyed them, and racing Rocket Man around three barrels at breakneck speed wasn't a solution to anything. She had grown up. She would stay home, do laundry, and learn to cook.

Back in Texas, the fifty miles from Midland International Airport to the outskirts of Salt Lick felt like five hundred. As soon as she dropped Edwina and C. J. off, going against all rational thinking and logic, she drove to the sheriff's office. When she burst through the door, a startled Tanya Metcalf looked up and informed her Buddy was out with his girlfriend from Odessa. "Oh, surely you've heard about them by now," Tanya said, looking smug. "They've been thick as pea soup for the past month. Guess he's got it pretty bad."

Debbie Sue had muttered something incoherent and backed out of the office, swearing to herself and God she would never come that close to humiliating herself again for Buddy Overstreet.

And she wouldn't.

It was over between her and Buddy. She had to deal with it, and what better way to do that than with a sexy, rich hunk like Quint.

She dropped an oversized nightshirt over her head, her thoughts flying to Pearl Ann and what Buddy had told her. She left the bedroom and checked the locks on her windows and both doors.

"Can you come by and pick me up?"

"I sure can, hon." Edwina's yawn came over the receiver. "What's wrong with Big Red? Throw a shoe?"

"It's at the Texaco. Buddy had it towed last night."

"Ohmygod. Did you have a wreck? Was anyone hurt? Were you arrested?"

"Ed, Ed, calm down. I had a flat out near Mom's. Buddy came along and gave me a ride home. He had my pickup towed because my spare was flat, too."

"You were alone with Buddy? Please tell me you bit him on the neck, right where he has that little scar under his chin."

Debbie Sue steadied herself, thinking of the position from which she had last seen that scar. "No biting. Not even close to his neck. Just as I thought we might be starting up a decent conversation, that whore of a schoolteacher called."

Debbie Sue repeated Buddy's telephone dialogue, filling in what she hadn't heard with what she imagined. She concluded with "You might know Odessa would hire somebody sorry and no-good to teach in their schools. How could Buddy not see right through her?"

"How do you know it was her?"

"Well, who else could it have been?"

"Why damn near anybody, from Tanya Metcalf to Liz Taylor. Buddy ain't chopped liver, you know."

Debbie Sue frowned. She hadn't thought of *that*. No, he definitely wasn't chopped liver. To her dismay, at thirty-one, he was even better-looking than he had been at twenty-one. Why couldn't he grow ugly?

A shower, a wrestling match with her Wranglers and boots, and a half hour later, she heard Edwina honk. She dashed out the door and into her pal's royal blue '68 Mustang where she was met by the reek of stale cigarette smoke. Debbie Sue cranked down the window to keep from gagging. Why would Edwina stink up a classic car with toxic fumes? They flew past Salt Lick's only drive-through eatery. "Times like this, I wish Hogg's opened before eleven. I'm starving. I had pickles and beer for supper."

"*Blech*. I'm surprised your mom didn't have something delicious for you."

"Chicken-fried steak and all the trimmings. It went home with Buddy." Debbie Sue related how her ex-husband's conversation with somebody with whom he obviously had more than a passing relationship had sent her into such a fit, she forgot her food and nearly fell out of his pickup.

"You poor thing. Don't worry. I can fix you up

with breakfast. What you need is to find a good man who can cook."

"What I need is to make enough money to hire a maid."

Edwina dug her cell phone out of her monstrous black and white cowhide purse and keyed in a number. "Hey, Poodle, could I ask you for a big old favor? If Debbie Sue and I pull up out front, would you bring us a couple of those biscuits you made this morning? And throw a sausage patty between them." She paused and turned to Debbie Sue. "Do you want an egg on that?"

"No egg and I don't want fries with that order, either, but I would looove some coffee, cream and one sugar."

Edwina placed the order, made a U-turn, and headed toward her trailer.

"I'm not believing this," Debbie Sue said. "I *would* say Vic has you spoiled, but that is such an understatement."

"Don't think it doesn't go both ways, hon. If I've learned anything in my forty-five years on this earth, it's how to give as well as take. Lord, I've run off a lot of good men with my hardheaded ways."

Debbie Sue couldn't tell if Edwina was making small talk or preaching. They pulled in front of a cream-colored double-wide with blue shutters. Vic Martin trotted out the front door with a small paper sack and a Styrofoam cup. He was a huge man, an ex-navy SEAL, complete with shaved head and muscles on his muscles. And right now his chest and belly were covered with a red ruffled apron that said "Kiss the Cook" in white letters. Seeing him deliver breakfast curbside made Debbie Sue giggle.

"I fixed one for you, too, Mama Doll." He grinned and gave Edwina's cheek a loving brush with his thumb. "Since I made you late this morning, it was the least I could do."

As they pulled away, Debbie Sue munched on a biscuit and mulled over Edwina's remark about hardheaded ways. Maybe the old smokestack had a point. "Now I've seen everything. Does he do windows, too?"

Edwina's mouth turned up in a sly smile. "You'd better believe it, hon, but that's not what he's best at."

"Don't tell me. I don't think I could stand it."

Well after six o'clock in the evening, Debbie Sue and Edwina washed and dried the last customer and locked the door. They hadn't had such a busy day since the high school prom. Weddings, funerals, and proms always bumped up the salon's gross numbers.

Most of the day's customers had come for gossip about Pearl Ann's death. Walking out with a new hairdo covering a head full of information was a bonus.

The five customers who had invested five dollars each in Edwina's pool, betting on when the murder victim would leave her husband, were especially eager to learn who had won the twenty-five-dollar prize. They agreed among themselves that whoever wrote "when hell freezes over," "when chickens need lip gloss," and "whenever" had disqualified themselves. "Before I sleep with George Strait" was the winner, hands down. Charlene had come close to winning with "When I grow a mustache," but menopause had sneaked in since she placed her bet and she was no longer eligible.

Edwina dragged out the push broom and began to sweep sand into a pile. Keeping the fine West Texas sand out of the shop on any day was impossible. When the door opened and closed as often as it had today, the white vinyl floor looked like someone had poured cupfuls of the tan grit on it. "When you saw Buddy last night, he didn't say anything about Pearl Ann, did he? It just haunts me why that woman would put a gun to her head."

"Just that he called in the forensic lab from Midland. I'm not sure, but I think he *has* to do that."

"Even if he didn't say anything, he's bound to *think* something. Last I knew, Buddy wasn't stupid. If I thought you were holding back on me . . ."

Debbie Sue gave her a shrug and upturned palms. She wouldn't dream of betraying Buddy's confidence, even to a good friend.

Edwina put away the broom, went to her station, and tapped a Marlboro from a crushed pack. "What I'm trying to say here, girl, is our reputation is on the line." She lit up. "On. The. Line. Think about it. When it comes to spreading the news, we've never been outdone. You don't need film at eleven if you've got the Styling Station twenty-four-seven."

Debbie Sue's mind wandered off to visualizing how that slogan would look on matchbooks. She could see the cover as a glossy pink, with burgundy letters and maybe a little logo. "Buddy said he'd hear something from Midland in a couple of days. We'll just have to wait. Every customer I had today thinks the whole thing is somehow Harley's fault."

"Too bad you missed Ruby Cantrell. She thinks aliens had something to do with it. Said they left a crop circle behind her house Monday night."

"When did a backyard full of dead weeds become a crop?"

"What can I say? You know Ruby. Sharon Douthitt said one of their pumpers told her husband he saw Harley going into the Starlite Inn in Odessa with a blond."

"Really? Somebody told me it was a redhead . . . Edwina, speaking of blonds, did C. J. ever say how she knew about Pearl Ann? I was so blown away by the news I didn't even think to ask her who told her so early in the morning. I mean, Pearl Ann must have just been found when C. J. raced in here."

"I asked her when you followed Buddy outside, but she just broke down and bawled like a baby. I never knew she and Pearl Ann were close."

On Friday the official story appeared in the *Salt Lick Weekly Reporter*, alongside Buddy's picture and a quote. Pearl Ann Carruthers had died from a single shot to the head by a 9mm automatic pistol, inflicted by persons unknown. Her husband had offered a fifty-thousand-dollar reward for information leading to the capture and conviction of the killer. The funeral was scheduled for Monday at the Calvary Baptist Church.

So much gossip flew through the Styling Station the thin white curtains Debbie Sue had hung on the windows didn't fall lax all day. She was half listening to the talk with one side of her brain, and focused on the reward with the other. Lord, with that much money she could pay off her debt to the bank and rid herself of the salon's monthly mortgage payment that was eating her lunch.

Soon after she and Buddy had divorced and he deeded the service station to her, the great State of Texas sent her a notice ordering her to dig up and either dispose of or replace the station's aged gasoline storage tanks. The bid for the clean removal of the tanks turned out to be staggering enough, but the cost of replacing them and upgrading the station to current EPA requirements was astronomical. The six-digit number put the quietus on her or anybody else making a living from selling gasoline from the old service station.

She couldn't think of any viable use for a limestone rock gas station building constructed in the forties. She couldn't think of a business she could operate in it or a service she could provide from it to compete with existing businesses in Odessa. The locals enjoyed making the forty-five-mile trip to the bigger town too much.

And worst of all, she couldn't think of a living person who would buy the relic from her. Buddy wouldn't even take it back for free. Ownership had passed to his mother when his father had dropped dead at age fifty from a heart attack in the midst of an oil change. Buddy had quit college to operate the station for his mother's benefit as well as to provide a living for himself and Debbie Sue, but he had hated the thing from the get-go. When the Salt Lick sheriff met an untimely death during his term, Buddy ran for the office unopposed. After being elected, he had closed the service station down for good.

A beauty salon was the solution Debbie Sue finally landed on, and she enrolled in the beauty college in Odessa. She had never been sorry, really. She found she liked the creativity required by hairdressing and cosmetology. The only difference from horse grooming or maintaining her steers back when she had been in 4-H was the horse and steers had usually been better company.

Converting the gas station to a beauty salon didn't prevent the state's demanding cleanup of the soil surrounding the old storage tanks when they were discovered to have leaked. Even if she tore down the building and pulled out the storage tanks, she would still have to clean the soil. Who knew the great State of Texas could be so mean?

As the company she hired out of Odessa worked at digging out contaminated dirt and replacing it with fresh, the cost soon exceeded the original estimate by more than double. Buddy had shown the better part of valor and assumed as much of the cost as he could. Even with that, her part amounted to over thirty thousand dollars.

She'd had no choice but to mortgage the station building. Her only other option was to walk off and turn her only asset over to the state, as many of the mom-and-pop service station owners had done after EPA legislation brought them bankrupting cleanup costs. Buddy urged her to do just that, but with typical Debbie Sue stubbornness, she refused.

After adding to the loan the cost of converting the interior, then purchasing salon equipment, she was fifty thousand dollars in debt and hadn't even torn out the antique pumps out front. Edwina solved that problem by dressing the pumps in women's clothes. She even went so far as to coordinate the costume to the season.

Nor did the salon have a decent sign. Debbie Sue quashed calling it the Styling Boutique as planned. With the words "Service Station" already visible in bright red letters, she simply bought a quart of white enamel and one of red. She covered over "ervice" with white, then in red, painted in "tyling."

No one in Salt Lick seemed to notice the mismatched or unaligned letters or even care. That was one of the nice things about living in a town as small and removed from urban culture. People didn't have high expectations.

So why *couldn't* she solve Pearl Ann's murder and get fifty thousand dollars? The chances she'd succeed were probably better than winning the lottery. Her instincts were good. Hadn't she had that gnawing hunch from the beginning that the woman didn't commit suicide?

Saturday dawned with Debbie Sue having cogitated all night. She left her bed determined to put Buddy Overstreet in a far, far corner of her mind where he belonged and concentrate on Quint Matthews. By hooking up with Quint, she wouldn't have to worry about solving a murder mystery to get enough money to pay off her debt. Despite the fact that the only time she had slept with him in more than ten years had conjured up her desire to reunite with her ex-husband, she had to admit Quint was an extremely capable and unselfish lover. Piles of money and great sex. What was not to like? *Solving a murder mystery? Phfft.* What had she been thinking?

Yep, hooking up with Quint was, by far, the smarter thing to do. With her mind set on the notion, all she had to do was convince her heart to follow.

She molded her breasts into her Wonderbra and pulled out of her closet a knit robin's egg blue shirt with a plunging V neck and her favorite Rockies, not too new, but not too faded, either. They fit her like a coat of paint.

Around her waist she wrapped a brown leather belt adorned with engraved sterling silver squares and enhanced it with one of her medium-sized trophy silver belt buckles. Then she pulled on beige Tony Lama boots and hooked sterling and turquoise drops in her earlobes.

A Navajo bracelet made of tortoiseshell inlaid with a coral cardinal and mother-of-pearl flowers cuffed her wrist. The piece was what they called "Old Pawn" in Albuquerque, and she considered it a treasure. Not just because it was old and it was against the law to make jewelry out of coral and tortoiseshell nowadays, but because Buddy had bought it for her. Last, she hung a silver chain holding a tiny turquoise heart around her neck. Buddy had bought it, too. The heart fell to a strategic place just at the top of her Wonderbra cleavage.

At three o'clock the last customer was sent out the door with new honey-colored frosting and a cut that had appeared on a model in *Glamour*. Debbie Sue locked the door. "Okay, Ed, this is it. With the commotion all week, I didn't get around to telling you Quint Matthews is stopping by and taking me out to dinner."

Edwina gasped. "He's not!"

"He is. He called me Tuesday night."

"Debbie Sue, I ought to take a hairbrush to your backside for depriving me of news like that."

"Just make me good-looking. It's plumb dumb for me to keep pining over Buddy. I need fresh meat."

Edwina gave her a sour look. "I'll try not to take that literally."

"I'm going for the *sophisticated bitch* look tonight, Ed."

"You got it, hon." The veteran beautician crushed out her cigarette and went to work. She shampooed Debbie Sue's long silky hair, then plopped her down in her styling chair, ignoring that the starched, tight Rockies made it binding to sit or bend. Edwina dried and combed and twisted and rolled. When she finished, Debbie Sue's red-brown hair was slicked back from her face in a smooth do with the blond highlighted streak showing down the middle and a sexy-as-all-get-out knot at the crown.

"Wow," Debbie Sue said. "I look like a fancy skunk."

"As long as you don't smell like one," Edwina quipped.

For a finishing touch to the topknot, Edwina added a little wispy hairpiece, then dragged out a satchel filled with cosmetics.

"No face makeup." Debbie Sue halted Edwina's hands. Except for a few freckles on her nose, her skin was flawless and smooth. "Just do my eyes and cheeks."

Edwina bronzed Debbie Sue's eyelids and mascaraed her naturally thick lashes. She added Antique Rose blush to her cheeks and Rosewood Frost lipstick to her full lips. When she finished, Debbie Sue almost didn't recognize herself. "You're a vision, girl. Want me to put some acrylics on those nails? We've got time."

"No fingernails. I won't be able to stuff my shirt-tail into these jeans." Debbie Sue rose and looked closer into the mirror, made a few brushes to her eyebrows with her fingertips, adjusted the heart hanging around her neck. She dug into her hand-bag, brought out a purse-sized atomizer of Paloma, and sprayed behind each ear and between her breasts. Family and friends called her a tomboy, but that didn't mean she couldn't smell like a sexpot. "Don't ever mention Buddy Over-street's name again, Ed. Tonight I'm going for the gold. I'm tired of this town, tired of this beauty shop, and tired of being broke."

"Um-um," Edwina said. "I can see it now. You'll be walking bowlegged for a week." She propped an elbow on the payout desk, gave Debbie Sue a head-to-toe. "Just don't make any sudden moves in those jeans unless you've got an extra pair somewhere."

Five

 At five o'clock a car door slammed and Debbie Sue's heart lurched. She felt seventeen again. Her pulse was racing, and she had a sudden urge to pee. She darted to the storeroom and peeked out from behind the burgundy and pink floral print curtain that hid the storeroom from the salon. "Ed, just act cool. I'll come out casually, as if I didn't realize he had gotten here."

She stood in the cramped area rehearsing an act of surprise. The last thing she wanted was for a bad boy like Quint to think her future depended on the outcome of this date. Some of her nervousness was for good reason. How often did a hick from Salt Lick go out with the Most Eligible Bachelor in Texas? Taking one last look in the mirror, she sucked in her gut and parted the curtains.

"Goodness, I didn't—" She clamped her mouth shut and tried not to gape. "Buddy. What are you doing here?"

Her ex laughed. "Between you and Ed I'm beginning to feel unwelcome. She 'bout jumped out of those funny-looking shoes when I came in. . . . Hey, Ed. You okay?"

Debbie Sue's gaze darted to Edwina, who had just lit the wrong end of her cigarette. A tiny flame burned beneath her nose. She tamped out the cigarette in an ashtray.

"You two sure are nervous. Somebody hiding out in the back holding a gun on us?"

"I'm, uh . . . we're just surprised to see you, that's all. Why are you here?"

"I got to feeling bad about not returning Virginia's food to you the other night. I forgot it was in the Tahoe until after ten o'clock. I figured it was too late to bring it back so I heated it up and ate it. Lord, your mother can cook."

Debbie Sue tried to block out the sight of Edwina waving her arms and pointing to her watch behind Buddy's back. It wouldn't be the end of the world if Quint came in, but she didn't relish the thought of being picked up for a date with her exhusband present, especially a date with Quint Matthews. Buddy knew she and the ex-rodeo star had once had a fling. She turned Buddy around and pushed him toward the front door. "Don't worry about it. I didn't need all those extra calories. Glad you enjoyed it."

"Whoa. I may be a country boy from a small town but I know when somebody's trying to get rid of me. Is everything really all right?"

"Dammit, Buddy, would you quit trying to find something wrong in every situation? Sometimes your insatiable need to fix everything is such a pain in the ass. Maybe I'm just plain ol' tired and want to get out of here or maybe I've got plans."

"Okay, I'm leaving. I came by to tell you Mack Humphrey's got some extra hay he'll give away. Thought you might could use it. Sorry I bothered you." He blatantly looked her up and down. "I can see you've got somewhere to go." He nodded to Edwina and stamped out the door.

He had no more than driven away before a shiny black Lincoln Navigator turned into the parking lot. "Ohmygod, he's here. Look at that rig he's driving." She made a mad dash for the back room again, then stuck her head around the floral curtain. "Ed, just talk to him for a little bit, then I'll come out."

Words were wasted on Edwina because she wasn't listening. She had her nose plastered to the window that took up the upper half of the front door. "Now there's a man who makes a woman feel proud to be female. Um-um. I'd be on him like cheese on nachos."

The bells on the door clattered as Quint entered. He swept off his hat and extended his right hand to Edwina. "I hope you remember me, darlin', 'cause I remember you. I'm Quint Matthews." The statement was on a par with "I hope you remember me. I'm Troy Aikman."

"Why, as I live and breathe," Edwina said and

fluttered her heavily mascaraed eyelashes. "Las Vegas wasn't it, Quint?"

"Yes, ma'am. Did Debbie Sue tell you I was coming by?"

"Seems like she mentioned it. I hope you didn't have any trouble finding the shop."

"It was hard deciding which service station with old gas pumps wearing dresses to stop at, but I finally just picked one and went with it."

Debbie adjusted her boobs in her Wonderbra and made her entrance with a gasp. "Why Quint, I didn't hear you come in."

Quint's gaze roamed her up and down and stopped at the little turquoise heart just as she had hoped. He broke into a wide grin. "Now that's what I'm talking about. You look good, Debbie Sue, real good."

Debbie Sue's brain shut down. Her tongue begged her to do something, but all she could produce was a giggle. She thought she heard Ed mutter "Pitiful" under her breath, but she wasn't sure.

Finally the gears clicked in, "I hope you don't mind if we drive over to Odessa to eat. I know a terrific restaurant, and it has a good house band that plays on weekends."

"Why honey, that sounds just great." He turned back to Edwina. "It was a pleasure to see you. I hope it's not so long before we meet again."

Buddy walked out of Nelson's Rexall carrying the latest edition of the *Odessa American* and a sack holding razor blades, shooting a glance across the street at the Styling Station's parking lot. A cowboy wearing a big hat was helping Debbie step up into a new black Navigator. And the man was? . . . Shit!

A pang sliced through Buddy's gut. Where in the hell had Quint Matthews come from? The last time Buddy saw him was at the Fort Worth Stock Show and Rodeo when a mean-ass bull named Bodacious had bucked his showoff butt in the dirt.

Buddy's queasy feeling made no sense. He had been divorced from Debbie Sue three years and he was seeing Kathy. His ex-wife was a beautiful woman. No reason why some guy wouldn't want to take her out, and she was free to see whom she wanted. But as hard as Buddy tried to rationalize, the cold hard truth couldn't be denied. The thought of her with Quint Matthews knocked the props right from under him.

He stood back under the drugstore's awning and watched the fancy SUV pull away from the Styling Station's parking lot, hoping Debbie Sue didn't spot him and think he was spying on her. The vehicle headed out the Odessa highway, and Buddy figured he knew its destination.

He threw his newspaper and sack into the Tahoe, scooted in and checked his watch. Kathy was expecting him in an hour. He scarcely had time to shower, shave, and change clothes. His original plan had been for a nice dinner somewhere, maybe a dance or two and a sleepover at

Kathy's apartment in Odessa. Suddenly the plan took on tarnish and his own empty bed in his tiny apartment held an awful lot of appeal.

The forty-five-mile drive in Quint's luxury SUV flew by as he caught Debbie Sue up on the last few months' rodeo news. He didn't mention Pearl Ann's murder, which Debbie Sue found to be a relief. It was all she had heard for the past five days.

The rodeo stock business was bigger than ever, he told her. Even parts of the country where rodeos had never been held, much less been popular, were now seeking him out for bookings. "I've been thinking ever since December, Deb. It'd sure be great to have you with me on the road. As much as you know about horses, you could find the best ones for me while I check out cattle. I fly first-class all over the country, darlin'. Stay at only the best hotels, got a bottomless expense account."

Debbie Sue felt herself grinning like an idiot. She didn't trust herself to comment for fear she might scream an exuberant "Yes!"

Following her directions, he drove them to Kincaid's. The well-known Odessa dining establishment was housed in a building designed to look like an old barn, inside and out. On the lower floor, small tables surrounded a dance floor and a raised bandstand. The serious dining occurred on the mezzanine, which could be reached by either elevator or a wide staircase rising up one side of the room, its handrails supported by massive carved balusters. The decor might be rustic, the dress code casual, but everybody in West Texas knew Kincaid's was no cheap steak joint.

Dining at Kincaid's with any man besides Buddy was a part of Debbie Sue's exorcism process. The restaurant had always been their special place. If she could manage an evening there without breaking down and weeping, she would wake up stronger for it in the morning.

Quint guided her into the packed foyer with a hand on the small of her back. Debbie Sue basked in the envious glances of women they passed. Not only was her escort a good-looking sonofagun, he might as well have had hundred-dollar bills sticking out of his pockets. Anybody in his (or her) right mind could see the shirt on his back had probably cost a minimum of two hundred dollars. And his boots . . . well, what he paid for the boots would buy her groceries for half a year.

Quint spoke to the maître d', and at the same time made a smooth move into his pocket, pressed something against the young man's hand. Immediately they were led upstairs to the mezzanine dining area that looked down on the dance floor below. The room's acoustics were so well tuned, meals were undisturbed by the band music.

The cocktail waitress appeared, and Debbie Sue ordered the restaurant's signature drink, a Margarita Mortal. Along with Jose Cuervo, grenadine, and triple sec, the concoction was topped off with a full jigger of Grand Marnier and served in a grandé margarita glass. Compared to the margaritas Debbie Sue made at home, it was an atom bomb.

Quint asked for a shot of Crown Royal. A large diamond mounted inside a gold horseshoe glinted from his left ring finger as he chose hors d'oeuvres from the menu. Debbie Sue gloated with wicked pleasure. Having money was so much fun.

They discussed the things they had in common, which mostly included livestock and rodeo. He picked up her hand and circled the back with his thumb, looking at her with a penetrating gaze. "I didn't drop into Salt Lick because I'm passing through, you know. I'm serious about wanting you to travel with me."

She felt both exhilarated and confused. Travel with him as what? A horse buyer? His mistress? Did a salary and benefits come with the package, or was her intended pay to be sleeping with him? "I don't know, Quint. I have responsibilities. And debt. I can't just walk off from everything. And I have Rocket Man."

"I can't believe you've still got that horse." He leaned back and finished off his drink. "Well, selling a horse is no problem. What kind of debt? Pretty good wages come with the job, you know."

Sell Rocket Man? Inside she scowled, but she made an effort to home in on the more positive parts of the conversation. She made a long-winded explanation of the service station's environmental cleanup and the expense of opening the salon, during the middle of which he ordered another shot of Crown.

"You mean ol' Buddy didn't help you pay for all that?" he said at the end of her story. "What kind of a chickenshit is he?"

Her spine jerked a little straighter. She had never heard *anybody*—except herself, of course, and she had a right to—call Buddy Overstreet a chickenshit. And as far as helping her, he had sold his horses and cows and paid every dime he had in savings toward the cleanup. "Of course he helped me. As much as he could. We were divorced, you know. He didn't have to do anything at all."

"I know why you married him, but how come you divorced him? I never heard."

"I didn't. He divorced me."

Quint's blue eyes landed on her cleavage again. "Well, if he isn't a chickenshit, he's at the least a dumb bastard. So tell me what happened."

How could he speak of Buddy in such a disrespectful way? Buddy had given up a lifelong dream to marry her. Her spine stiffened a little more. She went from sipping her margarita to gulping the last of it. "We had issues. It was my fault."

"I'll bet. If you hadn't been pregnant, you never would've married him in the first place."

"Why, that's not true. We loved each other. We wanted the baby, but I lost it. And afterward, I had this . . . depression. I made our lives so miserable, he couldn't live with me anymore."

What was she doing? Why was she telling Quint Matthews all of this?

He released her hand and leaned back, cocked his elbow on the back of his chair. "Jesus Christ, you're still in love with him, aren't you?"

"Well, no. I just . . . I just don't see what's to be gained by talking bad about him all the time. Can I have another margarita?"

"Sure." He summoned the waitress. "I still say he's a chickenshit. Let's go ahead and eat."

A chill settled between them. The conversation about her and Buddy's relationship had caught her off-guard, but she regrouped, keeping her eye on the prize. How could she have wound up defending Buddy to Quint? Had she lost her mind?

A different waitress came with menus, and she ordered a T-bone and a baked potato, but Quint ordered some kind of grilled gourmet chicken and a salad. When she gave him a questioning look, he patted his stomach and said, "Gotta watch my waistline. I don't get the exercise I used to."

They ordered more drinks while they waited for the food. Quint swallowed a sip of whiskey and leaned forward, resting his forearms on the table. "Debbie Sue, I haven't forgotten Las Vegas. I've been thinking about it for over eight months. Don't think I don't know why you hightailed it out of my room before sunup that morning. I said I want you with me and I meant it, but I don't want your ex-husband in bed with us again."

Help! Where was the waitress? She wanted a Margarita Mortal in each hand. It was one thing to spend the night with Quint on a lost weekend now and then, but to commit to a more permanent arrangement suddenly seemed like adding a fourth barrel to the barrel-racing course. She gulped a large swallow of her drink. "Bed?" she squeaked.

"Bed. We spent the night together, remember? And as I recall, you had a hell of a good time. I was thankful the room was soundproofed."

Yikes! Her scalp began to sweat. "Well, I—"

"Darlin', I can make you forget Buddy Overstreet ever lived. I can show you—"

"Why, Quint Matthews. I haven't seen you in years."

Debbie Sue and Quint looked up at the same time, and there stood Buddy.

And a woman. Without a doubt, the schoolteacher from Odessa. How *dare* he bring her to Kincaid's?

"Mind if we sit with you? The place is a little crowded tonight."

Before Quint could reply, Buddy dragged up two chairs and placed them at the end of their table. "Have a seat, Kathy," he said to the woman. She sank to the chair seat like a robot.

Buddy sat down himself and called the waitress over, ordered a glass of white wine and bottle of

Coors. "Bring these folks another round, too. Keep 'em coming." He winked as he instructed the waitress, "Put it on my bill."

Debbie Sue and Quint both sat speechless through the drink ordering process. Buddy made introductions—Quint, an old acquaintance. Debbie Sue, ex-wife. Kathy Something, a resident of Odessa.

Debbie Sue, Quint and the woman nodded to one another.

"Lemme see, Quint," Buddy said, grinning and pushing his gray hat back with his thumb. "I think it was the rodeo in Fort Worth the last time I saw you. You were trying to ride that mean sucker. I believe they called him Bodacious."

"Might have been," Quint said, unsmiling.

Buddy turned to Kathy. "Ol' Bodacious is the only bull they ever retired unridden. Isn't that right, Quint?"

"Might be."

Debbie Sue inhaled half her drink. The schoolteacher from Odessa blinked, and Debbie Sue stared at the bangs that crossed her forehead like a wide-toothed comb. Her dark hair brushed her shoulders when she moved her head. *Split ends.* The woman could use a hot oil treatment.

"Buddy tells me you're quite the horsewoman," Kathy said.

The first word from the woman's mouth, and Debbie Sue knew she wasn't a Texan. She managed a blurry glare at Buddy. "I know a horse or two."

"I've been telling Buddy he has to teach me to ride." Kathy batted her eyelashes at Buddy and squeezed his arm. "How hard can it be? Even children ride horseback."

Debbie plopped a forearm on the table and leaned forward. "I'll tell you this much—"

"You folks ordered yet?" Buddy's dark brown gaze drilled Debbie Sue. "Try the chicken-fried steak, Quint. That's my favorite. Beef's real good here."

Bastard. Debbie Sue ducked his eyes and pasted on a smile as wooden as the schoolteacher's.

The food came. Hers filled a platter, Quint's, a saucer. The steak was bigger than her hand and an inch thick. Her potato was the size of Idaho. No telling when she might get to eat here again, so she intended to ask for a doggie bag.

The waiter came for Buddy's and Kathy's orders. As Buddy started to order, Kathy placed her hand on his arm, stopping him, and began speaking to the waiter in Spanish. The young Mexican seemed delighted, and they carried on a conversation in Spanish for several minutes. After he left, Kathy turned to Buddy and told him their order would be done to perfection.

Big deal. A lot of Texans speak Spanish, especially if they teach school. "So, Karen," Debbie Sue said, "how long have you lived in Texas? Where'd you learn Spanish?"

"It's Kathy, dear. I've been here a little over a year. I'm from Chicago. Growing up, I learned

Polish and German. After those, Spanish came easily."

"Uh-huh." *Fuck.*

Buddy led the conversation into a discussion of fine performance horses about which he knew a lot, but Quint said little. The ex-rodeoer probably didn't know much about fine horses. His only real interest was broncs and bulls. In fact, she remembered from their rodeoing days, Quint hadn't much liked animals of any kind. His focus had always been only on winning money.

Kathy Something didn't say a dozen words. She mostly blinked until she turned to Debbie Sue and said, "Would you like to go with me to the little girls' room?"

Little girls' room? Please tell me she didn't say that. Debbie Sue wrinkled her nose and mouthed a no. When Kathy excused herself and crossed to the restrooms, Debbie Sue watched her backside. The woman was a bottle-butt, pure and simple. And she had on a *dress*. Where had Buddy found her?

The cocktail waitress appeared again with Kathy trailing behind. Debbie Sue opted to skip the middleman and go to straight tequila. Quint liked the idea so much he ordered a shot for himself. When the waitress queried Buddy and Kathy, they both declined. Buddy said he was on duty twenty-four-seven, like it or not, and Kathy never drank more than a glass or two of white wine, in case she ran into some of her students somewhere. Quint asked Kathy what she taught, and when she replied high school honors chemistry and yoga at night at the college, Debbie Sue ordered a double.

Her vision began to blur, and in her head, she was practicing Spanish verses she had learned in high school when a slurred statement from Quint interrupted her thoughts. "Let's dance, Susie. I promised you boot scootin'." He stood up and looked over the wrought-iron railing, down at the dance floor in the atrium below. He swayed forward. "Where the hell's the floor?"

Susie? Who the hell was *Susie?* "Downstairs. I'll show you." Debbie Sue scowled at Buddy and grabbed Quint's arm. "Excuso por favor," she said to their uninvited table guests. "We'll be backo uno momento."

Quint picked up his hat and set it on his head at a cockeyed angle. Debbie Sue led him from the table to the wide stairway. A few treads from the bottom, he missed a step, tumbled the rest of the way, and landed face-first on the empty dance floor. His hat popped off and skidded all the way to the foyer. Two waiters dropped their tasks and rushed to his aid.

Debbie Sue stopped, grabbed the rail above the melee, and called down to him. "Quint? Did you fall?"

He mumbled and muttered as the two waiters, babbling in Spanish, lifted him to his feet and escorted him to the men's room. Debbie Sue turned and climbed the stairs, hanging on to the rail with both hands as she started back to the table. Her surroundings seemed to be floating. She placed her steps with deliberate care as she returned to her chair and picked up her purse.

Buddy looked up. "That was quick. How's the band?"

She tossed her head so hard her neck popped. She lost her balance and wound up with her feet crossed at the ankles. "It was terrific, thank you. Now we're going home."

"Where's the champ?"

"He's waiting downstairs." She concentrated on uncrossing her feet.

Buddy broke into a loud laugh and slapped his thigh. "That landing at the bottom of those stairs was better than the one he made off of ol' Bodacious."

"Fuck you, Buddy Overstreet." Making a deliberate effort to avoid falling forward, she turned to Karen, or Kathy, or whoever. "It's very nice to have met you, ma'am."

At the bottom of the stairs, Debbie Sue found Quint doing something to his hat. The brim had a distinct impression of a boot heel. "Let's get the fuck outta here," he slurred.

Debbie Sue sensed a presence and turned. Buddy was right behind them. "Say, hoss," he said to Quint in a firm voice, "you're not planning on driving, I hope."

Oh shit. Debbie Sue opened her mouth to speak, but Buddy pointed his finger at her. "You're not driving, either."

"I'll get a cab," Quint mumbled.

"Doubt if you'll find a cab that'll drive you clear to Salt Lick." Buddy adjusted his hat and pulled car keys from his pocket. "I'll take you home myself."

Debbie Sue couldn't put two sentences together to argue. As if they were under arrest, Buddy herded them to the county's Tahoe and opened the back door. Quint fell onto the backseat and Debbie Sue followed him. Both knees of his Lucchese khakis were ripped and one tear had a bloody spot. She bent forward and took a closer look. "Ohmygod, Quint, you're hurt."

Even through the black mesh partition that separated them, Debbie Sue could see Buddy's eyes glued to Quint in the rearview mirror. "Where you staying, Slick?"

"My house. Just take us to my house," Debbie Sue said.

A moment of silence followed, then they peeled out of the parking lot with such a jolt their heads jerked backward.

"Why don't you drop me off first, sweetheart," Kathy said. "I can see you have your hands full."

"Shit," Debbie Sue muttered, staring through the black mesh at the backs of her ex-husband's and Kathy Something's heads. "Shit, shit, shit."

Edwina was looking at the TV, but her mind was miles away. Odessa to be exact. She intended to watch the situation between her good friend and Quint with a skeptical eye. Debbie Sue wasn't the type to sleep around, and it was real obvious Quint had ridden more at the rodeo than a few bulls.

Edwina's second husband and the father of her middle child had been a rodeo cowboy. He had never reached the lofty level of world champion. He had been involved more in the lower level of partying and carousing. She had always suspected he only married her because it was cheaper than having his Wranglers and shirts starched and ironed by the cleaners.

Even after all these years she still wished she had been there when he came home and found those precious shirts cut into confetti and his custom-made boots filled with cement.

The surface reasons to approve of Quint Matthews were all there—looks, charm, and money—but who knew what lay beneath? She had been lured by the same three demons herself and learned the hard way there was a big difference between having character and being one.

Six

 Buddy awoke at daylight horny, as usual.
For the past dozen or so Sunday mornings, Kathy
had been beside him, more than eager to assist
him to a pleasant satisfaction of his morning call.

This morning, he was glad to be alone. Debbie
Sue's memory filled the other side of the bed, and
a threesome had never appealed to him.

He hadn't slept worth a damn. All night, images
of her and Quint Matthews invaded his sleep.
And his nightmares. Without opening his eyes, he
yawned and stretched and locked his hands behind his neck, thinking about how it had poleaxed
him when he walked into Kincaid's and saw his
ex-wife and that showoff jerk holding hands
across the table.

And she was wearing the bracelet he had
bought her in Albuquerque when she and Rocket
Man won the barrel-racing competition and set a
record. After the show, they and the horse had

celebrated by sharing a six-pack. He and Debbie Sue celebrated in private later that evening and set what they had laughingly called a record of their own.

Sex between them had always been white-hot. Neither divorce nor time had diminished the memory of her body, honed and firmed by a life-time of athletic activity, pressed against him. Her mouth—sweet as a ripe plum—kissing, biting, sucking . . . *Shit.*

How could a man ever get a woman as vibrant as Debbie Sue out of his system? They went so far back, all the way to when she was a raw-boned lit-tle girl of eleven in an oversized hat and he was fourteen and they had been in 4-H. He had never seen a girl so good at handling horses, something he considered then to be the exclusive bailiwick of boys. She'd had no fear of an unruly knothead and soon had him nuzzling her pocket for a chunk of carrot. When the other boys weren't around to hear, he found himself consulting her about how to deal with his own mare.

By the time she had reached fifteen and he was a senior, anybody could see beauty would be added to her spirited personality and go-getter attitude. The same boys who teased him about the crush she'd had on him for four years were envious of the friendship he had forged with her.

She was competing and placing in barrel races in high school rodeo. Virginia hauled her from show to show in an old pickup, pulling a rusty, beat-up one-horse trailer housing a too-old horse that didn't even belong to them. The bay belonged to a ranching family who said Debbie Sue could ride him in exchange for grooming and training.

Everyone who saw her performance said all she needed was a good horse and she would be a champion.

It just so happened Buddy had what he believed was a good horse. He had been cowboying for a rancher up out of Lubbock when he came across one of the ranch's brood mares in trouble while attempting to deliver. He stayed with the exhausted animal and helped her leggy, wobbly offspring make his appearance at four o'clock in the morning. The rancher, on hearing Buddy had saved the mare's life, made him a gift of the foal.

Debbie Sue had been foremost in his mind even then. He countered the rancher's offer with a request the grateful man didn't even hesitate to agree to. Instead of the foal, Buddy asked for the five-year-old paint gelding the rancher's daughter had used for barrel racing. The girl had lost interest in the sport and the horse, and left the animal to roam the pastures. The horse's smarts, quickness, and speed hadn't escaped Buddy, and he had long known nothing was worse than a good, smart horse with nothing to do. With the right rider, the paint had the makings of a champion, and Buddy knew the right rider.

As if it were yesterday, Buddy remembered approaching Debbie Sue with his predicament. He would be leaving in the fall for college. "Fixin' to be a Texas Ranger," he told her. Would she like to have the barrel horse for her own?

When Buddy took her to see the brown and white horse he had named Pete, it was love at first sight. She laughed and cried and hugged the horse, promised to sleep in the barn with him. She renamed him Rocket Man on the spot. Then she threw her arms around Buddy's neck and said, "Buddy Overstreet, I will love you forever."

He winced. Forever had turned out to be too damn short.

For him, survival kept getting in the way of college, not to mention his dreams, and his education turned into a hit-or-miss proposition, punctuated by cowboying on cattle ranches and roughnecking on drilling rigs. He stayed in touch with Debbie Sue, using Rocket Man as an excuse for phone calls and visits.

Then Quint Matthews entered the picture. Buddy didn't know him personally, but he knew his reputation. A comer in bull riding, he had a showy style and in the arena, wore loud-colored shirts and bright red chaps. The buckle bunnies always went for the bull riders, and Quint took full advantage of that fact. It had taken some doing to win Debbie Sue back from a guy like Quint, but Buddy, in his typical plodding fashion, had done it and never looked back.

The question he faced today was, did he want to do it again?

And if he did, what was he going to do with Kathy?

He threw off the covers and sprang from bed. He couldn't lie in bed any longer thinking about old times and new problems.

"Aarrgh." The sound echoed from the bathroom.

Debbie Sue opened one eye to blinding sunlight and scanned the room. She was in *her* bed, in *her* bedroom. Her Rockies were folded and hanging neatly across the back of a chair. *What the hell . . . ?* She ran her hand over the mattress beside her. She was alone. *Thank God.*

Before taking the risk of raising her head, she lay there piecing together the previous night's events. She remembered getting up to dance, then being led to a backseat. Why would she and Quint be crawling into a backseat when he had driven his classy Navigator? Gradually things began to unfurl—stopping in front of her house, being carried inside and laid on the bed, jeans and boots gingerly removed, covers tucked around her body and . . . Buddy? Had Buddy kissed her?

Ohmygod. She had been brought home from her first date in years by her ex-husband. She threw back the sheet and saw, to her relief, she was wearing panties and her T-shirt.

A string of expletives from the bathroom vibrated the walls. She swung her legs over the side of the bed and pushed to her feet. Something dark, and fuzzy as a tarantula, covered her eyes. Just before she screamed, she remembered the hairpiece Edwina had stuck in her hair.

She stumbled to the narrow hallway and saw Quint in the bathroom doorway, hanging on to the doorjamb as if he had been crucified. He was wearing his wrinkled shirt and boxers. His hair looked like it had been combed with a skillet. Both his knees were cut, bruised, and swollen.

"Oh my Lord, Quint. Do you want something for that swelling?"

"Normally that's a question I can't wait to hear a woman ask early in the morning."

"I'm sooo sorry."

"Hellfire, Debbie Sue. You're more dangerous than bull riding ever was. I think my back's broke."

"Where did you sleep?"

"I woke up in the bathtub." He stared down at the tub with bloodshot eyes.

Debbie Sue bit her lip. He had to be looking at the orange ring of mineral rust that made a narrow circle around the white enamel sides of the old tub. No cleanser would remove it. The only way to get rid of it was to do away with the tub, but on her list of priorities, a long way from the top was a new bathtub to replace one that was perfectly good except for a little rust. "It's clean," she blurted. "You know how West Texas water is."

He grimaced and grunted. "What the hell happened to my pants?"

"You mean we didn't get home with them?"

"Fuck. I had to cut 'em off me with my pocket knife so I could take a leak."

"What?" Debbie Sue glanced at the floor and saw the wrinkled wad of khaki cloth. She might not survive bending over, but she took a deep breath and went for it, retrieved the pants from the bathroom floor, saw the ragged edges where the zipper had been carved out of the fly. She looked around. On the edge of the sink lay the khaki zipper with all its teeth interlocked. She picked it up and looked closer. It was sealed shut with something hard and clear. She lifted it to her nose and sniffed.

Fingernail glue!

Dammit, Buddy, I just hate you.

While Quint showered, Debbie Sue threw on a robe and padded to the kitchen. With every step, a gong crashed in her head. Her stomach rolled. She knew a country song from years ago about Jose Cuervo being a friend, but she intended to kill the sonofabitch if she ever saw him again.

She rooted around in a catch-all cabinet drawer looking for a safety pin for Quint to use to close his pants. All she found was an empty tube of fingernail glue and a pink plastic clothespin. Going back to the bathroom and hearing the thrum of the shower, she eased the door open and placed the clothespin on the vanity. "Quint, I couldn't find a safety pin, but here's a clothespin."

His soaked head jutted past the edge of the shower curtain. "A clothespin?"

"It's all I could find." She gave him a weak smile.

He grunted.

She returned to the kitchen, glad he didn't appear to be interested in a morning session of sex. She certainly wasn't up to it. Besides, seeing Buddy with a date last night had soured her on men in general and sex maybe forever. She didn't have a clear memory of everything that had happened, but she distinctly remembered hearing Karen Something call Buddy sweetheart.

She set coffee on to drip, then opened the refrigerator. She stood there studying the contents and letting the cold air cool her body. The morning temperature had to be ninety again.

She had bought bacon and eggs and frozen biscuits for this morning's breakfast, intending to do the domestic routine and cook for Quint. She even bought a half gallon of orange juice with the outrageous notion she would use the bottle of champagne aging in her cabinet since New Year's and make mimosas for breakfast.

Now the very idea made her want to hurl. She reached for the half-gallon jug of Tropicana, unscrewed the lid, and drank deeply. The cold orange juice hit her stomach like one big ice block.

Quint came out of the bathroom, sweating and trembling, and wearing his wrinkled khakis with the fly held together by the pink clothespin. When she told him it looked like a tiny penis, he tried to cover it with his wrinkled shirttail. "Do me a favor," he said, "and don't use the words 'tiny' and 'penis' in the same sentence." When she asked him if he wanted an egg for breakfast, he glared at her, turned and rushed back to the bathroom.

She drank more orange juice and ate a piece of stale bread. Then she squeezed herself into a pair of Wranglers, threw on a yellow T-shirt, and put her hair up in a ponytail.

They left her house in her pickup, headed for Odessa and Quint's Navigator. She had been forced to dig out her darkest sunglasses to combat the blinding white sunlight and focus her eyes on the road. By the time they reached the city limits of Salt Lick, Quint, leaning against the passenger door, was sound asleep and snoring like a foghorn.

When they reached the Navigator, Debbie Sue was relieved to see the luxury SUV hadn't been vandalized while spending the night in Kincaid's vast, empty parking lot. Quint limped to the driver's door, mumbling as he fumbled for keys that he would call her, and drove away. No doubt she had seen the last of him. It was just as well. Maybe she didn't have what it took to tie herself to somebody for the sake of money.

That, and seeing Buddy escorting a woman, reinforced that she *had* to collect that reward from Harley, pay off the bank, shut down the Styling Station, and leave Salt Lick, Texas.

It was past noon when she arrived back in Salt Lick, and she was hungry as a weaned calf. *Mom.*

Her mom always had something good cooked and ready to eat. She stopped off at City Grocery & Market and picked up a Rocket Man treat.

When she reached her mom's, the paint met her at the fence corner. He shied away when she tried to give him a hug, showing his independence. But when she dragged out the Cheerios, he couldn't resist. "You are such a pushover," she told him as she fed him handfuls of Cheerios.

As soon as she walked through the front doorway of Mom's house, she smelled food.

I would have made a lousy mom. I don't even cook.

She found her mother at the cookstove, an apron covering her church clothes, and Debbie Sue felt a twinge of guilt. As a good Southern Baptist little girl, she had always gone to Sunday school and church and even vacation bible school in the summers. Another lifetime, another world.

"There was a prayer for the Carruthers family before the sermon today," her mother said.

"Really?

"The women's auxiliary posted a request for food for the dinner after the funeral service Monday. I signed you up for a meat loaf."

"Mom, no. The last meat loaf I made, even Rocket Man wouldn't eat."

"I remember. I'll make the meat loaf. Do you think Edwina will want to bring something?"

"I wouldn't count on Ed. Until Vic came along, she used her oven for extra shoe storage."

They sat down to fried pork chops, fried potatoes, fried okra, red beans simmered with chili powder and a big hunk of salt pork, and hot fresh cornbread and a tub of real butter. Debbie Sue made a mental groan. Only in West Texas were bacon drippings as common an ingredient as salt and pepper. Someday she intended to have a conversation with her mother about health food, but not today.

"I wish I had known you were coming out," her mom said. "I've got some lemons. I would've baked a pie." She started to rise from the table. "I could—"

"Mom, I don't even know if I can eat all this. Where would I put a pie?"

"Oh dear. Are you having your period?"

Debbie Sue dropped her forehead to the tabletop, letting the cool Formica surface ease the fire in her brain. "Mom, do you have an aspirin?"

Her mother hurried from the room and returned with a bottle of aspirin tablets. "Your problem is you work too hard and you're under too much stress. Dr. Phil says—"

"I know, Mom." Debbie Sue washed down two tablets with iced sweet tea. She did feel better after eating and broached the subject weighing on her mind. "Bet you can't guess who was in town last night."

"Quint Matthews."

Damn small towns. "How'd you know?"

"Sweetie, when a celebrity comes to town, everybody knows. What's he doing in Salt Lick?"

"Oh, you know. Checking out livestock. Counting his money . . . Asking me to go traveling with him."

Her mother's brow arched. "Traveling where?"

"Everywhere. He thinks I'd be an asset to his business, helping him pick horses for rodeo stock."

"Of course you would. The only person I can think of who's better with horses than you are is Buddy."

"Well, trust me. Buddy won't be offered the job."

"Humph. I suspect a horse buyer is not what Quinton Matthews is *really* after. I remember him."

Her mother would never forget Quint was the male who deflowered her teenage daughter or that Debbie Sue and he had spent a summer screwing like rabbits.

"Oh, Mom. That was a long time ago."

"A leopard doesn't change his spots. Rodeo cowboys are all the same, all the time. Even if they get rich."

"He was a kid, Mom. We were both kids."

"Don't forget, I knew his daddy. I would hate to see my only little girl involved with a Matthews."

"Mom, he's filthy rich. Can't you overlook a few character flaws?"

"What answer did you give him?"

"None, I don't think. I may never hear from him again. You won't believe what Buddy did." Debbie Sue repeated the previous night's events.

Her mom laughed so hard her eyes teared. "That Buddy. I knew he still loves you."

"He got me drunk and humiliated me in public."

"But that doesn't mean he doesn't love you. I wonder if I could work that story into a song."

"Don't you dare."

On Sunday evening Debbie Sue called Edwina and told her that out of respect for the Carruthers family, she wouldn't be opening the beauty salon on Monday.

"Oh, come on. Tell me the truth. Quint's still there, isn't he? And you can't talk. I saw the chemistry between you two. Yesterday was the first time I saw Buddy Overstreet as past tense in your life."

Chemistry. Honors chemistry. As she thought of Buddy's date, Debbie Sue's stomach rolled again. "I met Buddy's schoolteacher last night. She's a Yankee. She's an honors chemistry teacher. Teaches yoga at the college at night. And she speaks perfect fuckin' Spanish."

"What does she look like?"

"Remember Ramsey's fifteen-year-old son, Todd?"

"She looks like Todd Ramsey?"

"No, she looks like Todd's horse."

"Now, now. Buddy wouldn't date someone who looks like a horse. Were you nice? Did you make a good impression?"

"Let's just say I, er, *we*, made an impression.

Buddy and Quint had a real pissing contest, and I think Quint lost."

She told the parts of the Saturday night disaster she could remember, including the details she had refrained from telling her mother. When she said Quint had left her house wearing his battered Resistol, wrinkled clothes, with a clothespin holding his pants together, Ed screamed with laughter for a full minute.

"It's not funny, Ed. He didn't even kiss me good-bye."

"Fingernail glue? Hold on. I have to tell Vic." Edwina yelled away from the phone. "Vic, Buddy didn't want Debbie Sue screwing Quint Matthews, so he glued his pants shut with fingernail glue."

Debbie Sue heard Vic's deep, rich laugh in the background and stared at the ceiling. "Maybe you should yell that again, Ed. I don't know if all the neighbors heard it."

"I can't believe Buddy did that," Edwina gasped between guffaws. "You gotta love a man with a sense of humor."

"I still have the zipper. I think I'll hang it on the rearview mirror in my pickup."

"If you don't, I want to," Edwina said and broke into peals of laughter again.

"I hate to change the subject when you're having such a good time," Debbie Sue said, "but have you talked to C. J. lately?"

"I haven't seen her since she came in the shop Tuesday."

"I've called her twice to see if she wants to go with me to Pearl Ann's funeral, but she doesn't answer. I don't know where she keeps herself these days."

"Hmm. Guess we'll see her at the funeral."

Seven

 Buddy and his deputy arrived at Wilkins Funeral Home at nine o'clock Monday morning to escort Pearl Ann Carruthers's coffin to the Calvary Baptist Church. Already, no empty space could be had in the old rock church building's small parking lot. A couple of troopers from the state Department of Public Safety were on hand to help unsnarl traffic.

Buddy was disappointed to see so large a crowd gathered so early. He had wanted to be positioned in time to watch the mourners as they arrived. Now, so many had arrived before him, he was forced to stand at the back of the church.

There were too many unfamiliar faces to learn anything new anyway. The Carruthers family tentacles reached far and wide, and friends from everywhere had come to pay their respects. The curious, Buddy suspected, outnumbered the grief-stricken by an embarrassing ratio.

Though the September day was hot, most of the attendees were dressed up. Not much occurred in Salt Lick that called for putting on dress clothes, especially on a ninety-degree day, but a funeral was just such an occasion. Debbie Sue arrived alone and sat with her friend Carol Jean. She actually had on a dark green dress and high-heeled shoes, clothes she rarely wore.

Buddy liked seeing her in a dress. She had great legs and slim ankles. Her dress wasn't frilly with bushels of billowing fabric like the ones Kathy wore. Debbie Sue's was plain and form-fitting. That thick, long hair he loved to burrow his hands in was piled on top of her head with a pretty clip, and she was wearing the little emerald earrings he had bought her once because they reminded him of her eyes. She looked every inch the woman who still haunted his nights if he didn't grab control of his mind, which was exactly what he had to do now.

She didn't glance his way. He guessed if she hadn't hated him before, Saturday night should have been the clincher. What he had done to her and Quint had been childish, but all he could think of at the time was keeping that bull rider out of her bed.

The eulogy was short, delivered by a preacher who had never seen Pearl Ann in his church. Nevertheless, as they did for any Salt Lick citizen, the women of the church auxiliary served lunch after the service in the reception hall. Buddy put in a cursory appearance.

Afterward he returned to his office in front of the jail and waited. The Midland CSI team had returned Pearl Ann's personal effects in a large manila envelope. Harley was due in to pick them up, and Buddy had questions for him.

The widowed man appeared on time, wearing a dress shirt and slacks and a loose tie. He hadn't changed clothes since the funeral. He looked pale and grim. Distress lines set off his mouth. At this moment he was Buddy's number one suspect. Hell, he was the *only* suspect.

Buddy dumped the manila envelope's contents onto the desk, and Harley sorted through the evidence of a well-heeled victim—a leather purse and matching wallet with fancy initials printed all over it. Driver's license. Credit cards from upscale stores. Three hundred dollars in cash. In addition, there was a diamond-faced Presidential Rolex watch, a diamond tennis bracelet, a wedding ring holding a diamond the size of a marble, a diamond and ruby cocktail ring, and gold and diamond hoop earrings. Robbery was obviously not the motive.

"Everything there?" Buddy asked.

Harley shuffled through the dozen or so credit cards. "I didn't even know she had all these." He turned his attention to the jewelry pieces and moved them around on the desk. "Best I can tell, it's all here. I didn't see her Monday evening, so I don't know what she was wearing. Nothing seems to be missing at home."

He picked up the tennis bracelet and studied it a few seconds. "Wait a minute. Was there a gold bracelet, with a charm on it? One of those cheap Texas things, had a diamond chip?"

Buddy assumed the forensics bunch had gone over the car's interior thoroughly. He shook his head, making a mental note to drive out to the landfill and look around. Even with crime scene tape stretched around where the car had been parked, so many people would have tramped through the site by now, his searching for a bracelet probably would be a waste of time, but he felt obligated to do it. "Guess they didn't find it. I'll take another look."

Harley walked over to the window, stuffed his hands into his pockets. "Are you going to call in some help on this?"

Buddy stayed in his seat, ignoring the slap at his ability to do the job to which he had been elected and wishing he could see Harley's face. "Before you start asking *me* questions, Harley, I've got a few for *you*."

The millionaire turned back, his expression startled. "Me?"

"You weren't home Monday night? When did you see Pearl Ann last?"

"Early Monday. She was still asleep when I left the house. I went to the Midland office. I came back when they called me Tuesday."

"Can anybody vouch for that?"

"I was at the condo. You know, the one I keep in Midland."

Buddy did know. He had been in the luxury condo. Harley had kept it for years to avoid the sixty-mile daily commute between Midland and Salt Lick. None of the Carruthers clan actually lived in Midland, even though their company offices were there.

Harley dragged a hand through his hair and looked at Buddy from under an arched brow. "I wasn't alone if that's what you're asking."

"That's part of what I'm asking. I'm gonna need your companion's name."

"No can do, my friend. It wouldn't matter anyway. She doesn't have anything to do with this."

"It's not her I'm asking about. She's not the one who needs an alibi . . . Or is she?"

"Goddammit, Buddy, just cool it." Harley strode back to the front of the desk and jabbed his finger on the desktop. "You've known me forever. You know I didn't do any harm to Pearl Ann. Jesus Christ, she did what she damn well pleased. Had everything money could buy."

"Simmer down, Harley. Who do you think *would* harm your wife?"

Harley laughed bitterly. "A better question is who wouldn't." His head tilted back, and he closed his eyes. "There were so damn many. I didn't even care enough to keep up with them anymore."

Buddy stood up and began to place Pearl Ann's baubles back into the manila envelope. "You might as well take this stuff on home. Give the matter some thought, 'cause I'm still gonna need that name."

As Harley left the office, Buddy stared after him, his mind traveling back to their school days. Buddy had been an athlete, played on Salt Lick's football team. Harley had been small and clumsy, a wannabe who mostly got in everybody's way and was the brunt of cruel jokes behind his back. The kids who hung out with him did so because he always had money to spend. The true poor little rich kid.

Feeling sorry for the way the jocks snubbed Harley, Buddy had been one of the few who tried to befriend him. Until the day the wealthy oil-man's son left home for college at A&M, he had hung on to the association with Buddy.

As was traditional, Harley, upon graduating from Texas A&M, took over the family's oil and gas business and managed it with ruthless finesse. He might be a "good ol' boy" who drank and caroused with the best of them, but no one laughed behind Harley Carruthers's back now. And they wouldn't dare laugh to his face.

These days, he and Buddy had so little in common, their relationship had to be defined as one of mutual respect more than friendship. But there was a connection nevertheless. Buddy's gut told him Harley hadn't murdered his wife, but who was the man protecting?

Buddy donned his hat and headed for the Tahoe. He might as well look for that gold bracelet with a Texas charm.

Approaching the landfill, even from a distance, he recognized a familiar red Silverado. "Dammit," he muttered.

He climbed up the dirt mound surrounding the landfill and looked down. The crime scene tape had been torn askew. Since the announcement that Harley intended to pay a fat reward, people had milled through the dump like cattle. Gawkers, busybodies, ghouls. Keeping the scene pristine had been impossible.

And standing right where the Cadillac had been parked, despite the warnings written on the yellow tape, he saw Debbie Sue and Edwina. They had no idea he was near. He blew out a long breath, then dug in his heels and hiked down. "What in the hell are you doing here, Debbie Sue?"

His ex-wife turned toward him. Her pointed chin hoisted. "Nothing. I'm just looking."

He gripped both her and Ed's upper arms and half walked, half ran them beyond the sagging crime scene tape. "You have no business behind this tape."

"Ow, ow," Debbie Sue said. "Who do you think you're manhandling? Get your hands off."

"This is a crime scene."

"Big deal. A heck of a lot of people were here before we got here. I'm investigating. I'm fixin' to collect the reward Harley put up."

"Debbie Sue, this is serious. It's murder, forgodsake."

Her eyes began to shimmer. *Tears?* "Please, Buddy. I have to. I need that money."

He had never been able to stay angry when she cried. He preferred her cussin' and spittin' and kickin' any day. He guided her and Edwina around the toe of the hill, to the Tahoe. He sat Debbie Sue, now engaged in all out weeping, down on the passenger seat and squatted in front of her. "Tell me the big financial emergency. What's happened?"

"I'm tired of slaving for the bank. I don't have a life. I work six days a week. I'll be an old woman by the time I get out of debt."

He reached back for his handkerchief and dabbed her eyes. "Everybody's in debt, Flash."

"It's more than the debt. I don't know if the shop's gonna make it. I can't lose the shop. I can't have another failure."

He pulled her to her feet and into his arms, rubbed her spine with his fingers. "You've never failed at anything, and I doubt if you're gonna fail at that beauty shop, either."

She wailed louder. He looked across her head at Edwina, pleading for help with his eyes.

Edwina stood there with a cigarette cocked between the fingers of one hand and the opposite fist planted on her hip. "It's been a tough week."

He set Debbie Sue away, wiped her eyes, and stuck his handkerchief under her nose. "Blow," he ordered, and she did. "Now you two listen to me." He stuffed his handkerchief back in his rear pocket. "I want you to stay out of this. You could do more harm than good. There's not a chance in hell you're fixin' to collect that reward. You could even end up like Pearl Ann. And I don't want to have to worry about you."

"We'll behave. We promise." Edwina dropped her cigarette into the sand and ground it out with her shoe. She reached for Debbie Sue's arm and coaxed her away from Buddy. "C'mon Debbie Sue. We've got fish to fry."

Buddy wasn't sure if he should take her last remark as a positive or a warning of things to come. The two women returned to the red Silverado with sobs still hitching from Debbie Sue's throat. Buddy watched them leave, a plume of white caliche dust spewing behind the pickup. God, what was he gonna do with the mess of feelings Debbie Sue aroused in him? He already knew he couldn't live with her, but living without had turned out to be just as hard.

He hadn't had his arms around her in over three years, had forced from his mind just how damn good he felt when he held her and when she acted like she needed him. She wasn't the type to cry over just any ol' thing. There had to be a lot of emotions running deep for her to show tears. She had always been so strong and independent, the very characteristics that made her both a pain in the ass and an irresistible partner.

He knew about her debt. Even after he had sold his scanty cow herd, his six horses, and the land he had made payments on for years to help her meet the expense for the service station cleanup, she had, against his advice, borrowed to the max.

Debbie Sue had never done anything half-assed. She had been determined to turn the sixty-five-year-old albatross into something profitable. He admired the effort and time she put into the task. Every time he drove past the beauty shop she was there, working. Her competitor opened only four days a week. Not to be outdone, Debbie Sue opted for a six-day week, taking Sunday as her only day of rest. No wonder she was emotional. She had to be exhausted.

If she was desperate enough to consider something as crazy as going after Pearl Ann's killer, would she consider attaching herself to someone as rich as Quint Matthews? The thought was unsettling, but quickly dismissed. *I know Debbie Sue*, Buddy told himself. Now that she was grown, she would never take up with somebody as shallow and egotistical as Quint.

"I know Debbie Sue," he repeated aloud. "I know Debbie Sue."

Each time he said it, the conviction seemed to dwindle.

* * *

Debbie Sue slashed away tears with the back of her hand. "I need your help, Ed."

"You know you've got it. What are we up to now?"

"Regardless of what Wyatt Earp says, we're fixin' to solve this crime. We can split the reward money. With twenty-five thousand dollars, I'll be able to pay down the loan on the shop. I can get the bank to lower the payment to an amount I can live with."

From the corner of her eye, Debbie Sue saw her pal shake her head. "I don't know, Debbie Sue. Buddy said—"

"Ed, it's more than the money. It's a matter of principle. He talked *down* to me, like I don't have good sense."

"Baby doll, sometimes you're your own worst enemy. Maybe you oughtta think about things."

"What ought I think about?"

"Buddy was awful nice to you just now. And what he said wasn't unreasonable."

Debbie Sue braked to a skidding stop as they reached the intersection with the highway. "Nice? He treated me like I'm ten years old. His concern is I might solve the crime and tarnish his image. And with a scratch on the great Buddy Overstreet's saddle, he might not get hired by the DPS."

"Hmm," Edwina said. "That's not the way I see it. He showed real concern. Besides, what do we know about solving a crime?"

Debbie Sue pulled onto the highway and barreled toward the Salt Lick city limits. "I already know more about this case than he does. If I tell you something, will you promise not to lecture me? And more important, promise you won't tell anyone, and I do mean *anyone*."

"I promise I won't lecture and I promise to keep this to myself. Now, is this the part where we cut our fingers and mix our blood?"

"Dammit, Ed, I need you to be serious about this."

"Sorry, hon. I can't help trying to turn a serious moment into something light. Dysfunctional upbringing, you know? Why don't you pull into Hogg's so I can get a Dr. Pepper and have a smoke."

"I'm fixin' to buy you nicotine patches for Christmas, Ed."

Debbie Sue wouldn't allow smoking in her pickup, but she knew Edwina's addiction. She careened into Hogg's Drive-In, barely missing the pink "Elvis Ate Here" sign out front.

No one of the current generation of Salt Lick citizens knew if Elvis had really eaten at Hogg's or what a rock-and-roll icon might have been doing in such a tiny, remote town in West Texas, but in honor of "The King," Barr Hogg kept the drive-in painted a vivid pink trimmed in black and had a jukebox that played *all* of Elvis's songs. Besides old-fashioned malts and milk shakes and other fattening treats, he served a unique array of hamburgers to consumers who drove from a hundred miles away to eat them. So maybe Elvis really *had* eaten there. Stranger things had happened.

Debbie Sue stopped at the drive-up window and ordered two Dr. Peppers, then drove to Salt Lick's community center where the city used precious water to keep a small lawn green. It was the closest thing to a park Salt Lick had. They left the Silverado and sat down at the one concrete table huddled under a spindly elm tree.

Edwina lit up, took a long draw from first her cigarette, then her Dr. Pepper. "Go ahead. I'm listening."

For the first time, Debbie Sue repeated the story Pearl Ann had told her about hiding money from Harley. Since Pearl Ann had gone to the great honky-tonk beyond, Debbie Sue figured an oath of secrecy no longer mattered.

"And all this time I thought she was dumb as a rock," Edwina said, shaking her head. "Where did she put the money?"

"That I don't know, but I know who does."

"You do?"

"Think about it. This is money only two people knew the whereabouts of, and one of them is dead."

Edwina's jaw dropped as realization struck her. "The accountant."

"Bingo."

"We gotta tell Buddy."

"Forget that. Don't you dare tell him. Or *anybody*. The reward is a big temptation, really big, but that's not all that's stuck in my craw." Debbie Sue stood up and began to pace around the concrete table. "Ever since I saw that woman with Buddy I've been thinking about how accomplished she is. She's college educated, she speaks several foreign languages, she teaches *advanced* classes and even knows how to do yoga, which takes concentration and self-discipline. Hell, I can't even spell self-discipline."

Edwina glared across her shoulder. "Don't you think you're being a little hard on yourself? Don't take this as an insult, but you were a professional barrel racer. You trained yourself and your horse to be champions in a tough, competitive business. You won money. You broke records."

"What's riding a horse around three barrels? Good Lord, Ed, a well-trained horse can do it by himself."

"Maybe so, but somebody has to teach him how."

"Even little kids can barrel race, Ed. I can't stand to have Buddy think a schoolteacher from Chicago is a step up from me."

"And how does solving this murder and collecting the reward change any of that? Not that I believe Buddy would ever think of you as a step down from anything or anyone."

"It would prove I'm no dingbat small-town nobody. It would prove a lot *to me*." Debbie Sue patted her chest with her palm. "I need to know I can start something and finish it. I need to feel like I've accomplished something besides having my husband divorce me and going bankrupt in a beauty shop. Until now, I've never felt ashamed of myself, and I hate it."

Edwina let out a gusty sigh and lit another cigarette. "So what are you planning? You and me going out chasing killers?"

"No. You and me are fixin' to go see that accountant."

"Hooo-ly shit! How do we find out who he is?"

"You've been sniffing too much spray net, Ed. Think. Who do we know who works for Carruthers Oil & Gas Company?

"Ohmygod." Edwina banged her forehead with the heel of her hand. "C. J."

"I don't want her to get suspicious though. We're going to have to be careful how we go about getting information from her."

"That'll be a trip you don't have to pack for. C. J.'s the most accommodating person I've ever met. She would've given Santa Anna the keys to the Alamo."

"If I recall seventh-grade history, I don't think he needed them. Anyway, that little personality quirk is why we can't let her in on what we're doing, which means we have to keep it a secret from *everyone*. Can you keep it from Vic?"

"You know I tell him everything, but I can try. But I won't lie to him, Debbie Sue. That's the quickest way to ruin a relationship. One lie leads to another, and before you know it your tongue's all tangled up."

Debbie Sue dropped back to the concrete seat at the table. "You know so much, Ed. You should put some of that wisdom to work for you. You should write one of those self-help books on relationships."

"Yeah, right. Everybody wants to read how a forty-five-year-old three time loser at marriage holds a relationship together."

"Is writing a book any more far-fetched than us finding Pearl Ann's killer?"

"I guess not. My downfall's always been not recognizing far-fetched when I see it."

Debbie Sue frowned and bit down on her bottom lip. "That's something we both could work on."

The drive back to the Styling Station was quiet. Debbie Sue couldn't stop thinking about how good it had felt to be in Buddy's arms. It was embarrassing she had cried and become so emotional in front of him. She had always prided herself on being strong and stoic, but it had seemed that everything came crashing down at that moment. Her debt, seeing him with a girlfriend, being in the place where Pearl Ann had died.

Buddy's girlfriend. He had moved on. Debbie Sue knew he had gone on a binge of women and sex after their divorce, but she excused him for that. He had been as lost as she. But having *one* girlfriend to whom he was loyal and with whom everyone associated him had to mean he was serious.

She had to move on, too. Somehow, like it or not, she had to move on, too.

But how?

* * *

Twenty-five-thousand dollars. Edwina couldn't wrap her mind around that much money. She dug in her purse and came up with a grocery store receipt and an eyebrow pencil. Scribbling figures, she calculated that if she put back a dollar bill a day, it would take over sixty-eight years to save twenty-five-thousand dollars.

Sixty-eight years. Motherofgod. The realization surged in her mind like a geyser. The reward took on new meaning. Good idea or not, she was now fully engaged in a new game, and the name of it was "Let's Spend the Money."

It would be nice to do something for her three daughters. Lord knew, there were more years than not when she hadn't been able to do anything but put three meals—*most of the time* three meals—on the table. Between sorry husbands, she had worked sorry jobs for even sorrier wages.

Billie Pat, Jimmie Sue, and Roberta Jean were the products of three separate unions. She had given them their respective fathers' names, and the men had given them little to nothing. Yet somehow all three had become well-adjusted, responsible women. They had met and married men who were good husbands and enjoyed productive lives. What more could a mother ask for?

How about three daughters who get really terrific souvenirs from their mother's trip to Barbados? *Now you're talkin'.* She and Vic had spent many nights talking about places they wanted to go and things they wanted to see. He had spent time there, tracking down bad guys. He spoke often about going back as a civilian.

Okay, that settles it. After everything Vic had done for her, the least she could do for him was to take him back to his beautiful island retreat. As a civilian. As a *first-class* civilian.

She would help Debbie Sue solve the mystery of Pearl Ann Carruthers's death and reap her half of the reward.

Eight

 A week had passed since the biggest funeral ever held in Salt Lick. Other than register in her brain every miniscule crumb of gossip she heard in the salon about Pearl Ann and Harley, Debbie Sue had done nothing toward solving the murder mystery. Well, not exactly nothing. She *had* watched or taped every episode of *CSI, NYPD Blue, Cops,* and all the *Law & Order* hybrids and studied the investigating techniques of the various TV detectives. She paid particular attention to the guilty characters and zeroed in on their mannerisms.

Buddy was outpacing her. Salon patrons reported daily on his investigative activities. With a badge and access to official reports, *he* had an overwhelming advantage.

Unidentified fingerprints had been found in Pearl Ann's car. When Buddy's deputy's wife came in for a trim, she revealed that the gun that killed

Pearl Ann had been her own. *Yikes!* How awful was that, being murdered with your own gun?

Buddy had questioned two dozen people, including all the hired help out at the Carruthers ranch. He had asked Harley to take a lie detector test with the Odessa police polygraphist, but Harley's lawyer had squelched that. Instead, Harley would hire his own technician. Salt Lick citizens awaited the results with held breaths.

Buddy was right about one thing. This was serious. If someone killed once, wouldn't he or, ohmygod, *she*, be likely to kill again if someone came close to discovering his or her identity? The ability to jump on a horse and gallop to safety didn't feel nearly as comforting as it had looked when Dale was helping Roy. Debbie Sue wished she had taken that Tae Kwon Do class when she lived in Lubbock.

Friday morning she decided she was as ready to begin as she would ever be. "It's time we did something," she told Edwina. Her sleuthing partner gave her a thumbs-up, and Debbie Sue called C. J. at work. "Hey, kid, where you been hiding? Ed and I were just talking about you. We haven't seen you in nearly two weeks. What's up?"

"Oh, Debbie Sue, it's so good to hear your voice. I've been trying to find the time to stop by the shop and I've been meaning to call, but crazy doesn't come close to describing the way things have been around here since . . . well, you know."

"I can only imagine. The whole thing seems like

a nightmare, doesn't it? Listen, Vic's on the road, so Ed's coming over to my house tonight after work for happy hour. I'm mixing a pitcher of killer margaritas." Debbie Sue laughed. "Killer, get it? We'll throw some burgers on the grill and kick back. You up for that?"

"Margaritas sound wonderful. I'll bring the rum."

Rum? Debbie Sue grinned. She had really missed C. J. "No, that's okay, sweetie. I've got a half gallon of tequila, and Ed's bringing the meat. See you around seven."

At the notion of interrogating a friend who was under the influence of tequila, Debbie Sue felt a twinge of guilt, but only a twinge. She didn't dare tell C. J. any of the plans she and Edwina had made. C. J. was loyal and trustworthy, but she blurted secrets without even knowing she did it.

By six-thirty Debbie Sue had donned cutoffs and a halter top and done the domestic thing—peeled off lettuce leaves, sliced onions, tomatoes, and cheese, and had them waiting under plastic wrap in the fridge. After dumping potato chips into a large wooden bowl, she walked outside to start the fire in the grill. Even with the house shadowing the eight-by-ten-foot concrete patio off the dining room, the ninety-plus temperature still had the whole backyard sizzling. Hell, it would probably be easier to just fry the meat on the patio's concrete.

The phone warbled. Probably Ed calling to ask if she needed to bring anything besides the hamburger meat. Debbie Sue picked up and cradled the receiver under her chin while she used both hands to squeeze another stream of fire starter onto the coals. "I had to start without you, but I can keep it hot 'til you get here."

"Darlin', I'm gonna call you for the rest of my life just to hear what you say when you answer the phone."

Fuck. She had to learn to check that damn caller ID. "Quint Matthews. I didn't realize it was you."

"Now don't go disappointing me."

"Are you in town?"

"I'm in Seguin at the ranch. I've been thinking about our last evening together. I'll say one thing for you, darlin', you certainly know how to keep a man guessing." He laughed. At least he was a good sport. "You know, I come across a lot better when the ex-husband doesn't show up and when my zipper's working."

She chuckled, too. "Well, I've come across a little bit better myself."

"I know. I haven't forgotten Vegas."

Debbie Sue felt a sudden flash as hot as the coals in the barbecue grill. She hadn't forgotten, either. "How are your knees? Were they badly hurt?"

"Nah, I've had worse injuries. Not as embarrassing, but worse. Listen, I've got to take a look at some calves up in Andrews in a couple of weeks. October fifth. How about I pick you up at your house, say seven o'clock two weeks from tomorrow night? We can finish our conversation. But let's find a one-story eating joint where we won't run into your ex-husband."

Debbie Sue chewed on her lip, deciding what to do. The Saturday night at Kincaid's hadn't been fair to Quint or her, either. He had always been a lot of fun, and she couldn't complain about him as a lover. And there *was* all that money, with which he was generous. "That sounds great. Two weeks from tomorrow, seven o'clock. I'm really glad you called."

Edwina arrived with the hamburger patties shaped and ready to cook and took over the barbecue grill. Debbie Sue made a pitcher of margaritas, carried it outside to the patio, and relayed the news about the pending date with Quint.

"Good, I'm glad," Edwina said. "I can't wait to hear what happens next."

"Hellooo." C.J.'s voice came from the front doorway.

"We're in the backyard," Debbie Sue yelled, "soaking up the heat."

The three friends went through their usual routine of hugs, kisses, and comments on clothes and hair and how good each one looked, as if months instead of two weeks had passed since they had seen each other. C. J. wore capri pants and a tube top that would have fit a Barbie doll. Debbie Sue noticed glittery studs bigger than pencil erasers stuck in her earlobes. "Hey, kid. New earrings. CZs, huh?"

"Uh, yeah," C. J. tittered. "Who can afford diamonds on *my* pay?"

Debbie Sue told C. J. of the disastrous date with Quint and the blond friend laughed until she cried. When Debbie Sue produced Quint's ragged and glued zipper, the three of them collapsed in laughter.

Edwina removed the cooked patties from the grill and Debbie Sue refilled C. J.'s glass. After gorging on hamburgers and gossip and plying C. J. with four margaritas, Debbie Sue felt the time was right. "So C. J., I was floored when Harley put up a fifty-thousand-dollar reward. I can't even imagine that kind of money. I knew the Carruthers were rich, but wow."

A loose spiral curl hung between the tipsy blond's eyes. She flopped one wrist. "Oh, rich isn't even the word. I'm surprised he didn't put up more."

"Any nibbles on that bait?" Edwina refilled C. J.'s glass with one more margarita.

"Not a one. One of the accountants assigned to handle the reward fund thought it would bring informs . . . informers, uh, ants out of the woodwork, but no one yet."

Uh-oh. C. J. was getting too snockered to talk. "One of the accountants? Just how many accountants does Harley have?" Debbie Sue shot a look at Edwina, who was holding her Bic lighter suspended beneath her cigarette.

"There's a dozen." C. J. began to list them on her

fingers. "One for land, one for oil, one for investments. Harley doesn't want to give the responsibility to just one or two. He says he doesn't want his whole empire crashing because one guy decides to make a career move."

"That Harley. Shrewd dude. No wonder he's rich."

"I don't think he's rich 'cause he's sssrude," C. J. slurred and leaned forward. "I think," she whispered, "it's 'cause his daddy gave him a lot of money."

"Hell of an allowance," Edwina put in, and the three of them cackled in unison.

"Pearl Ann told me once she didn't know a thing about the family business," Debbie Sue said.

"Guess it would have been tough screwing her way through a dozen accountants," Edwina cracked and they cackled again.

"Oh, Pearl Ann didn't have to do it with a bunch of accountants," C. J. said, sloshing her drink over the back of her hand, then licking away the wetness. "She had her own personal one. Harley wouldn't even dish . . . disscuss money with her. He just told her to see Eugene."

"No kidding? I'm betting Pearl Ann convinced Eugene to up the ante, if you know what I mean." Edwina's perfectly tweezed and shaped black eyebrows bobbed up and down.

"You mean sex? With Eugene?" C. J. giggled and held out her glass for a refill. Debbie Sue complied.

"You wouldn't think about Pearl Ann with Eugene if you saw him." C. J. sipped and licked her lips. "He's short as me and skinny. He has a comb-over that starts just a little above his right ear." C. J.'s finger pointed at her left temple. "His glasses look like bottle bottoms and he's chewed his fingernails to the nubs. I think his only intres' iss—iss hiss numbers." C. J. frowned, then giggled again. "Besides, he's swish . . . swissy. Naw, Eugene was safe from Pearl Ann."

"Are the accountants in the same building you work in?"

"Yeah, but different floors. I'm on two. They're on four, five and six. Hey, why don't y'all come see me sometime. We could do lunsh."

"Maybe we will," Debbie Sue said. "It's hard to get out of town when you work six days a week, but maybe we'll just mosey up there for lunch someday."

Debbie Sue excused herself, walked back into the kitchen and the notepad by the phone. "Eugene. Floors four through six. Short, comb-over, swishy nerd."

She returned to the patio, stepping into the middle of a conversation between C. J. and Edwina. C. J.'s eyes were round as marbles. "You mean you can do that with your mouth?"

Debbie Sue relaxed. For a split second she had feared Edwina had spilled the beans, but after C. J.'s comment, she knew her sleuthing partner was only lecturing on sex, which she was prone to do after she passed her margarita limit. Edwina the sex expert had the floor and the evening went forward without another word on the Carrutherses.

On Monday Debbie Sue canceled all appointments and hung a sign on the salon's front door. "Closed for Inventory." She drove to Edwina's trailer, twisting the radio knob until she found tolerable music—Merle Haggard singing about prison walls. She hoped Merle wasn't trying to tell her something.

Once Edwina was seated in the Silverado, Debbie Sue looked over at her and grinned. "Of all the adventures we've had, Ed, this may be the best."

"And if it's not," Edwina drawled, "it damn sure should be in the top ten. I just hope we haven't bit off more than we can chew. And I hope Buddy doesn't find out we're doing this."

"How would he find out? And what if he does? We have a right to go for the reward money."

"I know, but it makes me nervous. He told us to keep our noses clean."

"Look, we've already gone over it. Everything's perfect. This Eugene whatever-his-last-name-is had the perfect motive to murder Pearl Ann. Money. Green greed. The root of all evil. The path to destruction."

"Okay, now you're scaring me. You sound like the Baptist preacher."

"Sorry. I'm a little nervous, too. The thought of that reward money makes me crazy. What are you gonna do with your half?"

"I'm praying I don't have to use it for bail or a lawyer. If I get past that, I'm planning on a long romantic vacation for me and Vic."

Debbie Sue entered the Midland city limits and began looking for a pizza joint. She spotted a neon pizza whirling on the palm of an animated Italian chef. She stopped and ordered a large pepperoni. Twenty minutes later she walked out with the box.

"Lor-deee, that smells good," Edwina said. "I didn't think I was hungry until now. Let me just take a little peekie-poo."

Debbie Sue slapped a hand on the top of the box. "Oh no you don't. We don't touch the pizza, got it? Now start getting ready."

Edwina reached into a brown paper grocery sack she had placed on the seat between her and Debbie Sue and pulled out a bright orange shirt with "Pizza Slut" screen-printed in black across the back.

"Wait a minute," Debbie Sue said, spotting the back of the shirt. "What is this? I thought you said you had an old pizza delivery shirt?"

"This is it. What's the problem?"

"Pizza *Slut*? Where were you wearing this, a red-light district somewhere?"

"It's part of a Halloween costume. I don't think anyone'll notice. Have a little faith in me, sugar."

"You're right, Ed. No one will notice a skinny, five-foot-ten woman with a coal black beehive, cat-eye glasses, and leopard stretch pants. Especially if she's wearing three-inch wooden platforms and a shirt that says 'Pizza Slut'. I'm feeling better already." Debbie Sue sighed and shook her head. "It's too late to worry about it now. Here's the building."

She turned into the visitors' parking lot of the Carruthers Oil & Gas Company, a six-story building of reflective glass glittering in the sun. She looked one last time at Ed. "Okay, old friend, this is it. Are you ready?"

"Does a fifty-pound sack of flour make a big biscuit?" Edwina scooted out of the pickup, dug a crumpled pack of Marlboro Lights from her purse, pried out a bent cigarette, and lit up.

"Edwina! What are you doing?"

"I'm smoking, dammit. You won't let me smoke in the pickup."

Debbie Sue gasped and swung out the driver's door. "Well, hurry up. Someone may see us."

"Okay, okay." Edwina clamped the cigarette filter between her teeth and reached into the pickup cab for the pizza.

"Edwina, put that cigarette out."

"What, you want me to drop it right here, on this nice, clean concrete?" She tottered toward a butts receptacle outside the building entrance, balancing the pizza on one hand. Debbie Sue held her breath until Edwina dropped the cigarette into the receptacle, then the two of them passed through the wide entrance.

They stopped in front of stainless-steel elevator doors. "You know, Ed, we really should take the stairs. Someone we know could see us on this elevator."

Edwina stared down at her high-heeled shoes. "Are you out of your mind?"

"I keep telling you to quit smoking."

"Godalmighty." Edwina held up one foot and thrust it forward. "Even if I quit, I couldn't climb six flights of stairs in these shoes."

"Okay, okay. We'll take the elevator. We'll start at the top and work our way down. I've never liked starting at the bottom."

Debbie Sue kept her fingers crossed there would be a reception area. When they exited the elevator they found themselves peering across the hallway into a glass-fronted office suite where they could see burgundy high-backed chairs lining the walls and long, low-slung tables with magazines and elaborate floral centerpieces. A mahogany desk the size of a four-horse trailer was parked in the middle of the room, and a young woman sat behind it, staring intently at a blue computer screen.

"Okay, Ed, when you see me sit down and pick up a magazine, you come in with the pizza."

Edwina nodded.

On a deep breath, Debbie Sue opened the door.

"Good afternoon, may I help you?" The receptionist smiled, overfriendly. Even so, she succeeded in making Debbie Sue feel as if she had tracked manure onto the pearl gray carpeting. The scent in the air was woodsy potpourri, but Debbie Sue smelled money.

"I'm supposed to meet someone here, but I'm a little early. Do you mind if I just have a seat and wait?"

"No, not at all. May I offer you some coffee or other beverage?"

"No, thanks. I shouldn't be here that long." Debbie Sue picked up a *Newsweek* and began flipping through the pages.

When Edwina entered carrying the pizza box, the receptionist robotically looked up and smiled. "Good afternoon, may I help you?"

"I hope so," Edwina said between gum smacks. "I got a pizza for Eugene. The kid working the phones didn't get a last name."

"I'm sorry. We don't have a Eugene on this floor. Could that be the last name? We do have a Juan Eugenio. Let me call him."

The receptionist made a move to pick up the phone, but Edwina stopped her. "No, no, it was definitely a first name. I'll just try the other floors."

"Nonsense. Let me make just one call." French-manicured fingers lifted the receiver. "Hi, Carol Jean."

Debbie Sue's heart stuttered and Pizza Slut threw her a bug-eyed stare. Rapid-fire gum smacks carried all the way across the room.

"Someone's here looking for an employee

named Eugene," the receptionist was saying into the phone, "but she doesn't have a last name. Do you have the company directory in front of you? . . . No, you don't have to bring it to me. I've got a copy, but someone borrowed it . . . okay . . . un-huh, yes I have it, thanks." She hung up and smiled at Edwina. "You're in luck. There are only two Eugenes in the building. One on five, Eugene Thomas, and one on four, Eugene Grubbs."

"Thanks, hon, I really appreciate it." Edwina turned and breezed out as if she were wearing skates.

Debbie Sue stood up. "I think I'll go call the person I was going to meet. Thanks for everything."

She made for the door before the receptionist could offer to help her make the call. She found Edwina waiting in the hall, the pizza box braced against her hip.

"I thought I was gonna die, Debbie Sue. What if C. J. had come in? We didn't discuss that little detail."

"You're right. That was a close call. We'll take the stairs to five. You can make it. It's downhill."

Edwina's wooden heels clanged and echoed every step down the steel stairs until they reached the fifth floor. "I hope nobody heard us," she said.

Debbie Sue gave her a wry look. "I hope you remember the names."

"Hell, no, I don't. I'm concentrating on not losing my bladder." The same scene, minus the call to C. J., replayed on the fifth floor. Robotic receptionist, extremely helpful, informing Pizza Slut that Eugene Thomas had called in sick and wasn't available.

By the time they tramped to the fourth floor, Edwina's nervousness and impatience had tripled, a condition Debbie Sue had seen degenerate into disaster more than once. But it was too late to back out. She rejected the receptionist's syrupy friendliness again—apparently Carruthers Oil & Gas employed the Stepford Wives—and took a seat in the reception area. She held her breath as Edwina entered.

"Good afternoon, may I—"

"Help me?" Edwina dropped the pizza box on the receptionist's desk and bent forward, her palms on her knees as she heaved for breath. "Yeah, do me a favor, sugar. Tell Eugene his pizza's here."

Oh dear. Not only had Edwina run out of air, she had definitely lost some of her motivation for the required theatrics.

"Eugene?"

"Eugene Whoever. Don't you have a Eugene on this floor?"

With a puzzled expression, the receptionist picked up the phone. "Mr. Grubbs, there's a delivery person here from"—she waited while Edwina straightened and turned her back—"from, uh, Pizza . . . Pizza Slut? . . . Yes, maybe you should, sir. Thank you." She hung up, and the cheery demeanor returned. "He'll be right with you. Say, are you one of those singing messengers? You know, like they have for birthdays?"

Edwina shot her a wilting look. "Oh that's just part of my act. Wait 'til you catch my tap dance."

Before the conversation could turn into a scene, Mr. Comb-Over came out of a hallway to their right. "I'm Eugene Grubbs. May I help you?"

"Godalmighty," Edwina said, "you people are polite."

Debbie Sue mouthed for her to shut up.

Eugene was just as C. J. had described him. Short, skinny, thick glasses, but C. J. had failed to mention Eugene had a face so handsome, he could be called pretty.

"Here's your pizza." Edwina picked up the pizza box and shoved it toward him. Reflexively his hands came out and took it. "That'll be fourteen bucks," she told him.

"But—but I didn't order a pizza. There must be a mistake."

"All I know is some guy named Eugene at this address ordered a pizza and this is the third floor I've been to. You owe me fourteen bucks."

"I was planning to work through lunch, but—okay, what kind of pizza is it?" He opened the box and peeked inside. "There's a slice missing! You can't expect someone to pay for a pizza with a missing piece." He slapped the pizza box down on the receptionist's desk and prissed up the hallway from which he came. Yep, C. J. was right. He was definitely swishy.

Edwina shrugged at the even more puzzled receptionist and picked up the pizza box. "Looks like I'm out fourteen bucks. And a tip. You want a pizza?"

The receptionist shook her head.

Edwina shrugged again, scooped up a slice of the pizza, and chomped down on a big bite as she strode through the entrance doorway.

Debbie Sue followed straight to the elevators. As the steel doors glided shut, she opened her mouth to speak, but Edwina stopped her with a raised palm. "I don't want to hear it. If you'd said we had to take those stairs, I would've had to sit down on this pizza box and slide."

"Why in the hell did you eat a slice?"

"I got hungry. You made me leave the house so early I missed breakfast, remember?"

Debbie Sue scowled. "I doubt if it was *me* who made you miss breakfast, *Mama Doll*."

Edwina flipped a palm in the air. "Do we really care if ol' Eugene gets a pizza? We've got his last name and that's what we were after."

She was right. The last name was all they needed. They should have asked C. J. the night of the hamburger and margarita party, but unfortunately, their blond friend hadn't been the only one guzzling tequila.

She knew from C. J. that CO&G employees had reserved and labeled parking in the basement parking garage. On the elevator keypad, she chose "G." All they had to do was locate Eugene's slot.

As soon as the elevator doors opened again, there it was within their view, "Reserved for E. Grubbs." And occupying the parking place was an immaculate, new Mercedes-Benz.

"Wow," Edwina said. "Would you look at that? Instead of becoming a makeup artist, I should have taken some bookkeeping classes."

Debbie Sue dug in her purse and produced a note she had written earlier:

> *Meet me Sunday morning. 9 o'clock. Denny's on I-30. Don't worry about recognizing me. I know you. It's about a mutual friend, Pearl Ann Carruthers.*

A second look at the gleaming Mercedes revealed recessed wiper blades. *Rats.*

"Ed, give me your gum. I want to be sure this note doesn't blow away."

Nine

From the seat of his personal pickup truck in front of the CO&G building, Buddy made a phone call to Harley Carruthers's office. "This is Mr. Overstreet. I'd like to see Mr. Carruthers this afternoon, maybe around three-thirty."

"I'm sorry, sir, but his last appointment of the day is at three, and that time is already taken. May I take a message or may I offer you another time?"

"No, I'm from out of town. Maybe I can catch him after his appointment. Will he still be there at four?"

"No, sir. He leaves between three-thirty and four."

Buddy's dash clock showed two-fifty. "Guess I'll have to catch him later. Thanks for your help."

He had awakened determined to learn whom Harley was protecting. And he *was* protecting someone, of that Buddy was certain. He pulled into the visitors' parking lot and chose a slot that gave him the most advantageous view of the basement exit and took off his hat. Even if Harley saw him, Buddy doubted he would recognize him without his hat and out of the county's Tahoe. He left the motor running to take advantage of the air conditioning and put a George Jones CD in the player.

At precisely four o'clock, Harley's silver Lexus sedan pulled out of the parking lot. Dark tinted windows made it impossible to identify the passengers, but Buddy could see two silhouettes. Staying a safe distance back, he changed lanes and eased in behind the luxury car.

When the Lexus drove through the wrought-iron entrance into the gated condominium community where Harley owned a unit, Buddy swore under his breath. He badged the young woman at the security gate, and she waved him through without a word. Some security for a bunch of condos that were anything but low-rent.

He knew the location of Harley's unit in the warren of condos and townhouses. By the time he reached it, the Lexus had stopped in the driveway. Buddy parked behind a scrawny tree a comfortable distance back, but in perfect view of the two people exiting the vehicle. The woman had on sunglasses. Her long hair was the color of a roan horse he had owned once. A blue dress that looked like a work dress failed to hide a small but curvy body.

He didn't recognize her and was disappointed. He had figured Harley's mistress would be someone he knew. Now he realized she could have been his three o'clock appointment or one of his employees.

She and Harley kissed briefly when they reached the condo's front door, then disappeared inside. Buddy sat for another hour, but no one came out. He checked his watch. Kathy had invited him to dinner at her apartment, said she had something to discuss with him. He didn't want to be late. She insisted on punctuality.

A strain had been hamstringing their relationship ever since they had run into Debbie Sue and Quint Matthews at Kincaid's. They hadn't slept together since. He had been too busy to drive to Odessa for recreation.

For the whole thirty-mile drive from Midland to Odessa, he thought about the woman he had seen with Harley. He didn't know if it was her half-hidden profile, her walk, the curve of her backside, or what, but there was something familiar about her that he couldn't quite put his finger on.

Buddy arrived on time at Kathy's modest duplex apartment with a box of chocolates he had bought at a Midland drugstore tucked under his arm. Showing up for a date bringing candy was a new experience, but he couldn't think of anything else she might like, and he thought a gift might ease the tension between them.

She answered the door, barely giving him a

chance to remove his hat before both of her arms slid around his shoulders and her body pressed against his. Maybe things had settled down. He started to kiss her, but she turned her head. "Oh, careful. My lipstick."

Well, maybe things were still a little tense. He set her away and handed her the box of candy, accompanied by a hopeful smile. "Brought you something."

She made a little gasp and clasped her hands in front of herself. "Oh, thank you so much. I'm on a diet, but my students will love these."

Buddy was taken aback, but managed to laugh. "Gosh, if I'd known I was buying for students, I would've got a six-pack."

Her mouth tipped up into a smile. "Now, now. You don't want me to lose my figure, do you?"

Kathy was always concerned with her appearance, always wanted to look pretty. And she did. She kept her dark, shoulder-length hair neat, and she wore pretty dresses printed with flowers. She even smelled like roses. Tonight was no exception.

She smiled as she left his embrace and took his hat. "You look tired. Can I mix you a drink or get you a beer?"

She was always polite and hospitable. "Sure," he said, "beer will be fine."

She laid the box of candy beside a tall vase of flowers standing on a table by the front door, then placed his hat, crown up, on top of the candy box.

He winced. As soon as she turned her back and headed toward the kitchen, he turned the Resistol over to rest on its crown.

Delicious-smelling food aromas filled the apartment. "Sure smells good," he called to her. He walked over to the sofa, noting dark blue upholstery printed with big pink and white blossoms. At one end sat a little white table that looked like straw, holding a lamp and a bouquet of flowers. As he sank onto the puffy cushions, he felt like the grand marshal at the Rose Parade.

Her small living room looked nice. Cozy and feminine. A teacher's pay didn't afford expensive decorations, but the room was immaculate—as if something as messy as a person didn't live there. The gold lamp gave off light too dim to read by. He felt like a bull in a china closet in such fragile surroundings, but it beat the heck out of the bare one-bedroom apartment located above a garage he rented back in Salt Lick.

Soft, classical music that wasn't country-western played in the background. Yessir, he was a lucky man that a woman of Kathy's culture and refinement put up with him. She had come closer than anybody since Debbie Sue to capturing his heart. In fact, she was the first one to whom he had gotten close who didn't have something to do with horses or cows.

Kathy reappeared with a frosted glass of beer in hand. She placed a coaster on the table beside him and set the beer glass on it, then handed him a little square napkin.

"I hope you like lamb. I had a very difficult time finding it. The stores here don't stock it."

Buddy had never knowingly and willingly swallowed a bite of lamb in his life. "Sure," he said.

She took a seat beside him, her knees touching his, and set her own glass on a coaster on the table in front of the sofa. "I hate to hit you with this the minute you walk in, but I've been practicing what I want to say all day, and if I don't do it now I don't know if I ever will."

A tinge of worry flickered in Buddy's head. "You know you can talk to me about anything, Kathy."

Her lips tipped into a hint of a smile. "Okay, here goes. I've been thinking about us. Especially since we ran into your ex-wife at Kincaid's."

Buddy nearly choked on a gulp of beer. He grabbed his handkerchief from his rear pocket and wiped his mouth. "Nothing like good, cold beer on a hot day."

"It's clear Debbie Sue's getting on with her life," Kathy said, ignoring his cough.

Buddy felt a tic in his right eye. "It appears she is."

Kathy drew a deep breath. "But I wonder if *you* are."

"Me?"

"I don't know where I stand with you, Buddy." She rose and moved to the other side of the room.

"What I mean is, if you have unresolved feelings for your ex-wife, I'm wondering if maybe you want to explore those."

Buddy's mind raced. So that was the problem. Kathy felt insecure. They had been dating on weekends for almost a year, when he could get away from his job. He didn't mind driving to Odessa. In fact, he liked escaping the gossip and busybodies in Salt Lick. If he slept over at Kathy's apartment on a Saturday night, he didn't have to worry about somebody driving by and recognizing his pickup. He was content with the arrangement. He had thought she was, too.

"To be honest, I haven't thought too much about the future in the way you're talking about, Kathy."

Though she was standing a few feet away, he saw her eyes brighten with tears. She looked down, toying with her nails. "I've never told you," she said, "but I had a job offer to work in Austin the past school year. I turned it down, but now I don't know if I made the right choice."

He rose from his seat and walked over to her.

She looked up at him with eyes filled with emotion. "How can you be so obtuse? Don't you know I'm in love with you?"

Obtuse? Her hands slid up his chest and around his neck, but he grasped her wrists. "Kathy, I—" Her mouth covered his, stopping his words. She kissed him deeply, and he could feel the shiver than ran through her body. In spite of the panic mushrooming inside him, he returned her kiss.

"I feel so much better," she said, drawing back, "If you can kiss me like that, you must feel something, too. My parents are coming from Chicago for Thanksgiving. I'd like to be able to tell them we're talking about marriage."

"Marriage?" The tic in his eye grew worse.

"You plan for the future, don't you? We're both getting to the age we should think seriously about children we might want someday."

"Children?" The word came out a croak, and Buddy knew he wasn't carrying his end of the conversation. He didn't dislike kids, but the memory of losing one was stuck in his chest as permanently as a burr in a cow's tail. He had never been, and would never be, able to erase the image of a tiny white coffin and a tiny grave and a tiny human being he and Debbie Sue had called Luke. He hadn't had a driving desire to expose his heart to that much feeling again. For *any* woman.

"It's simple, really. When you think about your future, Buddy, am I a part of it? Do you or do you not see me in your plans?"

Buddy was having trouble seeing anything at all except a Texas Ranger's badge on his shirt and Salt Lick, Texas, in his rearview mirror. In rare moments, he had thought perhaps he should make some decisions concerning Kathy, but marriage wasn't exactly one of the things he had considered. So what *was* he considering? She had asked a fair question, but he couldn't force an honest answer from his mouth.

"Is this something you'd rather think about for a while?"

Her voice brought him back to the conversation. "Uh, Kathy, I don't want this to sound like a tired old saying, but I really do think the world of you. I'm caught off-guard is all."

"I thought the best part of our relationship is that neither one of us has to be on guard. No games, no pretenses."

"You're right. Just give me some breathing room, okay? I need to clear my head. I've got a lot going on."

"I know. I shouldn't have brought it up when you're so involved in this horrible murder investigation, but I have to think of myself, too." She paused for a few seconds. "You said breathing room. That doesn't mean you want to break things off, does it?"

"That's not what I mean." Buddy put his hands on her shoulders, looking into her eyes. "I just need some time. This is an important decision. We shouldn't be hasty making it."

"I don't want to lose you, Buddy." She began unbuttoning her dress.

Buddy checked himself to keep from groaning aloud. A cold shower couldn't have doused his libido any quicker than the conversation that had just occurred. Oh, he had to admit he had come here for sex, as much as anything else. He was human, wasn't he? He had anticipated a grilled T-bone, a relaxing drink or two, then a night in

Kathy's arms in Kathy's bed. The last had lost all its appeal, and he had no desire to eat cute little fluffy animals.

He headed for his hat. "Kathy, I think the best thing I can do is just go on home."

"But dinner—"

"I know you've gone to a lot of trouble and I appreciate it, but I'm feeling a little unsettled. I think it would be wrong if I stayed."

She looked up at him, her dark lashes blinking rapidly. "It's Debbie Sue, isn't it?"

"I didn't say that."

"But it's what you meant." In the low light, her eyes glistened with moisture.

He set his hat on and reached for the doorknob. "Don't be upset." He leaned down and brushed her cheek with his lips. "You've already hashed this out with yourself, but I'm a little slow. I need to do some thinking. Let me call you."

Rolling down the highway, Buddy chastised himself for getting into this situation with Kathy. She had asked how he could be so obtuse. Man, he had to agree with her on that one. He had been out of the dating game for a long time. In truth, he had never even been *in* it. He had known as a kid that Debbie Sue was the partner for him, and the encounters he had with women after her and prior to Kathy couldn't be called dating. It was more like buying a few drinks, then paying for a room.

He felt like a jackass for not seeing the signs Kathy had been putting up. He hadn't stopped to remind himself that most self-respecting women wouldn't be satisfied for an indefinite period of time with a casual arrangement built mostly on sex.

Maybe it wasn't fair to continue seeing Kathy if he didn't have plans to include her in his future.

His future?

That was another thing he hadn't succeeded in doing—putting together his future.

Introduced as a fiancé by Thanksgiving? Damn.

Well, it was still September. He didn't make snap decisions or form snap judgments. Even though he had to solve Pearl Ann's murder, there was still plenty of time before Thanksgiving to reflect about Kathy. He wasn't avoiding the issue, he told himself. He simply had time to think about it.

Debbie Sue was glad to see the name Maudeen Wiley on her appointment list for Thursday. Maudeen, who thought hair color was to be used like lipstick, came into the shop once a month, or more often, for a new shade.

Maudeen was just what Debbie Sue needed to lighten up the week. The octogenarian approached life full-throttle, didn't mind telling you she considered it her responsibility to dispense common sense, whenever necessary, to the less fortunate who appeared to have none.

Debbie Sue loved her attitude and always gave her undivided attention, extra time, and a special senior citizen's discount. She didn't mind lowering the fees because she enjoyed Maudeen's company and the hilarious words of wisdom the elderly woman left behind.

"Have you ever known someone you thought might be capable of murder?" Debbie Sue asked her as she applied a stripe of Fiesta Red color along Maudeen's part line.

"Funny you should ask. I went out with Bart Jenkins last week, and he has *killed* any chance he ever had of getting me in bed again."

Debbie Sue had to stop and think, searching for the link between the murder of a human being and Maudeen's social life. "Bart is such a sweet little man. What could he have done to upset you?"

"He told everyone at Peaceful Oasis I was easy. Every time I walk into a room, all the other women stop talking."

Debbie Sue stifled a grin as she parted the back of Maudeen's hair into sections. "Oh, they'll get over it. They're probably jealous. Maybe those ladies should come in and have their hair dyed. New hair color would give them something different to talk about."

"They already dye their hair. Pink, blue, purple. Looks like a damn Easter egg hunt when the old crows get their heads together."

Debbie Sue laughed. "You're a trip, Maudeen. I hope I still have as much fire as you when I get to be your age."

"Well, honey, I hope so, too. The worst part of getting old is how people think you *should* be acting. They want you dead before you die."

Debbie Sue spotted a gleam in the elderly woman's eye. "Tell me something. If you were going to go after this reward money Harley put up, how would you go about it?"

"Is that what you're thinking about? Lands, child, you do remind me of myself when I was your age. That's exactly what I would have done. Sounds like fun. First off, in your shoes, I'd make damn sure my evidence was rock hard before I gave it to the sheriff."

"I don't follow you."

"Why, honey, you're the sheriff's ex. You don't think you can just waltz in and claim the reward without everyone in town raising hell, do you? You'll have to all but catch the killer all by yourself and drag him up the road by the collar so it'll look like you're the one who really got him. Otherwise everybody will think you and your old sweetie are in cahoots."

Holy shit. Debbie Sue had been so focused on the amount of the reward money, she had never thought of what the town would think. She helped Maudeen from the hydraulic chair to a dryer chair and handed her *Globe* and the *National Enquirer.*

Maudeen had hit on something. It was like one of those sweepstakes drawings you enter where family members of the sponsor weren't eligible to win. Now she had one more reason to keep her activities a secret from Buddy.

After styling the older woman's bright red hair into a thick roll and lacquering it until it felt like plastic, Debbie Sue gave her favorite customer a kiss on the cheek and told her she would be hard for the men at Peaceful Oasis to resist.

"I do look good, don't I? Wish I could afford a boob lift. I'd go after that new guy that just moved into E-7. He's a younger man. Sixty-eight. And his grandson works for that company that makes Viagra."

"You don't worry about a boob job. If he hears you're easy, he'll probably be looking you up. Maybe even tonight when he sees your new hairdo."

"You're right. I'd better hurry back. It's almost four. Most of those old codgers will be shuffling into the dining room for supper. They'll all be in bed by seven, but if E-7 likes my new hair color and I'm lucky, I could be there by six."

As Maudeen was driven away by her great-granddaughter, Debbie Sue waved good-bye. As usual the sassy older woman had given her food for thought.

The remainder of the day was less entertaining. The Coca-Cola delivery man came and refilled the struggling seen-better-days Coke machine. A group of Boy Scouts came by selling raffle tickets for a drawing at Benton's Monuments and Home Accessory Emporium. The winner got either free headstone engraving or a silk flower arrangement. Debbie Sue bought three two-dollar tickets. What the heck? Where but Salt Lick could you go into a business to order a grave marker and come out with a toilet seat cover?

Ivalene Buchanan, the local Avon lady, made her deliveries. Ivalene felt her job called for her not only to sell Avon's products, but to be a walking billboard as well. Her eyelids were always at least four different colors. The deepest, richest shades of lipstick were always freshly applied to her lips, and her cheeks were wild with streaks of color and highlighter. Each wrist and bend of the elbow wafted a different fragrance, and she wore enough costume jewelry to sink an ocean liner.

Though nearing seventy, she proudly boasted that thanks to the miracle of Avon she didn't look a day over thirty-five. Edwina was always quick to agree, pointing out only to Debbie Sue that Ivalene truly didn't look *a day* over thirty-five, but she looked every bit of the twelve-thousand-plus days that she was.

Debbie Sue observed all of it with lazy amusement. She loved everything about her world. The eccentric octogenarians, the slow pace of life in a small town. Even the people who weren't her favorites fueled Edwina's mock standup comedy routines. Leaving Salt Lick forever wouldn't be easy. The only thing harder would be making the decision to do it.

Only two things were missing in her otherwise acceptable life—money and Buddy. She had two viable chances at money—the reward or Quint.

But she didn't have a chance in hell to recapture Buddy. Whoever said it was better to have loved and lost than to have never loved at all was a dumb-ass. A plain and simple dumb-ass.

Ten

Saturday night Debbie Sue went to bed early. She wanted to be rested and at the top of her game for the Sunday morning meeting with Eugene Grubbs. Edwina had promised to accompany her, then slide into a neighboring booth and listen. They had agreed early on to never leave each other alone with a suspect.

When sleep finally came it was filled with distorted images. A nightmare scared her awake and she sat up, her heart racing. In the dream, she had been sitting in a restaurant booth with a tall stack of hot pancakes in front of her. An unidentifiable man across the table suddenly grabbed her head and attempted to smother her by forcing her face into the pancakes. As she fought frantically for breath, the Odessa schoolteacher appeared in a waitress uniform and poured syrup on her head, ruining her blond highlights.

Oddly enough, she wasn't too worried about

the faceless person, but if she saw that bitch Kathy what's-her-name again, she would kill her for ruining her hair color.

Unable to return to sleep, she rose and showered and shampooed her hair. Though the morning temperature hovered in the high eighties, she dressed in black clothing—black Wranglers, black T-shirt, black boots. She banded her hair into a ponytail and tucked it under a dark blue "La-Mont's Feed & Supplements" gimme cap. To finish her disguise, she covered her eyes with a pair of sunglasses with mirrored lenses she had bought at The Galleria the last time she visited Dallas.

She left her house in plenty of time to pick up Edwina and reach the Denny's in Midland by nine. Her stomach was tied in knots. They rode in silence as the endless landscape of scrubby pasture, leafless brush, and sawing pump jacks flew by.

"Did Vic wonder where you were going so early on a Sunday morning?" Debbie Sue finally asked, breaking the tension.

"Vic's on a run to Phoenix. I don't expect to see him before Tuesday night."

The owner of an eighteen-wheeler, Vic was a contract trucker. He hauled everything from cattle to cabbage. Driving the interstate satisfied his need to be on the go, and Edwina satisfied all his other needs.

"Vic had a phone call from Brenda the other night," Edwina said suddenly.

Uh-oh. Debbie Sue already knew Vic's ex lived

somewhere in Southern California. To a trucker, a short hop from Phoenix. "Oh? Same situation as before?"

"Yep. She's drying out and wants to use Vic as a towel. I swear to God, if—"

"Ed, you can't be seriously worried about her. This woman doesn't mean anything to Vic. He's just being . . . he's just being Vic."

"And I'm just being Edwina. If she doesn't leave him alone, her next recovery program may be done from a hospital bed."

Debbie Sue didn't want to make light of Edwina's feelings, but if there was a better relationship around than Vic and Edwina's, she wasn't aware of it. Still, she couldn't blame her old friend for being concerned. If the shoe were on Debbie Sue's foot, she would feel the same way. Sometimes she wished it had been another woman whom she could blame for Buddy divorcing her. Maybe she could fight another woman and win him back, but how could she wage war against herself?

Denny's came into sight. "Tell me we're doing the right thing, huh, Ed?"

"Ab-so-fuckin'-lutely. I've already made a list where I'm gonna spend that money."

"I mean, you don't think anyone has ever been stabbed or had his throat cut with a butter knife, do you? Or what about a spoon or a fork? A fork could really do damage. A fork could put out an eye."

"Eugene doesn't look like he could stab *toast*.

Besides, it's broad daylight, and Sunday morning in Denny's is a mob scene."

"You're right. So all I have to worry about for the rest of my life is darkness and being alone. Terrific."

To be certain she could make a quick exit, she found a parking slot away from the view of other diners and backed into it with the skill of one who had backed a horse trailer into a tight spot uncountable times.

Inside, she and Edwina separated. She took a seat at an end booth near the emergency exit, and Edwina sat down at the next table over. No one but Edwina could overhear her conversation with Eugene.

A harried waitress came to Debbie Sue's table with coffee pot in hand. "Our special today is the all-you-can-eat pancakes."

"*No*. No pancakes. I don't want *any* pancakes. Just coffee. Here, you can take the silverware, too." Debbie Sue gathered up the knives, forks, and spoons arranged at four place settings and handed them to the waitress. "No pancakes, no silverware. Just coffee." To the pile of eating utensils in the waitress's hands, she added four pitchers of varied flavors of syrups. "Here, take these syrups. I don't need syrup because I'm not having pancakes."

The puzzled waitress left, arms laden with silverware and syrup pitchers.

At nine o'clock Eugene entered and looked

around. He was dressed impeccably. Beige shorts, starched beige shirt with a brown and gold scarf at the neck. He had a leather fanny pack belted around his waist and he wore loafers, no socks. He looked nervous and strung out.

It was then Debbie Sue knew she had *The Power*. She was suddenly self-assured and calm. She was suave, she was classy, she was Renee Russo in *The Thomas Crown Affair*. And he was *not* Pierce Brosnan.

Rising from her seat she approached her quarry, noting the look of bewilderment on his face, as if he were trying to remember where he had seen her before.

"Thank you for being prompt, Eugene. Won't you join me at my table?"

Before sitting down, Eugene pulled a handkerchief from his back pocket and thoroughly wiped the seat on his side of the booth. He reached into his fanny pack and brought out a squeeze bottle of gel hand sanitizer and rubbed it onto his hands and wrists, making sure the cuticles of each fingernail were thoroughly cleansed. It became even clearer what C. J. meant when she said Eugene was swishy.

Finally he turned his attention to Debbie Sue. "You knew Pearl Ann?"

"Yes, we were friends. For a long time."

"I doubt that. You might have thought she was your friend, but I guarantee you that little hussy was never a friend to anyone." He raised two fingers and wiggled them at the waitress.

"You don't sound like you liked her very much."

"I didn't dislike her. I was ambivalent about her. Mr. Carruthers gave me an assignment. She was part of it."

The waitress reappeared and poured Eugene's mug full of hot coffee, refilled Debbie Sue's. "Are you having breakfast, sir?" she asked Eugene. "Our special today is all-you-can-eat pancakes."

"Oh, no thank you. I'll have dry toast, whole wheat, and hot tea with a small sliver of lemon. And could I please have a spoon?"

Yikes! "Can you make that a metal spoon, not plastic?"

The waitress glared at Debbie Sue. "Sure I can." She stamped away.

Eugene's eyes darted about the room as if he feared someone might sneak from a hidden place and grab him. "What, exactly, do you want from me? Why the cloak-and-dagger routine? I've already told the sheriff from Salt Lick everything I know."

The last statement took some wind from Debbie Sue's sails. So it was true. Buddy *had* left no stone unturned.

The waitress returned with a full set of silverware for Eugene, along with his toast. Debbie Sue gulped and tried to discreetly examine the sharpness of the knife blade. "Did you tell the sheriff about the little kickback Pearl Ann's been tipping you all these years, or the getaway fund that is bound to be sizable by now?"

Small beads of sweat broke out on Eugene's forehead, and his left leg began bouncing hard enough to shake the table. *Yes!* She had hit a nerve.

"I don't know what you're talking about." His voice came out too shrill for an innocent man.

"Oh, come on. I know the arrangement. What did you do with the extra money, Eugene?" She leaned across the table and drilled him with a laser stare from behind her sunglasses. "Or better yet, what are your plans for the mother lode?"

"I've told the *authorities* all I know." He started to rise. "You're crazy. This conversation is over."

Debbie Sue whispered, "She made a tape. She had a file. And I have both of them."

Eugene sank back to the seat. "I don't believe you. I want to hear the tape. I want to see the file. Until I do, you're a liar and this meeting never happened."

"I'll let you choose. Who do you want present when you hear the tape, Sheriff Overstreet or Harley? The only way you're going to hear it is with one of them present. Besides, I don't even need the tape or a file." She tapped her temple with her forefinger. "I have enough details right here to set the law onto an investigation."

Eugene's shoulders fell and he looked down at his chewed fingernails. "What do you want from me? Is this extortion? Do you want money?"

Debbie Sue thought she might shriek with delight. Good Lord, this was easier than she had imagined. "Oh, I want money all right, but I don't want it from you. I want to collect the price on your head."

"Price on my—" He gasped. "Forevermore, you think *I* killed Pearl Ann?" He let out a nervous cackle.

Diners at other tables turned and looked, and Debbie Sue felt uneasy. She had expected him to break into tears and confess at this point. Then she would retrieve her cell phone, call Buddy, and ask him to come pick up the killer. That's how it happened on *Law & Order*.

"Maybe you did, maybe you didn't. In any case I think we have motive. Why don't I call Sheriff Overstreet? I think he'll be a lot more lenient if you turn yourself in. If he has to come after you, he might not be as civil. He's a big guy, you know."

"Oh, I know. And he is *sooo* yummy."

Yummy? She could think of a dozen adjectives to describe Buddy, but "yummy" wasn't one of them. "You could claim temporary insanity," she went on. "Harley would probably even back you up on that one. If the sheriff has to come after you, it's going to look bad for you. Premeditated." She pursed her mouth and nodded.

Eugene stared back at her, bug-eyed. Debbie Sue wished she could read minds because there was clearly a thought process in action. He sprang to his feet and glared down at her. "There's another legal term you might look for when you read your next crime novel. It's called 'circumstantial evidence.'" He turned and prissed to the front door, his mincing steps making his butt twitch.

Debbie Sue sat stunned. And confused

Edwina eased into the spot Eugene had vacated. "What was it he said about circumcision?"

"Circumstantial, Ed. He said my information is circumstantial. He doesn't think I have enough proof to do him any harm."

"He's just blowing smoke. I've seen a lot of men who were scared. Usually my exes when I threatened them with bodily harm, but that's beside the point. He was scared all right. When a man makes an exit that quick, it's because he doesn't want you to see his fear."

Debbie Sue looked at her friend with awe. "Ed, I am constantly amazed at your knowledge of the human animal, men in particular."

"Trust me, honey, it's both a gift and a curse. Speaking of blowing smoke, let's get out of here. I'm having a nicotine fit. Or did you want to have some of that all-you-eat pancake special?"

"I'd rather stop at Sonic for a breakfast burrito and a big Dr. Pepper. We should decide what to do next."

"Now you're talking."

Halfway to Salt Lick, Debbie Sue told Edwina she would call Eugene at work the next day and ask if he'd had time to think about their conversation. "You know," she said as an afterthought, "there's one thing about the meeting that really bugged me. It was all I could do to not stare at his eyebrows."

"Eyebrows?"

"Yeah, didn't you notice? They were perfectly plucked and dyed. Best job I've ever seen, too. And he thinks Buddy's yummy."

Edwina blinked a few times, then slapped her own cheek. "Well, rope my ankles and call me dogie."

By the next morning Debbie Sue had replayed her meeting with Eugene Grubbs over and over in her head. Her instincts told her he was guilty of *something*. At this point she wasn't sure it was murder, but then again, she didn't feel comfortable saying it wasn't. Being a detective was too hard. She couldn't wait to give up this second job she had taken on.

Before picking up the phone to call Carruthers Oil & Gas, she flipped over the week-at-a-glance calendar and let out a soft whistle. "Oh my Lord, Ed. I don't know how I let time slip by me, but homecoming weekend's coming up."

In Salt Lick, homecoming was more than a high school football function. It was a reunion of current and past residents. Starting on Thursday, parties would be slated in homes all over town. The weekend culminated Saturday night at a huge dance in the high school parking lot following the football game. "We're both booked solid starting Thursday, and right through to Saturday."

Edwina sighed and began to sort curlers in her tray. "Seems like it comes earlier every year. It won't be the same without the big to-do at the Carruthers place. Remember last year's party when C. J. and Pearl Ann got into that catfight over that really good-looking cowboy from San Angelo?"

Debbie thought back to a year ago and the dance at Harley's party barn. She had never seen mild-mannered C. J. so upset about *anything*. "Lord, yes, I'll never forget it. He wasn't a cowboy, though. Wasn't he the chef Pearl Ann insisted on bringing in for the party?"

"C. J. wasn't mad, as I recall. It was Pearl Ann who was fit to be tied. Poor C. J. was just defending herself."

"All I remember is when the guy and C. J. were dancing and Pearl Ann cut in. I thought Pearl Ann was going to pull C. J.'s hair out."

Edwina shook her head and sucked up a long drink of Dr. Pepper. "C. J. was so embarrassed."

"I know. She still doesn't like to talk about it." Debbie Sue propped her elbow on the payout desk and rested her chin on her palm. "You know, that's when I remember seeing another side to Harley, too. He was so nice to C. J. He took her outside and talked to her. He was trying to make her feel better. I'll bet he was always making some kind of apology for Pearl Ann's actions.

"Yep, Pearl Ann was always good for new gossip. Hell, what she *wore* was good for a week's worth. Homecoming this year's gonna be dull."

"Face it, Ed. Not only will there not be a party at Harley's this year, maybe there'll never be one again. But I can probably liven things up for you for a short while. I've got a date with Quint Saturday night."

"Shut up! Do you really?"

"Too bad he never made it to one of the Carruthers parties. He would have been right at home."

"So what're your plans? He's already been through the public humiliation routine. Why don't you save some time and just yank his dick off when he comes to the door?"

Debbie Sue fixed Edwina with a bland expression. "Why, Edwina Perkins. You act like what happened that night was *my* fault. I really want this evening to be calm and normal. I'm trying to convince myself I want to get involved with Quint, you know?"

"If you have to *convince* yourself, then do both of you a favor and forget it. I dated a really, really rich man once. He had so much money he misplaced more than most people make in a lifetime. I wanted to make things work so damn bad."

"So what happened?"

"I threw up every time he wanted to screw. Once or twice I made it to the bed, but every time I had to make him stop so I could throw up. Nothing shrinks a man's dick like vomit breath. I even tried telling myself I was allergic to him, and with enough exposure I would build up a tolerance."

"Good Lord, Ed, he *must* have had a ton of money."

"Well, I said he did. One good thing came of it though. I lost about fifteen pounds dating him, never looked better in my life."

"It's not quite that extreme with Quint. I really do like him and he does stir up some feelings in me. I just think he wants things to move a little faster than I do."

"If the man is really interested in you, he'll give you space. Look, Vic will be home this weekend. Why don't y'all come over? My honey can throw something on the grill that's sure to impress Quint. It'll be fun. We can eat early and still have time to go to the dance."

Vic could impress anyone with his home cooking and if there was any trouble, the six-foot-three martial arts expert could rip the instigator's heart from his chest. A man with those skills was a plus to have around at a drunken homecoming dance.

Besides that, with having dinner at a friend's house, she could postpone the inevitable decision about Quint—would she or wouldn't she? "Hey, thanks so much, Ed. He's picking me up at seven. We can be over soon after." She picked up the phone receiver. "Now don't interrupt me. I've got to make this phone call before anyone comes in." Debbie Sue keyed in CO&G's number.

A Stepford Wife answered. Debbie Sue asked for Eugene. A professional female voice told her Mr. Grubbs was out of the office ill. Debbie Sue swore under her breath. He was probably at home hiding behind the sofa.

"I'm a friend of his and thought I'd say hello. Do you have his home number handy? I'll call him there."

"I'm sorry, ma'am, but Mr. Grubbs has an unlisted number, and we aren't allowed to give out employees' phone numbers. If you'll leave me your name, when he retrieves his messages, I'll tell him you called."

"No, thanks. I'll just call back."

Okay, fruity hotshot, you've escaped me for now. She would allow him one day to make a decision. She would call again tomorrow morning, and he had better be there or . . .

Or what? Well, she didn't want to think about *or what* right now.

At the end of the day Edwina bid Debbie Sue a good evening and headed home. She had tried to put Brenda's message out of her mind but Vic was on the road, and what if he decided to just follow the interstate on out to California? In the commonsense recesses of her mind, she knew he wouldn't do such a thing, but in the battle-scarred regions of her heart, she feared he might. She knew the male animal only too well.

She had seen pictures of Brenda. Once when

helping Vic search for his discharge papers, among old military mementos, documents of commendation, letters to and from home, photos of a naval station, and numerous medals and ribbons, they found a snapshot of a young beauty, a stark contrast to his other pictures that were so military. Looking to be no more than eighteen, blond and tanned with a drop-dead gorgeous body covered only by a ruffled bikini, she seemed to be the perfect Valley Girl stereotype, lying on the beach, head propped on her hand to pose for the picture.

"Wow, is she one of your medals too?" Edwina had asked.

Vic looked at the picture for what Edwina felt was a little too long before answering. He explained the woman was his ex. Edwina had tried to imagine her after the ravages of time and alcohol abuse had taken their toll. But each time the image of the beauty on the beach assaulted her. Judging from the photo the only thing she and her live-in lover's ex-wife had in common was they were both females. And one other thing—they both loved Vic.

She decided right then and there, when she got home tonight if there was another message from Brenda, she intended to accidentally erase it. No sirree, she wasn't giving up Vic without a fight.

And if Miss California wanted to come and get him for herself, she'd better pack a lunch and bring an army.

Eleven

Buddy sat behind his battered desk in the sheriff's office and rocked back in the Naugahyde upholstered chair. He had drunk so many cups of coffee, he wouldn't blink for three days.

In front of him lay a yellow legal pad. On each line he had written the name of a person he had talked to casually or interviewed formally about the Carruthers murder. He had scribbled notes beside the names and in the margins.

Doodles and drawings of a Texas Rangers badge filled in the blank spots beside the names of the employees of Carruthers Oil & Gas. They had stonewalled him. Even Carol Jean had clammed up. He understood their attitudes. Working for CO&G was the best job in West Texas. Excellent benefits, outlandish perks, and a salary not even in shooting range of other area employers.

With flying colors, Harley had passed the lie

detector test arranged by his attorneys. Deep down, Buddy had never *really* believed he killed Pearl Ann anyway.

The only person he hadn't talked to was the mysterious redhead he had seen accompanying Harley to his condo.

He was at the end of his rope when it came to fresh ideas or clues. He reached for his hat and walked from his office into the reception area. "Tanya, I'm fixin' to run and take care of something. Be back shortly."

"I just put Kathy on hold for you."

Damn. He didn't want to get into a conversation with Kathy now. "Did you tell her I was here?"

"No, I told her I wasn't sure where you were."

"Good. Tell her I'm out. Thanks, Tanya."

Walking toward the Tahoe, he made a mental note to call Kathy later. He didn't know what he would tell her, but maybe an answer would come to him by the time he returned from his errand.

He pulled alongside the Styling Station, grinning as he passed the two gasoline pumps dressed in black and orange Halloween costumes. Salt Lick citizens didn't notice the oddity anymore, but it always made him laugh. A magazine in New York had even published pictures and done a small article about the pumps. Guess that was the kind of thing people up North liked to read about Texans.

Debbie Sue was just hanging up the phone

when Buddy entered. She looked up, hoping she had hidden a startled expression.

"Ladies. I didn't catch y'all at a bad time, did I?" He looked around the empty shop.

"Nope," Debbie Sue said, attempting to make her voice sound innocent. "We're just waiting for the herd to stampede. What's up?"

Edwina sauntered over to Buddy. "I think this boy's here for a haircut. Look at these curls." She lifted off his hat and combed her long red nails through his black hair. "How 'bout it, babycakes? Want me to give you a trim? Or how about something more personal?"

Buddy's face turned from tan to red. Edwina had always engaged in verbal foreplay with Buddy, and most of the time Debbie Sue laughed about it, but this morning it irritated her.

"Ed, one of these days I'm gonna put Vic in jail for about three days," Buddy said with a laugh, "and you and I are gonna get to know each other better."

"I'd ruin you for other women, cowboy. I'd give you two days, then break Vic out of jail and leave you heartbroken."

The two laughed. Debbie Sue tried to join in but sounded phony. "What are you doing here, Buddy? You don't usually come by just to say hello."

"I need your help, Flash. Is there someplace we can talk?"

"You can talk right here," Ed said. "I've got to

run to Kwik-Stop for some smokes and DP. I can't bear to face the day without them."

Liar. Debbie Sue knew Edwina came in every day with plenty of cigarettes and a gallon of Dr. Pepper.

"Always good to see you, hon." The skinny brunette trailed her fingers across Buddy's wide shoulders. "Come back when it's just the two of us. I want to show you some uses for these multi-position hydraulic chairs."

Debbie Sue didn't want to dwell on the mental picture that flew into her mind. She had imagined she and Buddy christening one of the salon chairs. She planted a fist on one hip. "Okay, you've got my full attention 'til ten o'clock. This doesn't involve Super Glue does it?"

Buddy frowned. "Huh? Uh, oh yeah. Sorry about that. It seemed funny at the time."

"Maybe to a sadist."

Buddy grinned and rested his forearms on the payout counter. His teeth were as perfect as new piano keys. Debbie Sue loved seeing him smile.

"Listen," he said, "I've hit a dead end on this murder. Pearl Ann left a string of people with a motive, but none I can find who would have actually killed her. Everybody's either got solid alibis or solid lie detector tests. All I've got is one fingerprint that doesn't match anybody's. That reward money hasn't raised so much as a whisper."

Despite her determination to maintain her silence about what she knew, Debbie Sue was moved by Buddy's straightforward admission. "So what do you want from me, a confession?"

"I don't mean for this to become beauty shop gossip, but Harley's got a redheaded girlfriend. Have you and Ed seen a woman around him with long red hair?"

"The only redheads I see are the ones who get their roots colored, and none of them are younger than sixty-five. Something tells me that's not who you're looking for."

"No, Harley's alibi is young and hot. He won't give me her name. I followed them, so I've seen her."

Debbie Sue couldn't keep her eyes from bulging. "You followed Harley and a girlfriend? Ohmygod, Buddy. This is serious. What if he finds out?"

"Murder *is* serious, Debbie Sue."

"Ohmy*god*, Buddy. Do you think Harley did it?"

Buddy's brow crinkled into a frown. "No, no, no, Debbie Sue. Don't blow this all out of proportion."

"Can't you use your authority? I mean, you're the sheriff. Don't you have ways to make him co-operate? Thumb screws? Electric shock?"

"Cut it out, Flash. This is getting to be a real problem. I wouldn't admit it to just anybody, but—"

He stopped and looked past her. She could see the tumult in his eyes. "What, Buddy?"

"I've pressed Harley as far as he's gonna be pressed. If I don't come up with a genuine suspect soon, he's threatening to bring in the Texas

Rangers or some other outside outfit. He's already asked why I don't call in help. I've got to find Pearl Ann's killer. I can't be known as the sheriff who couldn't solve the only murder that's happened in Salt Lick in sixty years. Christ, I'll never get hired by the DPS." He straightened his shoulders and gave her a direct look. "Kind of a selfish reason, huh?"

He look so beleaguered, Debbie Sue wanted to put her arms around him and whisper soothing words, but she struggled to maintain her grip on reality. "Don't be so hard on yourself, Buddy. We all do things for selfish reasons. Is the redheaded woman someone you think could be guilty?"

"Only because I can't find anybody else."

"If Harley passed the lie detector test, why is he still protecting his girlfriend?"

"That's my question, too. That's why the red-head has become my top suspect."

At that moment, the door opened and Edwina's first customer of the day entered. Debbie Sue directed her back to the shampoo area and told her Edwina would be back any minute.

"Looks like you're about to get busy," Buddy said. "I'll go. I didn't mean to bother you. It was a shot in the dark that you might know something that could help me."

"Hey, I'm not through talking, but you're right. It is about to get a little crowded in here. Can I call you tonight at home, say about eight o'clock?" She caught a quick little breath, fearing he might say no. "I might think of something between now and then."

"Sure, uh, I mean, yeah. Eight o'clock's fine. Hope you *do* think of something. And Flash?" He picked up her hand and kissed her palm. "Thanks."

A football-sized lump lodged in Debbie Sue's throat. Before they married and especially after, she and Buddy had been best friends, had always solved problems together until she screwed everything up. She felt the weight of the world on her shoulders as she watched him drive away. She had key information to the case and hadn't shared it with him.

Damn you, Buddy, for making me feel guilty.

By the end of the day Debbie Sue had made up her mind to tell Buddy everything she knew about Eugene Grubbs. Crime solving was best left in Buddy's hands anyway. At home, as she changed into cutoffs and a faded Dallas Cowboys T-shirt, she was surprised by a knock at her door.

It was only seven-thirty. Maybe Buddy was dropping by instead of waiting for her call. She hoped so. She had resisted the urge to kiss him this morning. He had been so open and honest, it had touched a deep place in her heart, and the thought of kissing him touched a deep place somewhere else. She intended to greet him with a kiss that would never end. Caution, pride, and ego be damned. Trying to rebuild her life without him wasn't working. One moment of kissing Buddy again was worth any price she might have to pay.

For thirty seconds, she worried about her appearance, then flung open the front door.

Kathy Something was standing on her doorstep, smiling like a possum. "Debbie Sue? Do you remember me?"

Debbie Sue's brain scrambled to recover from shock. "Sure, yeah, of course I do. It's Karen, isn't it?"

The woman was wearing black slacks, an old-lady blouse with seed pearl beading on a round collar, and black patent T-strap shoes. And she was clutching with both hands the strap of a small shiny patent leather purse. Where was she headed, Old Maid's Night Out?

"No, Kathy. Kathy Boczkowski. I was with Buddy at Kincaid's in Odessa the night we were introduced."

Kathy offered her hand, Debbie Sue shook it and winced. She hated pumping a hand that felt as if it had no bones.

"I'm sorry to drop by at this time of night. I went home from work to change into something more comfortable or I'd have been here earlier. I wonder, would you mind talking to me about Buddy?"

"Buddy? Has something happened to Buddy?"

"Oh no, nothing like that. Do you mind if I come in?"

Debbie Sue stepped back and gave Buddy's girlfriend entry to her home, trying to remember when she had last run the vacuum. *What in the hell kind of name is Bosh-cow-ski?*

As Kathy passed in front of her, Debbie Sue caught a strong whiff of roses. *Blech!* She rolled her eyes, slammed the door, and followed Kathy to the living room.

Her visitor perched on the edge of the couch, and Debbie Sue rushed to pick up scattered reading material—*Western Horseman, American Cowboy,* PRCA newsletters.

"It's very important to me that you and I have a good relationship, Debbie Sue. Buddy thinks the world of you, and I respect the years you've known each other."

Kathy might as well have been speaking Polish for all the sense her conversation made. Or for that matter, her visit. *What in the hell is she doing here?*

"I'd offer you coffee, but I only have instant. You want some"—Debbie Sue's mind inventoried what she had in the house to serve—"some orange juice?" She still had half of a half-gallon of Tropicana from when Quint came.

"Instant coffee would be fine. I sometimes resort to using it myself when I'm in a hurry."

Debbie Sue dredged up a phony smile and retreated to the kitchen. *What in the holy hell is she doing here?* As she rummaged through the cupboard looking for the jar of instant Folger's she had bought last winter, she sensed someone behind her and turned around, found herself nearly nose-to-nose with Kathy.

"I know you and Buddy went through a lot together and I'm not foolish enough to think, just because you're divorced, those years don't count."

What in the ever-loving, holy hell is she doing here? Debbie Sue found the coffee and placed a cup of water in the microwave. "I never drink coffee when the weather's hot." While the microwave ran, she set about searching a different cupboard. "Sugar. Want some sugar? Oh, here. I've got some of those little flavor pills you put in coffee. Um, let me see, I think it's Irish Cream. Yep, it's Irish Cream."

The microwave pinged and Debbie Sue dragged out the mug of hot water, dumped in a heaping teaspoon of coffee granules, then a flavor pill. She added a second one for good measure before handing the steaming mix to Kathy.

Kathy took the mug and went on talking non-stop. "Buddy and I talked about this and he agrees that when we run into each other again, there should always be friendship and warm wishes between us."

Friendship and warm wishes? When we run into each other again? Definitely not words that came from Buddy Overstreet's mouth. Enough was enough. "I'm sorry, but I don't understand where you're coming from or where you're headed. Let's cut to the chase."

"Well. You are upfront and forthright. Buddy said you would be direct. I assured him the best way to handle this was woman-to-woman. We thought you should be the first to know. He and I are going to be married. We intend to make the announcement at Thanksgiving."

All the air left the room. Debbie Sue felt as if her head had been injected with Novocain. "Oh" was the word that fell from her mouth.

"Are you all right? I'm so sorry. Can I get you something? You really don't look well."

"No, no, I'm fine. Just surprised. Uh . . . Buddy knows you're here?

"Oh, it was his idea that I come. He didn't want you to hear it like beauty salon gossip." She winced, a tight little frown squeezing between her brows. "Oh, I'm sorry. That was insensitive of me. You work in a salon, don't you?"

"Well, yeah. Actually I *own* it, but that's beside the point." Debbie Sue despised herself for feeling the need to offer a defense. "God love that Buddy, always thinking of my feelings. You know, I don't want to be rude, but . . ." Debbie Sue marched to the front door and opened it. She pasted on a smile. "I'm expecting company."

"Oh, well I don't want to intrude. Promise me you're fine."

Debbie Sue gave her a horse grin. "I promise."

After Kathy Bosh-cow-ski gathered her handbag and left, for what seemed like an hour Debbie Sue sat in the same spot staring at nothing in particular. She could feel her blood rushing through her body, hear her own breathing. Had she developed superhuman powers, or was the breaking of her very human heart what had brought on this phenomenon? She thought back to seeing Buddy earlier in the day. He had been so sweet, affectionate even. His kiss on the palm of her hand had almost made her faint.

She had bought his "poor me" routine, hook, line, and sinker; had nearly told him her fifty-thousand-dollar secret about Eugene Grubbs. And that wasn't all. She had made up her mind to . . .

Bastard!

She reached for the phone and stabbed in Buddy's number.

He answered on the first ring. "Hey you, I was afraid you might have changed your mind about calling."

"Buddy Overstreet, you're a limp-dicked motherfucker. If you ever come in my shop again, I'll poke you with a cattle prod." She punched off the call and threw the phone across the room.

As God is my witness, I will never understand women.

And just when he thought things had softened up between him and Debbie Sue, too. Buddy sat motionless holding the receiver to his ear. Until he heard a knock. He felt safe opening the door because his angry ex-wife couldn't possibly have made it to his house since she hung up in his ear just moments earlier.

To his astonishment there stood Kathy. "Kathy. What are you doing in Salt Lick?"

"I'm so sorry to bother you. I know you said you need some time, but I felt terrible about the way things ended yesterday. I feared you would think I was trying to use sex as a tool to sway your decision. I would never stoop to doing something so crude and unladylike."

"No need to apologize. I didn't think that at all." Buddy looked down at his socked feet. If he had known she was coming, he would've at least put on his boots.

"Oh good. I do feel better. Now I have a little confession. I went by Debbie Sue's house and—"

"You did what?" A mild panic zinged through his chest.

"I know, I know. It was a mistake. I only wanted to tell her I was glad to have finally met her and that you had all the respect in the world for her."

"Come on in," he said. "It's a little chilly out there on the porch."

"Oh, thank you." She stepped through the doorway, and the scent of flowers filled his small entry.

"Here, put your purse down." He took her purse, laid it on an end table by the couch. His place was a mess. Newspapers strewn all around, a plastic tray left from the TV dinner he'd had for supper, his boots lying in front of the couch.

She looked up at him with pleading eyes. "I also asked her for help. You know, tell me something about you that might help me improve our relationship. Since she's involved with another man, I didn't see the harm. I know it was stupid, but I felt so desperate after yesterday."

He felt a little desperate, too. Debbie Sue had called him names before, but he couldn't recall if she had ever called him the one he just heard. Cussin' was part of West Texas vernacular, even among women, but sometimes Debbie Sue took it to new heights. Clear back at age eleven, she'd had colorful language. When they were married, he had threatened a dozen times to wash her mouth out with soap.

"You're not angry with me, are you? I've already been thrown out of one house tonight."

"Debbie Sue can be a handful if you don't approach her just right. She can be . . . well, headstrong."

"Yes, I can certainly see that's true." Kathy smiled. "Living with her must have been trying. She's very juvenile for someone her age, isn't she?"

Juvenile? Buddy had never thought of Debbie Sue as juvenile, even when she had been one. As for living with her, when things had been good between them, he had never had so much fun in his life.

"I thought since I've driven over here, we might have some dinner together," Kathy went on.

Buddy was still lost in thought, and Kathy caught his attention only because he realized she had stopped talking. "I'm sorry, Kathy, you were saying?"

"Oh, silly, I asked if you wanted to go have some dinner?"

"Gosh, uh, wish I could, but I've already eaten. Plus I've got some things I need to look into, some phones calls to make."

She cocked her head and looked up at him from the corner of her eye. "Okay, I'll let you off the hook this time. But don't forget"—she rose on her tiptoes and placed a peck of a kiss on his lips—"I'm waiting for an answer."

Then her hands slid around his neck and she all-out kissed him. Her body came against him and she moved her pelvis against his fly. He could feel himself growing firm. Damn, this wasn't what he wanted. He took her wrists and unhooked her hands from behind his neck. "Kathy, I—"

She kissed him again, then gave him a teasing smile. "I know when I'm not wanted." She kissed the tip of her finger and touched his lips. "Bye, for now."

And she was gone.

He stood stupefied in the middle of the living room. He had a hard-on. Debbie Sue hadn't left his thoughts, but Kathy had turned him on. All he could do was sigh.

Experience had taught him that leaving Debbie Sue alone until she settled down was the best thing. He wished Kathy hadn't gone to see her, but it was too late now. Maybe it was fate.

He had no doubt the small kiss on Debbie Sue's palm had spawned a reaction, and he had made up his mind the next time the opportunity arose, he intended to give her more to think about. But Kathy stopping by her house probably had ensured the next opportunity was somewhere between next year and never.

Twelve

 Debbie Sue spent the greater part of the night vacillating between crying in despair and raging in anger. A part of her had known the day would come when Buddy would find someone and remarry, but another part of her refused to accept it. She couldn't remember much of life without him.

She stewed over two big decisions. With Kathy's announcement, she had no choice but to continue working toward collecting the reward money so she could pay off her debt and leave Salt Lick for good. She might go back to Lubbock to Texas Tech. Twenty-eight wasn't too old to start over in vet school.

If collecting the reward and reenrollment in college proved impossible, she would take Quint up on his offer. Either option would take her away from Salt Lick and a daily view of Buddy happy with a new wife.

She arrived at the salon uncustomarily late. Edwina's Mustang was already parked in its usual place. When Debbie Sue opened the door, she found the lights and the air conditioner on and she could smell a strong dose of brewing caffeine. A Toby Keith tune blared from the radio and Edwina was dancing in a circle with the broom, singing at the top of her voice.

Edwina froze mid-step. "What the hell happened to you? You look like you bawled your eyes out all night."

Debbie Sue rounded the payout desk and stuffed her purse in a drawer. "I don't want to talk about it, Ed."

"Only two things can turn a woman's eyes into road maps. Either a man or something she's allergic to."

"In my case I think they're one and the same." Debbie Sue sniffled. She walked over to her older, wiser friend, laid her head on her shoulder, and began to sob.

"Now, now, hon. It can't be as bad as that. Did you and Buddy get into a scrap again? Was it over this reward business? Was it Quint or Kathy?"

At the mention of Kathy's name, Debbie Sue's volume amplified. "She—she came by my house last night and—and—" Debbie Sue broke into racking sobs and couldn't continue.

"And—and what? You hit her? You threw her out? What in the hell does she mean coming to your house? She has no business—"

"She came to tell me she and Buddy are getting married."

"What? I don't believe it."

Between sobs, Debbie Sue recounted the story to Ed.

"Did you talk to Buddy?"

"Well . . . sort of."

"Uh-huh, I know what *that* means. I wouldn't believe it 'til I heard it from Buddy's mouth." Edwina set her away, yanked a tissue from a box on the payout desk, and handed it over. Debbie Sue dutifully dabbed her eyes.

"She wants you out of the way. Clear and simple. Hell, hon, one woman will say anything to another if she sees a threat."

Debbie Sue sniffed and blew her nose. Edwina stroked her hair. "Remember my ex Jimmy? I once told his girlfriend I had only a week to live and my last wish on earth was to spend that week with Jimmy. I had her going to the point she was bawling. She told me to have a wonderful week with him. I guess it was. We ended up married by Wednesday."

"Edwina, that's just awful. How could you do such a thing?"

"You've never heard the old saying, 'All's fair in love and war'?" Maybe that's what this Kathy person is thinking. Maybe she'll say and do anything to get the man she wants. I'd drive a tractor over one of my kin if—well, that's not a good example. I'd drive a tractor over *most* of my kin just because I had the opportunity."

Debbie Sue laughed a little. Edwina was good for a lot of things in life, including cheering up a friend.

"When you think with your emotions instead of your head," Edwina continued, "you always get the short end of the stick. We should talk about this later, after you've had some rest and a little more time to collect yourself. Don't make any decisions when you're heartbroken and haven't slept."

"No, Ed. I've been carrying that short-ended stick my whole life. I'm turning over a new leaf. From here on out, it's going to be about *me* and what *I* want." Debbie Sue squared her shoulders with renewed determination and went to the desk to check the appointment schedule.

The rest of the day went without interruption. She worked as if on automatic pilot. Customers came and went. She bleached, curled, teased, and sprayed nonstop, didn't even pause for lunch. Her first break came at two o'clock. She stepped into the back storage area for some privacy while she ate a Snickers bar and made her second call to Eugene in Midland.

After a transfer to Eugene's extension, a recorded female voice announced, "You have reached the office of Eugene Grubbs. Mr. Grubbs is no longer with our organization. If you care to leave a message please wait for the tone. If you prefer to speak with the operator please stay on the line."

What the hell? What had happened to Eugene?

Did he get fired? Did he quit? Was he on the run? Was he running in *her* direction?

Another voice broke into her scrambling thoughts. "This is the operator. May I help you?"

"I hope so. I'm calling Eugene Grubbs and I got a recording that said he no longer works there. There must be a mistake. I just spoke to him Sunday."

"I'm sorry, ma'am, but Mr. Grubbs submitted his resignation yesterday, effective immediately. Is there someone else who can assist you?"

Debbie Sue's head spun. She had the uneasy feeling that if she looked over her shoulder Eugene would be standing there. "If you can just tell me where he's gone, I'll call him there."

"I'm sorry, but he didn't leave a forwarding number."

"Can you give me his home address or phone number?"

"I'm sorry, ma'am, but that—"

Debbie Sue hung up. She had known the question was off-limits before she asked.

She must have had a dazed expression on her face when she walked back to the front of the shop, because Edwina said, "God, I have *got* to get you in a poker game someday. You look like you just saw a ghost."

"I've lost him. He's gone."

"Buddy's gone?"

"No, Ed, Eugene Grubbs. He quit his job. They don't know, or they're not telling, where he is. He was so scared Sunday he's probably in Canada by now. Or Mexico. Shit. My only suspect."

Debbie Sue sat down in her styling chair and rested her elbows on her knees, propped up her head with her hands. "I'm such a lousy sleuth. I didn't even get his license plate number. I have no way in hell of finding out where he lives, much less where he is."

"My sister's kid can find out anything you want to know on the Internet. He's a weird little sonofagun, but smart as a whip. Honestly, it would scare the stuffing right out of you if you saw what he can dig up on people. There's no such thing as not knowing where a person is anymore. If I'd had him and the Internet around fifteen years ago, I'd have saved a bundle on lawyers."

"Can you give him a call?"

"Sure."

"But be sure you don't tell him *why* we're looking for this guy."

Debbie Sue finished up the day and did her routine cleaning. She had never been so glad to see a workday end. When she stepped outside the shop to go home, she noticed for the first time the distinct smell of fall in the air. The summer heat still hung on, but there was the promise of autumn and lower temperatures.

And something else just as enticing—the aroma of burgers cooking on the grill at Hogg's Drive-In. All at once, her stomach didn't care about finances or love lost. It registered hunger with enough angst to get her attention.

Debbie Sue mounted the Silverado and wheeled into the drive-in, went inside to the front counter, and ordered a cheeseburger, a large order of onion rings, and a tall milk shake to go. Her bruised ego needed feeding, and there was nothing like grilled fat doused with ketchup and washed down with sweet ice cream to fill that ticket.

While she waited, she turned and gazed over the room full of tables and booths and diners and she saw him—Buddy, sitting at a table in the back corner with his deputy, Billy Don. She watched as he slipped a half teaspoon, never any more, of sugar into his coffee and lifted the cup to his lips. His tongue flicked a drop of coffee from his mustache. She felt light-headed, and the pain she had pushed to the recesses of her brain all day came full frontal.

She could hear his deep baritone voice, and when he tipped his hat back with his thumb and laughed, it became too much. She spun around and dashed for her pickup, fumbled the key into the ignition. She cranked the motor, backed up, and floored the accelerator. The Silverado lunged and came to a jolting stop. She had failed to press the clutch. Before every eye in Hogg's could land on her, she restarted the pickup, pulled away, and charged home.

Is this the way it's going to be every time I see him? I can't handle this. I simply cannot handle it. Yes, leaving Salt Lick was the right decision.

She parked in the driveway in front of her house and reached for her food. *Well, fuck.* She'd left it at Hogg's.

The minute Debbie Sue walked into the familiar surroundings of her home, before she even snapped on a light, she knew something was wrong.

Intuition in full gear, the hair stood up on the back of her neck and arms. She resisted the urge to turn and run and reached instead for the light switch closest to the front door. A small gasp passed her lips as she viewed the wreck that had once been her living room. Her reclining chair was overturned. Her sofa cushions had been thrown off, and the sofa bottom was cut into gaping openings with stuffing protruding.

Everything was in disarray. Drawers emptied, magazines and books scattered and torn. She found the same wreckage in every room. Even her bathroom had been trashed, and, most puzzling of all, some of her cosmetics appeared to be missing.

Instinctively she knew who had done this. Eugene Grubbs, looking for the fictitious tape. Well, he didn't find it, did he?

She spent the remainder of the evening putting everything back in order, adrenaline driving through her veins. It had been a while since she had done any deep housecleaning, so she incorporated that into the chore of straightening and reorganizing, which made for a really long day. By midnight she was spent. With exhaustion added to the sleeplessness of the previous night, she fell sound asleep as soon as her head hit the pillow.

The ringing of the phone seemed far away and dreamlike. She floated to the receiver. In her dream, Buddy was on the other end, calling her to thank her for a passionate evening together.

She giggled into the receiver. "Hi, sugarfoot—"

"Debbie Sue? Are you alone? Dammit, I must be getting old. I can't keep up with everything that's going on."

Oh crap. Edwina. Debbie Sue lifted herself from the haze. "What time is it?"

"It's late. Damn near eight o'clock. Still got time to have your coffee. I called to let you know what Curtis found."

"Did I know Curtis lost something?" She fought off the cobwebs clouding her thought process. "Who's Curtis?"

"My sister's kid. You know, the Internet geek?"

Debbie Sue was suddenly awake and alert. "Good, I'd like the chance to talk to that prissy little pissant again."

"When did you ever talk to Curtis?"

"Not him. Eugene Grubbs."

"Oh *that* prissy little pissant."

Debbie Sue explained to Edwina the condition in which she had found her home the previous evening.

"Did you call and report it to Buddy?"

"I wouldn't call Buddy if a whole damn wall

was torn down. It had to be Eugene looking for the tape, the one I told him I had."

"I've got his home address right here. You can make him a tape and mail it to him. Tell him you're gonna pull his ears off and stuff 'em in his pockets so he can hear you kicking his butt if he ever comes near your house again. You know, be subtle."

"This is serious, Ed. If he'll destroy my house, there's no telling what else he's capable of doing. I'm almost afraid to go into the shop today. He might have gone there, too."

"How does he even know who you are and where you live?"

"You said it yourself. There's no such thing as not being able to find out who someone is anymore. Now, tell me what Curtis told you."

To Debbie Sue's amazement, Edwina supplied Eugene's Social Security number, address, unlisted phone number, date of birth, education and employment history. He had no criminal record, not even a driving violation. One of his employers was Kisses Lounge.

Kisses Lounge? The only gay nightclub in Midland—or possibly in all of West Texas?

"Maybe you should give this information to Buddy," Edwina said. "I'm worried over your safety."

"I've been thinking about it, too. If we go into the shop today and the limp-wristed little shit has been there, I'll tell Buddy. If he hasn't, I won't. What do you think of that plan?"

"Like all your others, well thought out and clearly based on sound reasoning."

Debbie Sue arrived at the salon to find everything in the order in which it was left the night before. So what was her next move? Did she go to the home address provided by Curtis or try phoning again? She opted for the phone call. She would be braver over the phone. At this point, perceived bravery was all she had going in her favor.

After five rings she was ready to hang up when an answering machine picked up. "Hi! This is Eugene. If you want to tell me something, wait for the beep. If you're calling Janine, press two now."

Janine? Good Lord, was Eugene married? Did he have a female roommate?

"Surprise, Eugene," she said to the voice mail. "It's me again. You didn't find the tape, but then I guess you know that already. You didn't really think I'd be so stupid as to leave it at my house, did you? It's locked away in a safe place. It's time you gave up. I'll give you one day to think about it. I'll be waiting in front of the sheriff's office tomorrow night at six o'clock. We'll go in together, and you can turn yourself in. If you don't show up, I'm going in without you. I'll be giving the tape to the sheriff and I'm telling him everything else I know, too. See you tomorrow night."

She was shaking so hard, it took two attempts to hang up the receiver. The shakiness had to be from pure adrenaline coursing through her veins because she felt an odd sense of sudden strength and confidence.

The only thing to do now was decide what action she would take if he didn't show. All she had for evidence was a story relayed to her by a now-dead woman. If there was a paper trail of Pearl Ann's money and accounts, Eugene had probably disposed of it before he left the company. The tape would be the only concrete piece of evidence she had against him—that is, *if* she actually had a tape. The chance was looking good that the only thing she would collect in the way of reward was the dust the fund had accumulated.

Oh please, dear God. Let him turn himself in or I'm up one of your creeks without a paddle.

When Edwina arrived Debbie Sue told her about the phone call to Eugene.

"Janine? Who's Janine?"

"Maybe it's his wife or girlfriend."

"Nah, unless my instincts have gone south, I pegged that guy for being light in the loafers. Just for the hell of it, let's call back and listen to Janine's message."

"I don't know Ed, I'm—" Debbie Sue didn't finish her sentence because Edwina was already keying in the fifth number.

Edwina listened a minute, then pressed number two, keyed on the speaker phone, and waited. The soft strains of "Strangers in the Night" drifted through the phone, followed by a sultry feminine voice. "Well, hello. This is Janine. I'll be doing my show at Kisses tonight at nine. If you can't make it, please leave me a message. But trust me, honey, it'll be your loss if you don't come see me. Buh-bye."

Edwina hung up the receiver with a blank expression.

"That almost sounded like Eugene," Debbie Sue said.

Edwina's blank stare evolved into a big grin. "What're you gonna be doing tonight around, oh say, nine?"

"What am I ever doing any night around, oh say, nine? I'll be getting ready for bed."

"Not tonight. We're going to catch a show. I'm not sure, but I think we just might have located the elusive redhead you told me about."

Edwina's explanation of the voice mail message left Debbie Sue with a sick feeling in the pit of her stomach. Buddy's questions about a red-haired woman came back to her. Had the world gone crazy? Pearl Ann had been murdered, Buddy was engaged, and Harley was gay? "Eugene would recognize us. We'd be sitting ducks in a strange place."

"You don't get it, do you? We're going in drag. Dressed as men. The fort will be standing, but the little general and his troops won't be there."

"The fort? But why? Why do we need to do this?"

"What if Eugene goes underground and becomes Janine permanently? We have to know what he, I mean she, looks like, don't we?"

"Oh man. This wasn't supposed to get this complicated."

"You're right, there shouldn't be anything difficult about solving a murder. What a drag." Edwina chuckled. "Drag. Get it?"

"Ed, that's not funny. I'll go only if Vic goes with us."

"Ab-so-fuckin'-lutely. This would be like Christmas morning to him. Happy hour material for years to come."

Kisses Lounge was located in downtown Midland in an office building abandoned long ago by a defunct oil company. At eight-thirty Vic and his two new buddies walked in. The club was low lit with small tables and intimate booths surrounding a dance floor, with a stage at one end. Couples were in various stages of activity—dancing, sitting, or observing.

Looking around, Debbie Sue didn't see anything hugely different about this bar from any other she'd been in. The people, music, clinking drink glasses all looked and sounded the same until she looked closer and saw a day's growth of chin stubble barely visible beneath heavy makeup and chest hair instead of cleavage. The women were handsome men and the men had become beautiful women. Or something.

Debbie Sue and Edwina had achieved the

proper look without a lot of fuss. Edwina had trimmed some wisps of hair off an old wig and used her skills to make mustaches. Double-backed tape held the disguises in place. Once they scrubbed their faces of makeup, donned their usual weekend clothes, gelled their hair back and put on bill caps, the effect was startling in its authenticity.

Debbie Sue did go to the trouble of taking a couple of Ace bandages and pressing her breasts to a flat profile. Edwina achieved the same look without doing a thing. Vic suggested a more masculine walk for Debbie Sue and a rolled up pair of socks to stuff into her jeans for authenticity.

"I look like something crawled under my lip and died there," Debbie Sue complained.

"Well, excuse the hell out of me," Edwina retorted. "I did the best I could. I happen to think it looks real. Does *mine* look bad?"

"No, yours looks really good. Well groomed."

"Just listen to you two," Vic said with an eye roll. "Even when you're going out in drag you're worried about how you look. Unless you're hoping to get lucky it doesn't matter."

"Well, what's wrong with having a little pride in yourself?" Edwina whispered to Debbie Sue. Debbie Sue gave a thumbs-up.

"This place should be called Don't Judge a Book by Its Cover," Debbie Sue said.

"I never thought I'd hear myself complaining about a penis," Edwina said, adjusting the accessory in front of her jeans. "No wonder men are so hard to get along with." She grinned at Vic. "Excluding you, Poodle."

"I know," Debbie Sue replied. "If I had one of these things bunched up in the front of my pants all the time, I'd be disagreeable, too."

"Maybe that explains why they're always so eager to whip it out," Edwina said.

They chose an inconspicuous table that was private, but still allowed a good view of the stage. Vic ordered three beers just as the house lights dimmed from low to dark as a cave and the stage lights came to full voltage. A voice came on the sound system and announced that the lovely Janine would be making her appearance shortly and directed all to take their seats. The waiter—or was it waitress?—delivered their drinks and winked at Edwina.

"See," Debbie Sue said with a laugh, "I told you how good you looked. Maybe he or she will slip you a phone number before the night's over."

Edwina turned to answer, but just blinked instead. "What?" Debbie Sue asked. "What's wrong?"

"There's a hair in your beer."

"There is not. I just had a sip. You're being childish." She picked up her mug and it was all she could do not to squeal. Her perfectly formed mustache was floating on the surface of her beer.

"Don't worry about it," Vic said. "I'll lay odds that's not the first false anything that's been left in this joint at closing time."

Within minutes a ravishing redhead sauntered onto the stage. Her/his red sequined gown caressed her/his curves. Debbie Sue could see only a slight resemblance to Eugene, but to the unsuspecting eye she/he was all gorgeous woman.

Janine performed an ambitious routine of lip-synching to Aretha Franklin's "Respect," Peggy Lee's "Is That All There Is?" and brought the house down with Tammy Wynette's rendition of "Stand by Your Man."

At the end of the act, Debbie Sue and her coconspirators made a hasty exit. Vic drove them to a truck stop on the way out of town. Bored waitresses watched with no expression or reaction as the two men went into the ladies' room and emerged as women. Now, sans two "penises," they enjoyed strong black coffee and warm apple pie.

"Do you think you'll recognize Eugene again if you see him as Janine?" Edwina asked as they walked to Vic's pickup.

"I don't think I'll have a bit of trouble. He's one of the most beautiful women I've ever seen."

"Sweet baby," Edwina said to Vic, blowing a stream of smoke in the opposite direction, "did you ever find yourself alone with someone like that? You know, all promise and no delivery?"

Vic fished in the pocket of his jeans for his pickup keys. As he zapped the doors unlocked, his gaze shifted between Debbie Sue and Edwina. "Just once," he answered.

Something in the delivery of those two words

silenced Debbie Sue as well as Edwina for the ride home.

When Vic pulled up in front of Debbie Sue's house he volunteered to walk her to the door, but she declined.

"Just don't drive away until I get inside. No need for you to come in. Had fun, you two. Strange, but fun."

Debbie Sue blew them a kiss. As they pulled away, she waved one last time and pushed open the front door. She reached for the light switch. A hand covered hers. Before she could scream, pain exploded in the back of her head and her own lights went out.

Thirteen

Debbie Sue awoke disoriented and confused, with a dull pain in the back of her head. Her head felt cold. She reached to touch the tender spot and was surprised to feel an ice pack. "Sonofabitch—what the hell—where—"

"Oh thank God, you're alive. Lie still, don't move. I am sooo sorry," Eugene/Janine blabbed on. "I had no idea I had that kind of strength. You surprised me when you came in. I only wanted to stun you. Are you okay?"

The events of the evening began to unfold in Debbie Sue's crimped brain. She took note that she was lying on the floor, with a pillow under her head and her horse-design afghan across her body.

She twisted in the direction of the voice, and, despite the fact that she'd had the snot knocked out of her, she was taken aback by what she saw.

Eugene/Janine was dressed like a Ninja—black

running shoes, black sweatpants, and a black turtleneck top. He had removed the long wig but hadn't removed the stage make-up, the red lacquered nails or the four-inch chandelier rhinestone earrings.

"*I* surprised *you*?" She made an attempt to creak from the floor to the sofa and saw a gun in her attacker's hand.

"Don't move or I'll hurt you," her assailant warned.

"You've already hurt me, you little shit."

"Oh dear, I had this speech so well rehearsed. Now you've thrown me off. Give me a second." He cleared his throat as if auditioning for a part. "I got your little message. I'm not meeting you anywhere and you're not giving that tape to anyone but me. If you don't want to cooperate, maybe I'll have to make a call on your mother or your horse."

Under other circumstances Debbie Sue might have been terrified by the appearance of the intruder, the gun, and the warning, but her head hurt and it was hard to be too afraid of someone rehearsing a speech meant to instill terror in her heart while she watched. Still, she didn't want to underestimate him.

"Answer some questions for me first," she said. "Do you really think you're going to enjoy money you got at the expense of another person's life?"

Eugene/Janine gasped. "I've already told you, I didn't kill Pearl Ann. Just the thought of it—" He closed his eyes and shivered. "All that blood and . . . stuff. I can't even swat a fly. Are you sure you're okay? Can I get you something?"

For the first time Debbie Sue began to consider that he couldn't have murdered Pearl Ann, and he didn't have it in him to shoot *anybody*. She relaxed a little. "Okay, let's say I believe you. Why are you doing this? Why are you so afraid of the tape?"

His eyes teared and he began to sniffle. "I've worked for the Carrutherses since I left college. I have deep respect for all of them. They've treated me and the other employees in exemplary fashion." Debbie Sue reached for a Kleenex from the end table and handed it to him. He dabbed at the corner of one eye. "Oh dear, my mascara's running."

"You should use waterproof. Maybelline's the best. Finish your story."

"I *did not* respect or even like Pearl Ann. She was a greedy gold-digger. Why, Harley did everything in the world to make her happy. If I had someone who treated me just half . . ." His voice began to trail off, and Debbie Sue feared he might break into sobs.

He gathered himself and went on. "Excuse me, I'm trying not to be so emotional, but I've had one of those days when absolutely everything goes wrong. I've screwed up my entire life, and I can't seem to figure out how to stop this avalanche of despair closing in on me."

Avalanche of despair closing in on me. She had to remember that one for her mom. She fought the urge to lean forward and pat the knee of the man who had knocked her unconscious and was now holding a gun on her.

"When Pearl Ann approached me about helping her put back a little nest egg, I just couldn't resist the money. I'm so ashamed. The Carrutherses were so good to me."

"I can see where you'd be tempted. Five thousand dollars a month is a lot of money to anyone, but can we clear up one thing?"

Eugene/Janine looked up at her with a quizzical expression.

"Pearl Ann told me part of the payoff was sleeping with you."

He sprang from his seat as if he had been goosed. "That cheap, overdressed, over-made-up tramp. Why, the very thought makes me want to just put this gun to my head. I swear it does. How dare she besmirch my reputation."

"Calm down, Eugene. At this point, I don't think your reputation is what's at stake here."

"You're right." He dropped to the couch. "Oh God, what a mess I've made." He laid the gun on the cushion, hid his face in his hands, and burst into tears. Debbie Sue scooted closer and put her arms around him, patting his shoulders and saying an occasional there, there.

With her free hand she picked up the gun. Its featherlike weight told her it couldn't be real. Had to be a stage prop. On closer examination she saw it was plastic.

Her only suspect was no killer. *Fuck!* Now *she* felt like crying.

"The worst part of this whole thing, Debbie Sue, uh, may I call you Debbie Sue?"

She flipped up a palm and shot a glance at the ceiling. "Sure, why not."

"The worst part is—do you have another tissue? I hate it when my mascara runs."

Debbie Sue plucked a bouquet of tissues from the box and handed them over. "What's the worst part?"

He blew his nose with a loud snort. "I didn't stop with hiding the five thousand a month from Mr. Carruthers. I embezzled the nest egg for myself. That tape will start an investigation, and I'll end up in jail for embezzlement or a murder I didn't commit." He began to sob again.

"There, there," Debbie Sue said again and patted his shoulder. She couldn't keep from wondering just how much money Eugene/Janine had stolen.

"I'm too pretty to go to jail," he wailed. "I have delicate features. I don't want to end up as someone's prison bitch. I have a Ph.D. in finance from SMU, forgodsake." He placed a fist against his mouth and bit down on his knuckles.

"Give the money back. And what you can't give back, Harley will probably let you pay back. Don't you think that's worth a try?"

"It's gone. Not a cent is left."

"All of it? I mean, we must be talking thousands here."

"All of it. I've given it to a team of surgeons, the best money can buy, in Las Vegas. I'm going, or I *was* going to have a sex change operation."

"No shit?" It was all Debbie Sue could think of to mutter.

"Yes. I've known for as long as I can remember I was trapped in the wrong body. Can you imagine what it's like walking around as the wrong sex? It is hell, a living nightmare. I've spent my whole life in love with men I can't possibly have."

"Well, honey, who hasn't? I mean, really."

"When I saw the financial opportunity, I couldn't resist it. It's not like I really hurt anyone." Eugene/Janine burst into great gulps of weeping. "Damn these hormones. I've been taking hormone shots for weeks now preparing for the surgery. I cry all the time, and when I'm not crying, I'm eating. I'm not so sure being a woman is such a great idea after all. Oh, my life is crap."

If the scenario were not so tragic Debbie Sue could have burst into laughter. "Just so you'll know, I caught your show tonight at Kisses Lounge, and I thought you were terrific."

"You did? You thought the show was good? Do you think they'd like me in Las Vegas?"

"Why not? You knocked everyone out at Kisses, and you looked stunning."

"Really? You're not just saying that? You didn't

think I went a little overboard on the eye shadow?"

"It worked great under the lights."

"The hair, you didn't think the hair was too big? I could get another—"

"The hair was fabulous and the dress was to die for."

"You're just so nice to say such sweet things. You know, my mom made that dress."

"Get out."

"No, *you* get out." The two fell against each other in laughter, like old college roommates.

"Seriously," Debbie Sue said, "you need to come by the salon and let us do your colors for you. With your blue eyes and fair complexion—"

"Debbie Sue, are you in there?" The voice was Edwina's and she was yelling and pounding on the front door. "Debbie Sue, if you don't answer me, Vic's fixin' to tear this door off of its hinges. Debbie Sue, are you all right?"

"Ed, I'm okay," she shouted to the closed door, then turned to Eugene/Janine. "You better scram. Go out the back while I keep Ed and Vic busy. Trust me, you don't want to mess with either one of them. Vic's got a *real* gun. He knows how to shoot, and Ed will tear your arm off and beat you with it."

"Oh my gracious." Eugene/Janine covered his mouth with his fingers. "No offense, sweetie, but maybe you should find some new friends." He stood. "You're right. I'd better dash. Thanks so much. You're such a lamb. I'm so sorry I hit you. Oh, about the tape . . ."

"Don't worry. There never was a tape. Or a file. I only told you that to get your attention."

"Why you little hustler. You're quite the tease, aren't you? I could get really angry at you if I didn't feel like I've found a new friend." Eugene/Janine made kissing sounds in her direction and headed for the patio door leading to the backyard.

As soon as he was out of sight, Debbie Sue went to the front door and opened it. Edwina and Vic stumbled through.

"Where is he? Where'd he go?" Edwina pushed past her carrying a flowerpot of dead begonias from the front porch, poised to whack somebody. "Are you all right?"

"What are you doing here?"

"Your neighbor Mrs. Sanders called us and said she saw a man or a woman, she couldn't be sure, holding you at gunpoint. Why are you hanging on to an ice pack? Are you hurt?"

"I'm fine. Eugene Grubbs was here. I accidentally hit my head. Things are fine now. He didn't hurt me."

"See, Vic? I told you it wasn't necessary to call Buddy."

Oh no! "You called Buddy? Why would you do that? I don't want to see him. I have nothing to say to him."

"You have nothing to say to who?" Buddy entered the room in full professional mode. He looked around the room, his deep brown eyes taking everything in, his hand resting on the pistol riding on his belt. One eyebrow climbed up his forehead at the sight of the pot in Edwina's hand.

She looked down at the brown dried plant, too. "This needs water. I was just bringing it in to give it a drink."

Buddy strode toward the patio door Eugene had left open a few inches. Before reaching it, he stopped, bent over, and picked up something lying on the floor. He turned back to them, dangling a glittery long earring between his thumb and finger. "This belong to anyone here?"

Vic stood by, no expression at all, chewing on a toothpick. Edwina and Debbie Sue spoke in unison. "It's mine."

Buddy's eyes shifted between them. "So which is it?"

"It's hers," Debbie Sue and Edwina said in harmony and pointed at each other.

Buddy's fists jammed against his belt. "Okay, you two, I'm in no mood to play games. I want to know what's going on here. Debbie Sue, are you all right? I got a report a man and a woman were holding a gun on you. I want to know who and why?"

"It's a misunderstanding. You can see I'm fine. There was no gun. It was a hair dryer. I was fixin' a friend's hair."

"But your neighbor—"

"Mrs. Sanders is blind as a bat. Last Wednesday night she watched her aquarium for an hour before she realized it wasn't the TV."

Edwina flipped a wrist at Buddy. "Yeah, she's failed the eye exam at the DMV the last five times she's gone to get her driver's license renewed."

Debbie Sue could see Buddy wasn't buying it. His posture showed no hint of muscles loosening.

"Okay, that's enough," Vic said. "I'm not letting this go any further." He fished a small piece of notepaper from his jeans pocket and handed it to Buddy. "Here's the name, address, and phone number of the man who was here this evening. This is probably the second time he's been here. The first time he broke in and trashed Debbie Sue's house. I'm not sure what happened tonight."

Every drop of blood in Debbie Sue's body drained to her feet. She forgot her anger and that Buddy had hurt her heart. She forgot he was marrying the schoolteacher from Odessa. Truth be known, she'd come close to forgetting her name. She was a wreck.

Buddy studied the name on the notepaper for what seemed like an eternity. Debbie Sue could see he was so mad his hands were trembling. He folded the note and slid it into his shirt pocket, turning to face her. "Anything you want to tell me?"

"Eugene is a friend of mine. Since when did it become a crime to have a friend over? My house was broken into, but I don't know who did it. Nothing was taken. It was probably some kids looking for beer."

"Rest assured, all of you, I'm gonna get to the bottom of this. I'm gonna call the police chief in Midland and tell him to pick up this Eugene for questioning. If there's nothing to hide, then there's no problem, but if I find out you've kept something from me—"

"Oh and you'd be just the one to recognize someone keeping secrets, wouldn't you, *Sheriff* Overstreet." Debbie Sue glared up at him. "Yep, let's just all tell the secrets we're keeping."

"I don't have a clue what you're talking about, but I'm not finished with you." Buddy turned to Vic. "Thanks for the information. I appreciate your help." He touched his hat brim. "Ladies," he said, and strode into the night.

"Saaay," Edwina drawled, "that went real well."

Debbie Sue explained Eugene's visit to Edwina and Vic. By the end of the story, they were all in agreement that Eugene most likely had nothing to do with Pearl Ann's murder.

The moment the friends drove away from her house, Debbie Sue called Eugene and warned him he would soon be picked up by the Midland police. "Just stick with the story that we're friends and I was doing your hair." Debbie Sue pictured Eugene's bald head and bit down on her lip. "Believe me, if you can carry this off, you'll be getting that surgery."

"Thank you so much for your faith in me. I don't know how I can ever repay you." He/she burst into sobs.

"I didn't even ask if you have an alibi for the night Pearl Ann was killed."

"I *do* have an alibi. I was performing at Kisses. I had three shows and didn't leave there until almost daylight. It'll be easy to check out. We had a full house that night."

"You'll have to lie to the sheriff about taking the money. Do you think you can manage that?"

"Oh, honey, my whole life is a lie. Did you say the sheriff, the Salt Lick sheriff? Is *that* who I'm going to be talking to? Oh honey, put the cuffs on and take me in. That man is gorgeous."

"That man is a chickenshit. And my ex-husband."

"Are you kidding me? Uh-oh, I see lights flashing. Oh dear, I see two men in uniform coming to my door. Guess I better go. Let's keep in touch, sweetie." He made an exaggerated sigh. "I'm ready for my close-up, Mr. DeMille."

Driving away from Debbie Sue's, Edwina sweet-talked Vic into stopping by Hogg's for a pint of ice cream. It had been a stressful evening, and she wanted a diversion before returning home. Four cars were ahead of them in the drive-through line, leaving them time to talk.

"What's your take, Poodle? Do you think Eugene had anything to do with Pearl Ann's murder?"

"He sure had the motive. That's a lot of money, but the guy is no killer. If he was, he would have taken Debbie Sue out instead of looking for the tapes. Removing her from the picture would ensure that no one would know."

Taken Debbie Sue out? The gravity of those words struck Edwina hard. What in the hell had she and Debbie Sue been thinking, trying to find a murderer? Godalmighty, she couldn't find the remote control half the time. With Eugene/Janine being cleared, it pretty much put them out of the bounty-hunting business. That was fine with her. Nothing was worth one of them getting killed.

The next morning Buddy drove to Midland and interrogated Eugene Grubbs for two hours. He felt like a bully. The accountant was no bigger than a bar of soap after a hard day's washing. When Debbie Sue had first said she was doing a friend's hair, Buddy hadn't believed her, but he did believe she could have been doing the guy's, er, the girl's, uh . . . well, makeup.

Eugene was honest and upfront about the animosity he felt for Pearl Ann. He had an explanation for the sudden departure from his employment and the visit to Debbie Sue's house. When the call came in from the manager of Kisses verifying that Eugene had performed on stage the evening in question, Buddy had no choice but to erase him from the list of suspects.

"Say, Sheriff Overstreet," Eugene said as Buddy departed. "You should come by the club and catch my show sometime."

"Yeah, well, I don't get to Midland—"

"I'll do a special number just for you. Got a request?"

"Yeah, I do, Eugene. How about, 'From Now On, All My Friends Are Gonna Be Strangers'?"

"Ooohh, Merle Haggard. You've got it, cowboy." Eugene looked up at him like a bull yearling turned loose in a herd of heifers. "That and anything else you want, cowboy."

Buddy wasn't sure, but he thought Eugene batted his eyelashes.

Fourteen

 Debbie Sue came to semiconsciousness the next morning with memories of waking beside Buddy drifting through her mind. When they had been married, mornings had always been special. She would snuggle in close to him, he would wrap his strong arms around her, and even if they didn't make love, they would hold each other until they both were fully awake.

Her arm flopped over to the empty opposite side of the bed and found the unused pillow. Whispering his name, she pressed the pillow to her body. She imagined her hand wrapping around his hard, thick penis, teasing him awake with her thumb and hearing his soft groan. She imagined his work-hardened hands kneading her bottom and her sliding her leg across his belly. She shifted positions, waiting for the next part of the vignette when he would pull her astraddle him and . . . ohdeargod. She had forgotten how Buddy felt inside her. She could remember his intense eyes locked on hers, remember his outcry when he came and her own earth-shaking orgasms, but she couldn't remember how he *felt*.

She opened her eyes and sat up in her misery, wiping away tears with the corner of the bed-sheet. Why couldn't someone magically appear and give her the date and time that Buddy Overstreet would no longer haunt her dreams? If she knew that five, ten years from today, his memory wouldn't arouse her body or stir emotions in her heart, she would buck up and endure until that date. It was the daily ache that left her depleted, the fear that this pain might never end, that it had become part of her unchosen destiny.

The thought of him waking beside Kathy Bozo and doing with her what Debbie Sue had just imagined sent a pain so sharp through her brain, she couldn't bear to lie in bed any longer. Well, she simply wouldn't allow herself to think about it, she told herself in the bathroom mirror. She would fill her head with all forms of minutiae. If she needed to whistle "Dixie" and tap dance, she would do that, too. Whatever it took. Her heart couldn't stand this overload of grief.

In keeping with that strategy, she stopped at a produce stand a family of migrant workers had set up on the side of the road between her house and the salon and bought a couple of pumpkins to carve into jack-o'-lanterns.

Then she made her way to the Kwik-Stop a

block from the salon. With Eugene Grubbs cleared of the murder of Pearl Ann, she had decided she had better resort to Plan B for her retirement portfolio: lottery tickets. Saturday night's pot was up to twenty-four million. A win, coupled with a date with Quint Matthews, wouldn't be a bad way to end the week, especially considering the week's beginning had been a chapter right out of a Stephen King novel.

At the salon, lifting the pumpkins out of her pickup bed and positioning one under each arm, she kicked open the front door, ready for another day of glitz and glamour. The jingly bells on the doorknob whacked the door with a vengeance.

Under Edwina's watchful but wary eye, she placed the pumpkins at her work station, then marched to the back of the salon. She donned her smock and returned to the front. "Ed, you and I are fixin' to do some carving."

Edwina inhaled a puff of smoke and shifted her weight from one leg to the other. "A few days ago you were crying your eyes out. Yesterday you were assaulted by a cross-dressing fruit, and today you want to carve vegetables. You're either handling things really well or you've gone clear off the deep end. Which is it?"

"Eugene is not a fruit, he's a woman trapped in a man's body, Ed. A pumpkin is a fruit, not a vegetable. Now, listen carefully. I cannot, I *will* not, talk or think about Buddy and Kathy Bozo. If I do, I'll lose my mind. Do you want to see me lose my mind, Ed? Is that what you want? Are you interested in helping me carve these friggin' pumpkins or not?"

"Okay, okay. I woke up this morning with a driving urge for a horticulture lesson. You think I can work miracles with hair? Wait 'til you see what I can do with *fruit*. I haven't done one of these since my kids were little."

"It'll be fun. When I was in high school a bunch of us would ride out to Fiddler's Road on Halloween night. The guys would build a big fire and we would all sit around telling horror stories while we carved jack-o'-lanterns. Times were so simple then. Buddy would help me with my pumpkin because he always had a sharp knife and—"

Before she knew what hit her, Debbie Sue was crying. Buddy had been a part of those Halloween festivities for two of her high school years. How do you stop thinking about someone who penetrates every memory you've stored in the past seventeen of your twenty-eight years?

Edwina came over and smoothed strands of hair from Debbie Sue's forehead. "I know you don't want to talk about him, but since you're already crying, there's something important I have to ask."

"What?"

"Vic feels real bad about calling Buddy into that situation last night. He wouldn't do anything to upset you, but he thought the report of someone holding a gun on you was no joking matter. He hopes you're not mad at him."

"No, I'm not mad at Vic. Please tell him being mad at him never even entered my mind." Debbie Sue pulled herself together.

"Good, that's a relief. We're both looking forward to having you and Quint over Saturday night."

"Do you think Vic will like Quint?" Debbie Sue plucked a Kleenex from a box on the end of the payout counter and dabbed her eyes.

"Hell's bells, hon, you know Vic. He pretty much treats everyone the same. He thinks the world of you, and if Quint is someone important to you, then Vic will treat him as such."

Debbie Sue had to admit, at this point Quint *was* important to her. He could be holding the key to her future. Or she could be holding the winning lottery ticket. Either way, the gamble held comparable odds.

Buddy stopped in the middle of the main street to allow a carload of teenagers to pass. Jaywalking wasn't a concern in Salt Lick. To find a crosswalk, you'd have to drive clear to Odessa. The driver honked and all the teens shouted and waved. Buddy smiled and tugged at his hat brim.

Being a teenager—high school homecoming, football games, Halloween—man, what a great time that had been. The teenage problems that had been typical then seemed small and insignificant compared with what he faced now. He wondered if, in twenty years, he would feel the same way about his current predicament. Something, probably the dull headache that had not eased up since Pearl Ann's body was found, told him her murder would never be small and insignificant, but his most fervent prayer was that it didn't remain unsolved.

Buddy thought back on this morning's interrogation of Eugene Grubbs. If the man's alibi hadn't checked out, Buddy would have been tempted to arrest him on the spot and bring Debbie Sue in on general principle. She hadn't told him the truth about her relationship with Eugene. Buddy had no proof to back up his gut feeling, but the fact that Eugene was Pearl Ann's accountant smelled of trouble. Be it fornication or cooking the books, there wasn't a better dealer at the table than Pearl Ann had been.

Thinking about the victim made him remember there would be no get-together this year at the Carruthers party barn following the football game, a first in a good number of years. One year he remembered in particular when homecoming fell on a Halloween weekend, Harley announced the party would be a masquerade ball. Debbie Sue and he hadn't been married long, and he wasn't sheriff. Partying had been more fun when he was only a law-abiding citizen and not the law.

Debbie Sue was pregnant and couldn't drink alcohol, but they hadn't needed booze to have fun.

They had gone to the party as a football player and a cheerleader, only they added a twist. *She* dressed up like the football player and *he* the cheerleader. He took a lot of teasing about his hairy legs and the enormous prosthetic boobs that kept traveling from the front of his sweater to his shoulder blades. They both had laughed until they cried. She had gone a little overboard in painting him up with eye shadow and gluing on false eyelashes. The final touch had been the addition of a wig of long red—

Buddy stopped dead in his tracks. He felt as if someone had just put a fist in his gut. *Good Lord. The red wig.*

The sudden recognition of the elusive redhead nearly toppled him. Retracing his steps, he crossed the street and hot-footed to the Tahoe. A glance at his watch told him she should be home in twenty minutes, providing she didn't have a rendezvous planned with Harley. He drove to his office, grabbed some notes off his desk, and headed out, intending to be there when she pulled up.

Debbie Sue carved on her pumpkin between customers. She cut an opening in the top and scooped out the insides, all the while making sounds and exclamations of disgust. She had forgotten what a yucky job pumpkin carving was. Edwina dove into the project wholeheartedly. She chose painting a face over carving one and with the cosmetics on hand, was able to produce a jack-o'-lantern face worthy of a prize.

Just as they were admiring their artwork, the Christmas bells on the front door jangled and Eugene/Janine entered with the subtlety of a wild bucking horse. He/she was wearing designer clothes with all the accessories and looked every bit the part of a rich, well-kept woman.

"Eugene! I didn't know if I'd ever see you again. You look fabulous." Debbie Sue rushed over to meet him and kissed air beside his cheek.

"I just couldn't leave without saying good-bye," he said.

"Ed, c'mere. I want you to meet someone. Eugene, this is one of my best friends in the world, Edwina. We all call her Ed."

Edwina advanced slowly as she and Eugene/Janine sized each other up.

Eugene/Janine let out a gasp of recognition. "Well, my stars. If it isn't the Pizza Slut."

"I'm surprised you remembered me. We met only the once." Edwina actually blushed. Debbie Sue couldn't believe her eyes.

"Why, how could I not remember you? You have one of the most original looks around. I haven't seen anyone wear cat-eye glasses with rhinestones in years. You are truly one of a kind."

Debbie Sue glanced at Edwina, who today was wearing black and orange striped leggings, a black oversized sweater, and black high-heeled boots to her ankles. In addition, she had on orange glass bead earrings the diameter of a Dr. Pepper can and a black and orange cha-cha bracelet. Debbie Sue had become so accustomed to Edwina's colorful dress, she scarcely noticed it anymore.

"That's true enough," Edwina said.

"You're leaving?" Debbie Sue asked Eugene/Janine.

"Oh, sweetie, I'm on my way to Las Vegas. To be born again."

"I've heard people give a lot of reasons for going to Vegas," Edwina said, "but being born again wasn't one of them."

"I'll explain it later, Ed," Debbie Sue said.

"Oh my goodness. Who did the makeup on the pumpkin?"

Edwina spoke up. "That would be me."

"Oh my heavens, girl, you are so good. You certainly answered your calling as an artiste, didn't you?"

Debbie Sue broke in. "So Eugene, I guess everything went okay with the questioning by the sheriff. You're cleared?"

"Oh yes. I just left Sheriff Overstreet about four hours ago. My alibi was airtight. Kind of a shame, too. I wouldn't have minded spending a little more time with that luscious man. For whatever reason you two broke up, get it behind you, girl. That man is a keeper."

"That man is a—"

"Now listen to me, Debbie Sue, I've had more experience with men than both of you. Well"—he hesitated, looking in Edwina's direction—"maybe not *both* of you, but I know a real gentleman when I meet one. I've heard every homophobic remark in the book, and Sheriff Overstreet treated me with the utmost courtesy. Believe me, in this cowboy corner of the world, he is a rarity."

Debbie Sue was anxious to change the subject. She didn't want to talk about Buddy and she sure as hell didn't want to talk about his outstanding virtues. "You left one of your earrings at my house. I wish I had known I'd be seeing you. I would've brought it to the salon today."

"Don't worry about it. When I get settled in Vegas I'll send you my address and you can mail it to me. I guess I'd better go. I'm flying out tonight at seven forty-five. I just wanted to thank you again. Wish me luck?"

"You know I do."

He opened the door, then stopped and turned back. "Debbie Sue, you were right about paying Harley back. I will, as soon as I become a star. Or maybe I'll fall in love with a rich man."

"Wow," Edwina said when he/she had left. She dug a cigarette out of her pack at the payout station. "He's happier than a hog sleeping in the sunshine."

"Yeah," Debbie Sue muttered. "He did steal the money. I feel guilty. Should we tell somebody?"

"The money was gone a long time ago. At this point, what difference does it make whose saddlebags it's in?"

"But, Ed—"

"Shh."

She wasn't at home as Buddy had hoped. Not wanting her to see the Tahoe, he circled the block a couple of times and waited a safe distance from the house. Nothing about this investigation had gone by the book, but he was determined to fit at least one piece of the puzzle into place.

Approximately thirty minutes later her Camry approached. As soon as she disappeared into the house, he pulled into the driveway, took a deep breath, and slid out of the Tahoe. Walking up to the porch, he straightened his holster, removed his hat and punched the doorbell. The woman who opened the door did a poor job hiding her startled expression.

Buddy nodded. "Carol Jean, may I have a few moments of your time?"

He saw her quick intake of breath. "Has something happened to Mom or Dad?"

"No, nothing like that. I'm here in a professional role to ask you some questions."

"Professional role? Questions? About what?"

"I've talked to Harley several times about circumstances surrounding Pearl Ann's—"

"Circumstances surrounding—I'm sorry to be

so dense, but I don't understand. Harley's not in some kind of trouble, is he?"

"No. Listen, can I come in for a minute?"

"Oh, of course. I'm so sorry to be so rude." She stepped back and allowed him entry into her living room. "Please sit down." She led him toward her sofa. "Here, let me take your hat. Can I—"

He hung on to his hat, holding it against his stomach. "I'm not gonna be here long. Look, Harley submitted to a lie detector test and passed, but he won't give me the name of the woman he was with the night Pearl Ann was murdered. I need to know who the woman is and why he's trying to protect her."

"I don't see how I can be of any help. I don't know anything about Harley's personal life." Her enormous sky blue eyes grew even larger.

"You don't?"

"Why, no. I'm pretty low on the flow chart at CO&G, so to speak. I hardly ever see Harley. I answer to several people who may eventually answer to him, but I—" She smiled, showing a dimple. "Could I offer you something to drink? I've got everything from beer to Kool-Aid. How are you, Buddy? Are you still seeing that teacher from Midland? Or was it Odessa?"

She was talking faster than he had ever heard her, so he patted the air with his palm to calm her down. "Look, Carol Jean, we go a long way back. You stood up with Debbie Sue at our wedding. I'll never forget the song you sang at our baby's funeral service. I'm not gonna play games with you. I've followed Harley a couple of times when he left his building and took a redhead to his condo. I'm thinking the redhead is you."

Her eyelids flew open even wider. "Buddy, you know I date a different guy every three months. Once men figure out I don't put out, they dump me. Up until a couple of weeks ago, Harley was a married man."

"Maybe so, but I know his marriage to Pearl Ann wasn't made in heaven. It wouldn't surprise me to hear she cheated on him during their honeymoon. And if she didn't, it wasn't long afterward. I'm not passing judgment. I've talked to every person in this town and beyond about the murder. The redhead is the only one I've missed."

Tears suddenly welled in her eyes. She sank to a chair and ducked her chin. "I'm so ashamed. You mustn't misunderstand about Harley. He didn't care who knew we were seeing each other. It was me who made him lie. He was trying to protect me." She looked up at him with troubled eyes. "You know my folks. They would be so humiliated if they knew I had been seeing a married man, especially Harley."

Buddy took a seat on one end of the sofa and laid his hat on a sofa cushion beside him. This could be a long, fruitful conversation. "They don't care for Harley?"

"It's not that they don't care for him. But he has

a reputation for prowling around and they wouldn't want me to be included as one of the prowlees. They have higher ambitions for me, I guess."

"Have long have you and Harley been seeing each other?"

"A little over a year. He's so different from what people think. Pearl Ann told such awful stories about him, and we all believed her." She hunched forward, her fingers tightly interlocked. "Why do you suppose we believed her?"

"I don't know, Carol Jean, I really don't." He leaned forward, too, resting his elbows on his knees. "Can you tell me what happened? Start with the night of the murder."

She shuddered and wrapped her arms around herself as if she felt a sudden cold wind. "I'll never get used to hearing that word linked with Pearl Ann." She looked off into the distance as if she were seeing an instant replay. "He and I left the office about seven that evening. We always waited until no one was around or we would take off before everyone started leaving for the day."

She stood up and began to pace. "The wig was my idea. It's the same one you wore to the Halloween party that year you and Debbie Sue . . . Well, anyway, we went to the condo and I fixed supper for the two of us. It's such a novelty to him to have a woman other than a Mexican cook make a meal for him. The first time I did he was astonished. I think I fell in love with him that night."

She returned to her chair and sat down again, appearing to be less agitated. "His brother Justin—he and I are the only ones who have Harley's cell phone number—called early the morning Pearl Ann was found and told Harley."

Buddy had called the Salt Lick ranch house that morning and spoken to Justin, who assured him he knew how to reach Harley and would do so immediately.

"So Harley was with you the entire evening?"

"Yes. We didn't go out. We watched TV and read. Some evenings we just sat on the couch and talked all night long. You know how that is, don't you?"

Only too well. Buddy could see that Carol Jean was deeply in love with Harley, and judging from the reaction he had received from Harley when he questioned him, the feeling was mutual.

"They had no marriage. I'm not being the naive other woman. I've heard many conversations between the two of them. She didn't care what he did and he didn't care what she did, either. So many infidelities killed anything he felt. He actually hoped she'd meet someone and run off with him. He thought that would have solved his problems. I think she was too smart to do that. She liked having money and being named Carruthers."

"You've never heard Harley mention anyone he thinks could have killed her?"

"He said the list is so long it would probably never be solved. Honestly, I think she finally met up with someone a little meaner than she was. I'll always believe she told someone to kiss off one time too many." Her jaw tightened. "I only wish I did have a name," she said with more vehemence than Buddy had ever heard from her. "I wish this were all over and behind us. If Pearl Ann's murder goes unsolved, the stigma will hang over Harley's head forever. And mine."

Buddy didn't doubt it. A story as juicy as Harley and Carol Jean's would travel through Salt Lick faster than bad news at a church social. "I have one more question, Carol Jean. Why didn't Harley just get a divorce?"

"Being married to Pearl Ann didn't keep him from doing what he wanted to until he met me. I believe he would have divorced her eventually."

They sat in silence for a minute or more. Finally Carol Jean spoke in her childlike voice. "Being in love can be both a blessing and a curse, can't it?"

Buddy only nodded. She had said it all. There was no need for words from him.

Fifteen

 Buddy plopped onto the seat behind the Tahoe's steering wheel. The weeks of twenty-four-hour days wondering and speculating, theorizing and deducting had taken its toll.

With no other leads and no other suspects he was stopped as surely as a wagon with a broken wheel. He sat with his fingers on the key, just a motion away from turning the ignition. *What now? Start over? Throw in the towel, call the Rangers and turn the case over to them, admit I can't solve Pearl Ann's murder?*

On a sigh, he started up the Tahoe. What he needed most was a decent night's sleep. Maybe he could manage that much now that he knew the redhead's identity. No, he couldn't give up. Tomorrow he would go at it again with a rested mind. It would take more than a dearth of clues and suspects and nowhere else to turn to make him quit.

He pulled into the uncovered parking space near his small upstairs apartment and clomped up the stairs, the mystery a lead weight on his shoulders. Inside he dropped his keys in an empty ceramic bowl adorning the center of the dining table, walked over and turned on the air conditioner perched in one of the living room windows. On the end of the kitchen counter, the red signal on his answering machine flashed persistently. He groaned, pressed the button, and listened to a computer-generated voice while unbuttoning his shirtsleeves. "You have seven messages."

Seven. He had spent the week talking to people, even some he usually avoided. How could there be seven people he had missed?

First things first. He retrieved a cold Coors from the refrigerator, pried off his boots, and sat down to hear what he hoped was something new.

The first call was from his mom, from somewhere up north. Devastated by the death of his dad, she had been Buddy's financial responsibility for four years following his dad's sudden death. When she remarried a high school boyfriend from Abilene, Buddy approved. Since their marriage, the two traveled the country in their RV. She called from time to time to give their location and to tell Buddy she loved him.

He said, "I love you too, Mom," to the answering machine and pushed the button for the next message. Two calls from telemarketers, two hangups, a quick "Call me" from Kathy.

The last message chased his exhaustion right out the door.

At first he thought the caller must be one of his old friends from his younger days, and he replayed it. There was the unmistakable sound of voices and Tejano music in the background. Bar sounds. He heard what he suspected was the fumbling of the receiver.

"Shit," somebody muttered. Then the caller was talking. "Hey . . . hey, Sheriff Overstreet? I wanna tell you something." The deep male voice slurred, but the touch of Spanish was unmistakable. "I luffed Pearl. She luffed me, too. She was sooo beautiful. . . . Need to tell somebody I'm sorry. I gafe her a Texas bracelet and—"

"Please deposit two dollars and twenty-five cents for one minute," a computerized female voice said.

By now Buddy was on his feet, hovered over the answering machine. He heard more fumbling and swearing, then the line went dead. "Goddammit!" He slammed his palm on the counter. He did nothing for a minute but breathe hard and cuss himself for not having subscribed to caller ID. The machine told him the call had been made at two o'clock in the afternoon, but not from where.

Buddy was certain he had never heard the caller's voice. Until the mention of the bracelet, he thought it might be a crank call, but only three people knew about the missing bracelet—himself, Harley, and Pearl Ann's killer.

The TV remote was in Debbie Sue's hand, but her mind was at Midland Airport. She looked at the clock above her TV. Seven twenty-five, Eugene/Janine would be boarding soon for his/her trip to Vegas and a new life.

A new life. Debbie Sue envied anyone who had found the path to a new life. And the money to take them there. She felt lonely and thought of calling her mom. Nah. A heart-to-heart would only keep her mother awake all night. Edwina? Nope. Edwina's wisecracks wouldn't cheer her up tonight. Besides, Edwina was probably snuggled up to Vic, and why ruin a good thing someone else had going?

Then she thought of a voice she hadn't heard in a while.

Debbie Sue had strict telephone etiquette. She never called anyone after ten o'clock in the evening and she never allowed a phone to ring more than four times. An answering machine would pick up by then and if not, well, the conversation wasn't meant to be. Just as she was about to hang up, her old friend's soft voice with its Texas twang came on the line with a sweet hello.

"C. J., did I bother you? I was ready to hang up."

"Heavens no, I was running a bubble bath. How have you been?"

C. J. had always reminded Debbie Sue of a kitten. Everything about her was delicate and soft. Even her voice sounded like a kitten's mew. "Oh, you know. Same old, same old. Sometimes blond, sometimes red, sometimes a permanent wave."

"It's eerie that you called. I was just thinking about you."

Debbie Sue smiled. When they were teenagers, she and C. J. had often been awed that they shared the same thoughts at the same time. "Same wavelength, remember? If I called every time I thought about you I'd be on the phone all day."

"Oh, I know. I haven't been a very good friend lately. I don't even know what's going on in your life, I've been so absorbed in keeping my own on track."

Debbie Sue thought she heard a rueful tone. "Well, that sounds intriguing. You've *always* had your life on track. Since we were little kids you were on track and *I* was running *up* the track barely ahead of the speeding train."

C. J. laughed. "You managed to stay ahead of it, though. I'm afraid this time it's me who's running up the track. In fact, I feel like I've just been mowed down by that locomotive."

This kind of talk was uncharacteristic of C. J., the eternal optimist. C. J. had pulled Debbie Sue out of a quagmire of anxiety too many times to count. Having the tables turned left Debbie Sue speechless. Her reason for calling seemed selfish and petty now. It was clear that her friend was in need also. "C. J., what's up? Is there anything I can help you with? Do you want me to just listen?"

"Oh, Debbie Sue, I've done something I'm so ashamed of. Everyone in town will know about it soon. You know how Salt Lick is. I don't know how I'm going to handle the rumors, the backbiting and stares."

Debbie Sue allowed a moment of silence for C. J. to continue, but no words came from the receiver. "So what is this terrible thing you've done? Let me guess. You didn't take a book back to the library on time."

More silence, except for the sound of an occasional sniffle.

"I'm sorry. Don't mind me. You know I have to make a smart-ass remark about everything. I didn't mean to hurt your feelings. Are you still there?"

"Buddy just left my house, and I told him something I swore I would never tell another living soul. I won't be able to hold my head up around here. Once this gets out, Harley's life and mine will be as good as over."

"Buddy? Harley? C. J., maybe you just better tell me—Motherofgod, don't say another word to anyone. We'll get you a good lawyer."

"What are you talking about? I don't need a lawyer."

"Are you sure? The combination of Buddy, Harley, and admitting a secret isn't a good sign these days."

"Debbie Sue Overstreet, if you will just give me a minute, I'll explain."

"Well, you said you'd done something awful. Sorry. Jumping to conclusions is the only exercise I get anymore. Why don't I just shut up and let you do all the talking. Now, plain and simple, what's up?"

C. J. filled Debbie Sue in on the events of the past year. She told her how Buddy had figured out that she was the mysterious redhead and had come to her house to talk to her earlier.

Debbie Sue was stunned. She had never known Carol Jean Anderson to step outside the box. The overdue library book would have been an adequate surprise, but what Debbie Sue had just heard was a bona fide shock. "Did Pearl Ann know?"

"No, she rarely saw or talked to Harley. The only thing she knew about their marriage was what she wanted out of it. I don't know what you think of Harley, but he truly is a wonderful man. A lot of bad things have been said about him, but they're not true. Despite everything that's happened, this past year has been the happiest of my life."

"Hey," Debbie Sue said softly, "you don't need to defend your man to me. I always took what Pearl Ann said about him with a grain of salt. I've known the Carruthers family all my life. We all have. They're good people. I don't like to judge a person unless I've seen them do something with my own two eyes."

"Thanks, I really appreciate that."

"As far as what people will be saying, just remember it'll only be until the next juicy story comes along. You haven't done anything most of them haven't done or wish they could. People know you, they know you're no home wrecker. More important than that, they know Harley had no home to be wrecked. The only person's happiness you need to worry about is your own."

A long pause. A longer bout of sniffling.

"So just how serious is it between you and Harley?"

"I want to wait a respectable amount of time and then we're getting married. I hope the murder will be solved and we won't have to worry about it the rest of our lives. He wants children as soon as possible. Can you see me as a mother, Debbie Sue?"

"I can't see you as anything but."

C.J.'s crying resumed. "It's been so hard not telling you or Edwina. Thank you so much. I really do feel better. I knew I just needed to hear you say it's all going to be okay."

"Well, that's because it is. You, Ed, and I have to get together soon. I'm being nice and supportive tonight but I can assure you we're going to grill you for details of this lurid year you've been living, you hussy."

C.J. laughed and made promises Debbie Sue

knew she didn't intend to keep. "You're sure you're okay with this?"

"Okay with one of my best friends becoming one of the richest women in Texas? Yeah, I'm okay with that."

After hanging up, Debbie Sue sat quietly, letting C. J.'s conversation sink in. Suddenly it all made sense. The long stretches of time when they wouldn't see her. The lame excuses she came up with for her scarcity. Diamond earrings the size of aspirin tablets. Once Edwina had even said perhaps C. J. was involved with a married man, but then they had laughed it off as just too preposterous for somebody as innocent as C. J.

It just goes to show, things aren't always what they seem.

By midmorning Buddy had tracked the number and location of the pay phone from which the guilt-ridden murderer had placed the call. Unfortunately, he had paid with cash instead of a calling card.

Buddy wrote down the information, thanked the operator, and hung up. The call had been placed from a bar in Dallas called Luna de Neón. The Neon Moon. He intended to go to Dallas. With any luck, Luna de Neón would be a hole-in-the-wall bar, one of those places where the bartender knows everyone who comes and goes. He knew the chances were slim, but less than twenty-four hours ago they had been nonexistent.

He called Harley and asked him to stop by his office and listen to the tape. Harley listened several times, but admitted he didn't recognize the caller. As Harley headed for the door, Buddy stopped him. "Harley, I had a long talk with Carol Jean last night. I know she's the woman you've been protecting."

Harley dropped to the seat of the straight-back chair in front of Buddy's desk. "Thank God, that much is over. I promised her I wouldn't tell anyone. I hope you can understand why we didn't want anyone to know about us."

"You should've come clean from the beginning. It would have made everything easier all the way around for both of us. There's nothing anybody could tell me that would make me think ill of Carol Jean."

"You're right. We're old friends, Buddy. I should have trusted you more . . . But I just love her so damn much and I don't want anything to hurt her."

"It would've hurt her a lot more if I'd wound up having to throw your butt in jail."

Harley looked at the ceiling and shook his head. "Women drive us to do dumb things, don't they? Did I hear you say you're going to Dallas tomorrow?"

"Yeah, but first I want to go out to your place with this tape and let your housekeepers listen. Maybe one of them overheard this guy before."

"Juanita and Gloria? Go ahead. Good idea." Harley rose to leave. "Tell me something, how did you figure out it was Carol? I thought we were being pretty careful."

"It was the red wig, Harley. I wore it one year to a Halloween party out at your place."

"Damned if you didn't."

With those few words Harley was gone.

In the afternoon Buddy drove out to the Flying C and found both of the Mexican domestic helpers at the Carruthers ranch. They agreed the voice was not one they knew. Buddy thanked them and returned to Salt Lick to make arrangements for a quick trip to Dallas.

As he passed Virginia Pratt's place he scanned the pasture for a glimpse of Rocket Man. As if the horse knew Buddy would be coming by, he was standing at the fence facing the highway. While in the motion of slowing and pulling over to the shoulder of the road, Buddy scolded himself because of the daunting tasks that lay before him and the time constraints. But he had to say hello to an old friend.

He climbed out of the pickup and walked up to the fence. Rocket Man nickered and sawed his head up and down. Buddy rubbed a hand down the horse's sleek neck. "Hey there, ol' pal. How you doin' this evening?" Rocket Man snorted and sniffed Buddy's pockets. "I don't have anything for you today. Your mama has spoiled you rotten." Buddy scratched the horse's ears. "She's mad at me again. Take care of her while I'm gone."

Returning to the Tahoe, he made a mental note to call on Virginia when he returned. He had been too busy to drop by of late, and he didn't want her to think he had forgotten about her.

On the way to town, he radioed the office. "Tanya, is Billy Don anywhere to be found?"

"Yessir. He's out front roping the fire hydrant. Want me to get him for you?"

God, he wished Billy Don wouldn't do that. Having the citizens of Salt Lick see the deputy with nothing better to do than practice roping didn't give the sheriff's office the air of professionalism and serious law enforcement Buddy would have liked.

Buddy had inherited Billy Don. He had been hired by the former sheriff right out of the oil fields. Buddy had to remind himself that Billy Don didn't see his job as a career. To him, the job of deputy brought him a considerably smaller paycheck than the one he had earned on a roughnecking crew, but he would be the first to admit the hours were better and the work was safer.

"No, just tell him to stick around. I want to talk to him when I get in. Shouldn't be more than twenty minutes."

The thought of leaving Billy Don in charge of the citizens of Salt Lick for more than a day was worrisome. The deputy was a good enough kid. His heart was in the right place, but his heart wasn't what worried Buddy. His *head* was what Buddy could never quite figure out the location of.

Billy Don managed to muddle through day by day when most of the calls into the sheriff's office involved family disturbances or drunkenness. With Buddy never more than a short distance away, he had always been able to undo Billy Don's bungling. But on a homecoming weekend, the town would be filled with revelers, and few of them would be sober.

A look of panic spread across his deputy's face when Buddy explained he would be out of town from early Saturday until Monday. "It's important that I make this trip to Dallas, Billy Don, and I need to know you can handle any situation that comes up while I'm gone."

"You can count on me, Sheriff. I won't do anything stupid like I've done before, neither."

If the statement was meant to be a cradle of comfort, it missed its mark. "There'll be a lot of people in town for the homecoming. Lots of parties and drinking. All you have to do is keep the peace. Make sure everybody's safe."

"Keep the peace. Make sure everybody's safe. Got it."

"I'll be around 'til tomorrow morning, but I plan on leaving before sunup. Is there anything I can help you with before then? Any questions?"

"Just a couple."

Buddy was relieved and impressed that Billy Don showed enough initiative to have inquiries. "Sure thing. What?"

"Where do you store the riot guns? And are you going to leave me any bullets?"

Buddy didn't dare blink. If he did, he might cry.

"There's not fixin' to be any riots and you're not gonna need to shoot anybody."

If the deputy survived 'til Monday, it would be a miracle.

Sixteen

 Debbie Sue awoke Saturday morning
after a marathon night of bizarre dreams and restlessness, the tangle of her bed linens evidence of
the aerobic workout. The bottom fitted sheet lay
piled on the floor. The top sheet was rolled in a
ball and tucked into the folds of the bedspread.
One pillow was at the foot of the bed, and her left
foot was stuck into the other pillow cover, along
with the pillow. The last time she had seen a bed
this tossed was when—*stop it*!

Thinking of Buddy in *any* context had to end.
Thinking of him *and* sex in the same thought was
suicidal. Why in God's name did she have to wake
up every morning thinking of a man she could no
longer have?

She was a firm believer in the powers of the
mind. She had a perfectly good brain, well condi-
tioned. She would turn that old memory off and

turn on a new one. C. J. and Harley—now *there* was something to think about.

C. J. had always had her pick of beaus. Three or four had proposed, but the petite blond hadn't even come close to accepting. Debbie Sue and Edwina had speculated many times on what it would take to capture C. J.'s heart. Now they knew.

They? Holy shit! Edwina didn't know about C. J. and Harley.

Debbie Sue glanced at the clock and wondered if she had time to call Edwina and tell her the big news. No, telling it in person would be better. She headed for the shower.

Half an hour later, having applied a scant amount of makeup, secured her hair with a large clip, and squeezed into jeans, T-shirt, and boots, she grabbed her purse and was on her way.

In the drive through town, she noted more activity than normal for a Saturday morning. The Steers, Salt Lick's six-man football team, were enjoying a winning season, which added to the number of alumni returning for homecoming.

Years ago, during oil's heyday, Salt Lick had been busy and bustling. These days most of the graduating youth left and didn't return, choosing instead jobs that had livable paychecks and fashionable addresses in Austin, Houston, and Dallas.

It was hard for Debbie Sue to imagine herself anywhere but here, but if she elected to go with

Quint on his whirlwind stops around the country, this time next year, she herself could be one of the former citizens returning for homecoming.

A powerful need she couldn't ignore hit her. She was starving. She thought about the sugar-laden offerings from the Kwik-Stop, but dismissed them when she remembered the delicious sausage biscuits served by Vic. She still had an hour before time to open the salon. She could go by Edwina's, tell her the latest news, and if she was lucky, she would be offered breakfast. Even if Vic wasn't in town, a piece of toast sounded better than high-calorie pastries. She made a sharp U-turn and sped toward Edwina's trailer.

There was only one way in and one way out of Edwina and Vic's cul-de-sac address. Debbie Sue had no choice but to drive by the garage apartment Buddy rented on the corner. She wasn't worried about running into him though. He would have left for his office at least two hours earlier.

The radio DJ announced the next classic tune was a favorite from Dolly Parton, "Old Flames Can't Hold a Candle to You." *Well, that's appropriate.* She reached for the volume knob, cranked it up and sang along . . .

And nearly zoomed right past Edwina's and Vic's street. She stomped the brake and yanked the steering wheel. Before she knew what happened, the pickup skidded and fishtailed. When it corrected itself and came to a stop, a white cloud of caliche dust and dirt hung in the air like fog. "OhmyGod! Shit!"

As the thick dust settled, she saw a person in front of Buddy's place, covered in fine white dust. "Oh, shit." The mystery person was bent over beside a black Mazda Miata, coughing and sputtering. It was—*yikes!*—Kathy Bozo-whatever.

Maybe she didn't notice me. Debbie Sue eased past the dust-covered car. She pulled up in front of Edwina's trailer and dashed to the front door. When it opened, she practically fell in on top of her friend.

"Hey," Edwina said, "what's going on? You being chased by somebody?"

"Quick, c'mere. I want you to see something." Debbie Sue rushed through the living room to the window, pulling Edwina with her. "See that woman?"

"That's a woman? She looks like one of those tribal people from Australia. What are they called? I got it on the tip of my tongue . . ."

"Aborigine."

"No, that's not it."

"Yes, it is. Dammit Ed, I didn't come over here to give you an anthropology lesson.

"Well, professor, what's so interesting about an albino coughing up a lung?" Edwina parted the curtains for a better look.

"That's Kathy Bozonowsky. The woman Buddy's gonna marry."

"What?" Edwina pushed Debbie Sue out of the way for a better look. "What happened to her?"

"I turned the corner too fast and—"

"I swear to God, sweetie, if you'd been alive when they built the *Titanic*, they would've called it the *Debbie Sue*."

Debbie Sue stared with wide-eyed astonishment at her friend and coworker. "Why, Ed. You can't think I did that on purpose."

"No, you're right, if you'd had a purpose, you would've run over her. What the hell kind of a name is Bozonosky?"

"Not Texan, that's for sure. She must be just leaving." Debbie Sue felt a tiny sting behind her eyelids. "Do you think she stayed over?"

"Naw, Buddy left out of here around five this morning. He and I hollered at each other when I walked Vic out to his truck. That car wasn't there then. He looked like he was going out of town. He had a piece of luggage and some hanging clothes."

"Really? If she'd known he was out of town, she wouldn't have come by, would she? That's a good sign, isn't it? The fact that he went out of town and she didn't even know. Maybe they had a fight."

"Now there you go again getting ahead of yourself. Did you ever talk to Buddy about this engagement?"

"Well, no, I've been meaning—"

"The two of you make my ass wanna eat a biscuit. It's clear to anyone who comes in contact with either one of you that you're crazy about each other."

"*Were* crazy about each other, Ed. *Were.* What you're seeing between me and Buddy now is nothing but a lifetime of knowing each other. Concern and friendship. It's not so much his getting married that bothers me, but he's marrying a snotty goody-two-shoes. That really ticks me off. She'll make his life miserable."

A pang of conscience hit Debbie Sue. How could anyone make his life more miserable than she had made it with her cussin', dish-throwing fits, days at a time of bawling and bitching, and finally her absences of weeks at a time rodeoing, something he opposed. Well, she wouldn't think about it right now. If she did, she would wind up in tears.

"Oh, so that's how it is? Concern and what else? Oh yeah, friendship."

"I don't want to talk about it anymore. That's not why I came over in the first place. I have some really big news, Ed."

"Really big? Okay, shoot."

"Nope. First I want something to eat. I was hoping Vic was home."

"He went to El Paso, but I'll scramble you up some eggs. The coffee's still hot."

"I've got a nine o'clock. Let me have just some

toast and coffee. I'll tell you while you're getting dressed."

Perched on the end of Edwina's bed with toast and coffee, Debbie Sue told her pal about the phone conversation she had the night before with C. J.

Edwina stopped lining her eyelids and gaped at her in the mirror's reflection. "Why, I flat-out can't believe it. Why didn't you call me and tell me last night?"

"It was late and I didn't want to disturb you. I figured only one of us needed to lose a night's sleep over it."

"Well, no kidding. I wouldn't have slept a wink. How in the hell did we miss that?"

"I guess because it was the last thing we expected. We were so intrigued by Pearl Ann's love life, we didn't stop to think Harley might have one, too."

"And they're getting married?"

"As soon as a respectable time has passed."

"Respectable? Given what Pearl Ann knew about *respectable*, I'd say about thirty minutes should be enough."

"Ed, don't speak ill of the dead. She'll come back to haunt you."

"I wish ol' Pearl Ann would come back to haunt me. It'd be worth it just to tell her about C. J. and Harley."

*   *   *

Buddy's plane landed at Love Field and he rented a car. Salt Lick's budget wasn't flush, so he asked for the cheapest vehicle. He ended up with a compact he had to crawl in and out of and in which he couldn't wear his hat.

He headed for the Dallas Police Headquarters. As a professional courtesy and for the sake of safety, he wanted to let Dallas PD know he was in town and for what purpose. And since he had no idea where he was or where he was going, he hoped for some assistance from his fellow officers in finding Luna de Neón.

He parked in the slot assigned for visiting peace officers and joined the mass of pedestrians standing at the corner waiting for the traffic light to change. He was the only person dressed in Western-style clothes, and stood out like a sore thumb. In Fort Worth, he figured no one would have given him a second glance, but in downtown Dallas . . . well, he was *not* part of a pedestrian's normal day. He felt a tinge of sadness. Dallas had become so cosmopolitan it had lost the look of Texas. Most of the oglers were transplanted Yankees and foreigners who had never seen a real cowboy. Maybe they had never even seen a horse.

Buddy climbed the steep stairs and entered the law enforcement building. A real pretty young woman was sitting at a reception desk in the middle of the foyer helping some Asian tourists with a map. The moment she spotted him she diverted her attention and eyed him up and down. "Why, hello cowboy. Are they filming a movie downtown or are you with the rodeo?"

"No, ma'am." Buddy touched the brim of his hat in a gesture of greeting. "I mean, there *could* be, but I'm not part of it, the movie, that is. I've been in rodeos though."

"Really? I'll just bet you have. I wouldn't mind watching you perform in the saddle."

With Edwina, Buddy would have joined in the exchange of sexual innuendos, but with this beautiful stranger, who was obviously more worldly than he, a slow panic crept up his spine.

"I was wondering if you'd be good enough to show me—"

"I'll be happy to show you anything you want to see." She leaned forward just enough to give him full view of ample cleavage. "Do you see something I can show you?"

Buddy gulped so hard he thought he heard the sound vibrate in the elevator shafts. She was having a good time at his expense. He wished he could think of something glib and smart, but the truth was, he felt like a fifteen-year-old kid on a 4-H trip. "Could you please tell me where the office of the chief of police is?"

"Sure thing. Use the elevator just behind you. Go up to the fifth floor. When you exit, turn to your left and it's the third door on the right." She gave him a big red grin.

"Thank you, ma'am." Buddy tipped his hat and nodded in her direction. As he walked off, he heard her remark, "Now *that's* what I moved to Texas for." Women. He would never understand them.

When Buddy reached the police chief's office, much to his relief, seated behind the desk was a woman who couldn't be more opposite of the younger woman in the lobby. She weighed at least three hundred pounds and had frizzy gray hair. She was busy filing papers in an accordion folder and barely looked up when he entered.

"How may I help you?"

Buddy noted that the nameplate on her desk said "Ethel Price."

"Miz Price, my name is Sheriff James Russell Oversteet."

"Do you have an appointment, Sheriff?"

"No ma'am, I'm in town be—"

"Are you picking up a prisoner?"

"No ma'am, I'm in town—"

"Are you testifying in a court case today?"

"No ma'am—"

"If you don't have an appointment and if you don't have official business here, I'm afraid—"

"Miz Price, with all due respect, if you keep interrupting me neither one of us is gonna get what we need." Feeling ill-at-ease in canyons of tall buildings and throngs of rude people had worn Buddy's patience thin.

She stopped her filing and peered at him over

the top of her half glasses. A big smile replaced the sullen expression she had been wearing. "You're from West Texas, aren't you?"

"Yes ma'am, Salt Lick. Have you ever heard of it?"

"Sure have. A big unsolved murder took place there. Pearl Ann Carruthers. Salt Lick has the best six-man football teams in Texas and there's a beauty shop in that town that's located in what used to be a gas station. The owner put dresses on the old pumps out front. Do you know the place?"

"Yes ma'am, I sure do. Two women work there. You'd like both of them."

"I'm sure I would. Maybe I'll just drive out west one weekend and check it out. It'd be good to get out of the city. Kinda closes in on you after a while, know what I mean? Now, how may I help you, Sheriff Overstreet from Salt Lick?"

"I only want to report my presence here today. I'm headed to a place called Luna de Neón to ask some questions. Do you happen to know anything about the place?"

"Enough to know you need to give me more details. They don't pay me to just sit here and look pretty, you know. I decide when the guys in the back get involved. Why don't you just tell me why you need to go to the Neon Moon."

Buddy explained.

"You did the right thing coming by here first," she said. "I've worked twenty-five years in the police department. I could tell you some stories. Most yahoos come to town and don't check in. First thing you know they've gotten themselves into hot water and when they call us we don't know who they are, where they're from, or if the call is even legitimate."

"I don't want to end up as one of your stories, Miz Price. I surely don't."

"Well, Sheriff, it's too late now. Let me step into the back for just a minute and I'll get someone who can help you."

When Miz Price emerged, she had a young Hispanic man in tow. He looked to be seventeen or eighteen, but the detective shield around his neck meant he had to be at least ten years beyond that. He was dressed like a gang-banger, with the walk and posture fitting the role. Even through his disguise, Buddy sensed a strictly business attitude about the young cop.

"Sheriff Overstreet, this is Detective Efrain Gomez. He works undercover. He's going to accompany you to the Neon Moon."

Sober-faced, Detective Gomez extended his hand.

"It's good of you to offer, but I really don't need anyone to go with me. I have directions, and I think I'll be fine." Though it would be nice to have someone help him find the Neon Moon, Buddy wasn't eager to share his investigation with a stranger, detective or not.

"I understand what you're *not* saying, Sheriff Overstreet," the detective said, "but trust us, Luna de Neón is not a place you want to go into alone."

"I appreciate your concern—"

"Sheriff Overstreet," Detective Gomez broke in, "do you speak Spanish?"

"Enough to get by."

"Getting by won't cut it in Luna de Neón. The place is one-hundred-percent Mexican, ninety percent illegal. If they so much as smell *law*, they'll scatter. You gotta lose the gun and the badge. We'll go in my car. I'll explain on the way over how this is gonna go down."

The detective clearly had a grasp of the situation. Buddy believed a wise man knew his limitations. He decided it was time to follow the more experienced detective's advice.

"Miz Price, would it be okay if I leave my gun and badge here with you? I don't want to lock them up in my car."

"In town less than an hour and you're already thinking like a city boy. We'll make one out of you, too, if you hang around long enough."

"Thank you for the offer, ma'am, but I'll finish up my business and be heading home."

"One more thing, Sheriff Overstreet," the receptionist added. "How'd you get past Yvette?"

"Yvette?"

"The young gal who works the information desk in the lobby. She always has an eye out for a good-looking man. You want my opinion, *she's* the most dangerous thing you'll come across today."

Buddy laughed. "I hope you're right about that, Miz Price."

Standing beside Detective Gomez, Buddy rode the elevator to the underground parking garage in silence. The detective seemed to be concentrating on his own thoughts, and far be it from Buddy to disturb him.

Once in the garage, he led the way to a late-model Chevy. The car had been red at one time, but was now faded to a pinkish hue. The driver's door was turquoise. Duct tape secured the flattened side of a cardboard Clorox box to the passenger window.

The detective's wardrobe, the car, the cryptic warning—it all seemed a little melodramatic to Buddy. After all, it was still broad daylight. "Detective Gomez, is all of this really necessary?"

"All of what, Sheriff, the precautions? Trust me. I've done undercover work in the area around Luna de Neón for the past eight years. You do not fuck with these people. They would just as soon kill you as swat the gnat. Now, do me a favor." He opened the Chevy's trunk. "Please put your hat and wallet in here, roll your shirtsleeves up, and pull your shirttail out. You are going in as a jealous husband."

Buddy hesitated, reminded that it had been jealousy that prompted his behavior at Kincaid's when he saw Debbie Sue with Quint Matthews. Of all times for that notion to raise its head.

"Oh," the detective said, "and put a hundred bucks in your pocket."

Seventeen

 Debbie Sue arrived at work Saturday with a swarm of people and thoughts colliding inside her head—Buddy, Kathy Bozo, Quint, Eugene/Janine, Pearl Ann, Harley and C.J., Edwina and Vic.

She almost groaned when she saw Maudeen Wiley waiting for her, sitting in her great-granddaughter's mini-van parked in front of the Styling Station. Debbie Sue had always maintained a policy of "walk-ins welcome," partly for snagging last-minute customers, but mainly because a majority of the Styling Station's patrons were elderly. Since they couldn't remember if they had made an appointment, they often showed up as if they had.

As she helped Maudeen out of the mini-van and into the salon, the granddaughter pulled away in a cloud of caliche dust, leaving her grandmother in Debbie Sue's care.

The octogenarian settled into the reclining chair in front of the shampoo bowl. "I think we need to tone down this red color. I look like an Irish setter. And besides, the men won't leave me alone."

Debbie Sue draped her with a black cape, removed her thick bifocals, then eased her back to the sink. "I thought you wanted the men to be attracted to you."

"It gets tiresome fooling with them. They're too old to get it up. I told the cook at the home she should put Viagara in the oatmeal."

Constantly surprised and amused by Maudeen, Debbie Sue hid a grin. "What did she say?"

"Who knows? She can't speak English."

The cowbells whacked the front door, followed by the clomp of Edwina's platforms, and the day began with four people showing up at once. If Pearl Ann's murder had done nothing else, it had boosted the Styling Station's business considerably. One by one new customers had drifted from the competitor down the street to the Styling Station to hear the latest scoop.

As had become the norm since the murder, the first question every customer asked was "Have you heard anything new?" They assumed the sheriff's ex-wife had an inside track to the investigation.

Out front, Edwina was sorting and organizing and offering a free conditioning or a free set of acrylic nails if at least two of the women would make an appointment to come back on Monday.

Among the voices Debbie Sue recognized was Edwina's twin sister from Big Spring, Earlene. She hadn't been in for a free hairdo since Pearl Ann's corpse had been found, but like kudzu creeping over Georgia, the grapevine's fingers had had time to crawl over the scrub grass and sand dunes of West Texas. They must have reached Big Spring a hundred miles away because Earlene, whose visits were always accompanied by an ulterior motive, had come all the way to Salt Lick for some spicy tidbit to take back to her friends and coworkers at Wal-Mart. Earlene was about as welcome as a cloudburst at a rodeo.

Maudeen recognized her voice, too. "I remember when those two girls were born. Their folks came from Oklahoma, following oil field work. It was right after the war, I think."

"Which war?" Debbie Sue rinsed the last of the shampoo from Maudeen's hair and covered her red curls with a towel.

"Why, honey, the big one. And I can tell you their daddy, Art Elrod, didn't spend the war fighting Germans and Japs. He'd already screwed himself out of a seat at the table when he got to Salt Lick."

Debbie Sue giggled.

"Him and Edna had six kids," Maudeen went on. "All boys, and Edna was pregnant and big as a horse. When twin girls popped out, she was in a state of shock. Why, she didn't even have names for them."

Debbie Sue knew Edwina had older brothers, but they were seldom mentioned. They were scattered over Texas, Oklahoma, and New Mexico. Not much more was known about Earlene except that Edwina and she had nothing in common, and sharing the womb was the last thing they had done together. Debbie Sue helped Maudeen to a sitting position. "Ed hates her name."

Maudeen slid her bifocals on. "I don't doubt it. Why, Edna had picked out boy names so many times she just naturally gravitated to Ed and Earl. I expect Edwina and Earlene was the best she could do in the exhausted state she was in." On a sigh, Maudeen shook her head.

Debbie Sue helped her to her feet and offered her arm for Maudeen to hang on to. "You're probably one of the few people in town who even remember Ed's got a twin sister."

"Who'd want to remember Earlene? I'll bet tonight's dessert she's green with envy Edwina's captured that sexy-looking truck driver."

As Debbie Sue guided Maudeen from the shampoo room, she wondered if Edwina *had* captured Vic, and how brokenhearted would she be if he made up with his former wife?

Looking around the salon's front room, Debbie Sue saw a half dozen more waiting customers and wished she had rescinded the "walk-ins welcome" policy for the day. A heated argument had arisen about whether Elvis had really dined at Hogg's Drive-In.

Maudeen stopped in her tracks and planted bony hands on her nonexistent hips. "Why, I know he did. Why, he tried to pick me up right there in the dining room and take me off to the motel, but I turned him down."

Debbie Sue directed her to the styling chair in front of her station before a catfight among eighty-year-olds erupted.

"I want something special for homecoming," Maudeen said as Debbie Sue ran a comb through her wet hair.

"You're going to the homecoming festivities?"

"Why, of course. It's the only thing that happens in Salt Lick and this may be my last year to go."

"You're not moving out of—"

"Lands, no, but two of my friends croaked this year. I may be next."

"Nonsense, Maudeen. You're gonna live to a hundred."

Earlene, parked in the next chair and waiting for Edwina to retrieve some supplies from the back, piped up. "Well, I for one doubt if Elvis ever ate at Hogg's. I wish they'd take down that ugly pink sign. I mean, really. A pink and black plywood sign? It makes Salt Lick look tacky. I'm embarrassed to tell people I grew up here."

Edwina remained unusually quiet, as she always did when her sister was around. Earlene hadn't been in the shop an hour yet, and already she had flaunted to the audience of six her husband's good job at the post office. Jobs with regular pay and benefits were scarce as hen's teeth in the declining West Texas economy.

Earlene had also thrown out a remark or two about her successful twenty-seven-year marriage compared to Edwina's three matrimonial failures and boasted about how well *her* kids were doing without so much as asking about Edwina's three offspring.

In addition, she had reported how her ten-year career as a cashier at Wal-Mart was really taking her places, and she and her husband had paid cash for a new Crown Victoria.

No wonder Edwina was so quiet. Long ago, Debbie Sue and C. J. had determined Earlene thought herself better than Edwina. Well, for that matter, Earlene thought herself better than Debbie Sue and C. J., too. Lord, wouldn't she just die if she knew C. J. was on the verge of marrying Harley and taking Pearl Ann's crown as one of the richest women in Texas. If it weren't for violating C. J.'s trust, Debbie Sue would love to tell it.

"Edwina," Earlene said, "don't take this the wrong way. You know yourself I was overdue a visit to you, but I promised the girls I'd come back to work Monday with the low-down on Pearl Ann Carruthers."

"There's no low-down. She was found shot in her car. We're all waiting to hear who and why."

"Oh come on. You *have* to know the facts. This is such a small town and one of your best friends is the sheriff's ex. Let me tell you what I've heard. I heard she was found naked, robbed of all her jewelry, and r-a-p-e-d." She whispered loud enough for everyone to hear.

Maudeen spoke up. "Well, you heard r-o-n-g, Earlene. Pearl Ann was one of our own. The *fact* is, she's dead. The *fact* is, no one knows who killed her but the one who killed her. And while we're talking about facts, I'll tell you another one—"

"Now, Maudeen," Debbie Sue said, lifting the old woman's red curls and examining them and hoping to hush her salty tongue, "this deep red isn't going to be easy to change. If we try to go blond, it's liable to turn pink. I could apply a dark brown rinse, which would give you brown hair with copper highlights."

"That's fine, honey. You do whatever you think is best. And while you're doing it, tell me about your love life." Maudeen raised her voice loud enough for Earlene to hear. "Been getting any lately?"

"Maudeen!"

"You kids think you invented sex? How do you think you got here in the first place?"

"For your information, I do have a date tonight, but I don't know if I'll sleep with him."

Earlene couldn't help but hear, especially when

she was straining so hard to do just that. "You shouldn't be planning something like that ahead of time. Why would a man buy the cow if he can get the milk free?"

Maudeen threw her head back and cackled. "I never cared where he got the milk, long as he didn't forget the liquor."

Well, there you go, Debbie Sue thought. If there was ever anyone to give it back to Earlene in spades, it was Maudeen. And on that note, she retreated to the back room to find a brown rinse.

When she returned, Earlene was speaking loud and slow to Maudeen. "You really shouldn't be drinking liquor at your age."

"Have to, honey," Maudeen said. "Can't afford cocaine on a fixed income."

Earlene's chin dropped. "You're teasing, right?" She tittered and glanced at Edwina in the mirror. "She's teasing me, isn't she?"

Quick as lightning, Edwina answered. "Naw. She's snorted three husbands' life insurance right up her nose."

A great sigh came from Maudeen. "Nose candy. Nearly killed me in '68."

"Nose candy? . . . Well, my good Lord. I never . . . I don't know why I waste my time coming over here. You people are all crazy."

Nose candy? Where did an eighty-seven-year-old woman learn such lingo? But at least Earlene stayed silent for the rest of her visit.

Debbie Sue walked Maudeen to the door when her great-granddaughter arrived. The older woman pulled her down close and whispered. "Get yourself some of those lacy pants like those Victor Secret women wear. Your ass looks as good as theirs. Nothing makes a man hotter than sexy pants."

Debbie Sue laughed and hugged her favorite customer. "Shh. And by the way, thanks for shutting Earlene up."

"Why, honey, it was fun. I always enjoy taking on rookies. Hope I didn't hurt Edwina's feelings."

"Don't worry. She's in the back calling Vic. She had to wait 'til she stopped laughing to dial the number."

Buddy was glad Detective Gomez was doing the driving. He moved along the city streets with the ease of someone long accustomed to doing it. Buddy had been given some directions, but they didn't say anything about streets closed for repair, a fire engine denying access to an avenue, or street markers ripped from poles.

"You lived in Dallas all your life, Detective?"

"I came from Los Angeles about eight years ago. I worked undercover. Got injured in a drug bust. My wife thought it was a good time to move closer to her family. Even as a little kid, I wanted to be a detective. Coming here allowed that to happen."

Buddy looked with respect on the profile of a

man who had a lifelong dream and had actually achieved it. "Any regrets?"

"Never. Well, maybe one. I hate I waited so long and let so many things sidetrack me. But better late than never, right?"

"Yeah, right."

They had reached a part of the city that evidently had fallen on hard times. The houses that were still lived in had iron bars on the windows, and wary onlookers moved in and out of doorways. Car carcasses decomposed in front yards. Among them, wild-haired, skinny children ran and played as if oblivious to their surroundings. Scowling people, mostly Hispanic, seemed to be everywhere, and day laborers lined the street waiting for contractors to hire them.

It looked more like a Third World country, Buddy thought, than a neighborhood in the shadows of a wealthy American city, and he found himself appreciating Salt Lick and its sparse population anew. He was struck with the perplexing question of how anybody associating with a woman married to one of the richest men in Texas could come from this environment.

"Here we are. Now, Sheriff, once again, let me do all the talking."

Luna de Neón was a square, windowless stucco building painted mustard yellow. From any angle, it was in dire need of repair. The words "Luna de Neón" were painted in red uneven letters on the building front. A Mexican flag served as a curtain on the wooden entry door's windowpane.

Detective Gomez pushed open the weather-beaten door, and Buddy followed him into a gloomy room that reeked of body odor. October had brought cooler temperatures. Buddy could only guess how the joint had smelled in July.

The bar, located on the left, was lit by multicolored Christmas lights draped nail to nail from the ceiling. It looked to have been a drugstore counter in another time. A pool table crouched on the immediate right. Beyond, in the back of the room's dark recess, was a small dance floor anchored by an ancient jukebox blaring a Tejano tune.

When Buddy's eyes became accustomed to the dim light he could see the place was full of men who looked as if they had survived the roughest blows life could deliver. The few women present looked no better.

He followed the detective to the bar, feeling the cold stares of dark eyes glued to him, though no one paid attention to the detective. He said a prayer of thanks he had listened to Gomez. Had he let his ego prevail, right now he could be in a lot of trouble. Of this he had no doubt.

Standing beside Gomez at the bar, he feigned a relaxed stance and listened intently to the conversation between the detective and the bartender, who had a thick black mustache that reminded Buddy of pictures he had seen of Pancho Villa. All he needed was a sombrero and a couple of bandoliers crisscrossing his chest. Buddy's knowledge of the Tex-Mex language was barely good enough to make out the exchange between the detective and the barkeep.

The detective explained that Buddy was *un buen hombre y un buen marido.* Buddy deciphered "good man and good husband."

Buddy was married to Gomez's girlfriend's sister, Maria, the detective continued, and some guy had called her from the pay phone in here yesterday afternoon around two o'clock. Buddy was looking to find out anything he could. He added that Maria was a *puta* who had cheated before and Buddy wasn't putting up with it any longer. He wanted three things—the name of the caller, revenge, and a divorce.

The bartender nodded solemn-faced, said he understood the situation completely. He gave Buddy the head-to-toe, then told Gomez he wanted fifty dollars for information.

Buddy nodded and reached in his pocket for the bills he had stuffed in it back in the parking lot at the law enforcement center. He sorted out two twenties and a ten, tore them in half, and handed the three halves to Gomez. The detective passed them to the bartender and told him, "If he thinks you're telling the truth, he'll give you the other halves."

The bartender said there was a man in yesterday he had never seen. Mexican, but not from the neighborhood. He was present less than an hour.

He came in very, very drunk. He asked for a shot of a brand of whiskey not kept in the bar. He used the phone. The waitress helped him put money in the coin slot. He fumbled and dropped the receiver. The waitress heard him tell someone he loved her.

Buddy nodded and Gomez relinquished the remaining torn halves of the bills.

The bartender went on to explain that the caller was well-dressed, looked like he belonged in downtown Dallas. He was very tall, as tall as Buddy. Several of the women tried to hit on him, called him handsome. He left shortly after making the phone call.

Gomez asked if he saw the man's car, and the bartender answered he did not. Gomez thanked him and turned and addressed the room. In a loud voice he told them he was looking for the *hombre* who had made a phone call in here yesterday. *"Muy, muy borracho, bien-vestido, hermoso. Alto,"* he added and pointed at Buddy, which left Buddy confused. He thought *alto* meant halt.

Only stares came in response, wary and suspicious.

"They will not talk to you," the bartender said and chuckled as he wiped the bartop.

Gomez thanked him and they turned to leave. As Buddy reached the door, a hulking man stepped between him and the exit and placed a palm on his chest. He stood eye level with Buddy. His dark eyes glinted. Buddy took in the muscular arms covered with tattoos, a wide scar running along the right side of the stranger's face and disappearing into a black beard. Greasy hair hung past his thick shoulders.

The ominous stranger sneered, lifted his chin, and sniffed the air. "*Huelo el cerdo. Es usted un hombre del cerdo?*"

Buddy picked up on the words "smell," "pig," and "man," and that was enough. He knew one thing from working with wild horses. The biggest mistake you could make was showing fear. The same could apply to humans. He looked down at the hand impeding his movement and answered in the best street Spanish he could manage. "I smell an asshole. Are you an asshole?"

The big Mexican's black eyes bored into his, but Buddy refused to flinch. Suddenly the man laughed, showing gold front teeth. He turned to the room and raised both palms. "*Bastardo resistente,*" he declared.

Everyone cheered, threw back drinks, and slammed shot glasses on tables. The big Mexican threw his thick arms around Buddy, pressed him in an aromatic hug, and invited him to have a drink.

Buddy said no thanks and backed out of the bar.

"What'd he say to me?" he asked Gomez once they were back in the car and headed for the law enforcement center.

"The first time he said, 'I smell a pig. Are you a pig?'"

"I got that part of it. What'd he say that made everybody cheer? I understood bastard, but not the second word."

"He told them you were a tough bastard."

Buddy laughed. "Well, as long as they didn't know the truth. I was damn glad not to be there all by myself."

Gomez laughed, too. "It went okay. You did good. I don't mean to be disrespectful of where you came from, but have you ever thought about leaving Salt Lick? Pursuing law enforcement elsewhere?"

"I've had a dream of being a Texas Ranger. I can't remember ever wanting to be anything else."

"So what happened?"

"Life mostly. I was in college when my dad died of a sudden heart attack. He owned a service station. He and Mom hadn't been able to put much money back, especially helping me go to college and all. I quit school to run the service station and help my mom. About four years ago the sheriff in Salt Lick died in a car wreck, so I ran for the office."

"You still helping your mom?"

"Nope. She remarried."

"You married, got any kids."

"Divorced. No kids."

"How long did you go to college?"

"Two years."

"Then what's holding you in Salt Lick? You got enough college hours and experience to apply with the DPS now. Four years with them and you could be promoted to Trooper Class Two. Then you could ask for consideration for a Ranger position. You're what, in your early thirties?"

"Yeah, something like that."

"The average age of a Texas Ranger is forty-five. You're way ahead of the game."

The detective hadn't said anything Buddy didn't already know. "How do you know so much about the Rangers?"

"I looked into it myself. It didn't appeal to me and I didn't want to do four years with DPS. Like I said, I wanted to be a detective in a metropolitan area. Guess it comes with our upbringing, huh?"

"How's that?"

"A kid from LA wants to be a detective. A kid from Texas wants to be a Texas Ranger. Maybe we watched too much TV growing up."

Buddy laughed. "Maybe you're right."

The remainder of the ride back to the law enforcement center, Buddy was silent. He didn't want to disclose to anybody that the thing holding him back was really Debbie Sue. He didn't even like admitting the fact to himself.

All trainees with DPS had to complete a twenty-six-week training course in Austin. Once training was complete, consideration would be given to a request of assignment to a specific area in the state, but bottom line, a DPS trooper was sent where he was needed.

He had never been totally apart from Debbie

Sue, even when she had gone to college in Lubbock. Now, though they were divorced, he saw her often and usually knew of her activities. He hadn't been able to make himself leave her, and Salt Lick, behind.

Eighteen

 The Styling Station's last customer for the day was Debbie Sue's mom. The minute Debbie Sue began telling her what a hectic day she'd had, in typical fashion Mom said she would schedule for another time.

"No, please. I've looked forward to seeing you. Don't cancel on me now."

"Well . . . I'll leave you a good tip."

Debbie Sue said it was a deal and urged her mother to the shampoo room. She had no intention of taking a tip or even charging her mother. Still, she knew she would find a ten-dollar bill stuffed in her purse or her smock pocket at day's end. It was a game they played.

"Have you noticed all the commotion at the sheriff's office?" her mom asked.

"Nope. Haven't paid any attention." Debbie Sue cradled her mother's neck with a towel and tested the water temperature "You want coconut or strawberry?"

"I had coconut last time. I'll take strawberry. I heard the FBI released a flyer on a suspected terrorist who might have crossed over from Mexico. Billy Don's pulling everyone over to do a photo check. There must be a dozen cars parked in front."

The pleasant fragrance of strawberry-scented shampoo filled the small space as Debbie Sue washed her mom's hair. "Good Lord. Well, I guess it keeps him out of any real trouble. I can just imagine Buddy's reaction when he gets back in town."

"Back in town? How do you know if he's out of town? Have you two been talking?"

"Don't get your hopes up, Mom. Ed saw him leaving at the crack of dawn with clothes hanging in the back. Must be official. He was in the Tahoe."

"Hmm, I find that interesting. Aren't you just a little bit intrigued?"

"Nope. Am not." Debbie Sue rinsed away shampoo suds and placed a towel around her mother's head. "Now, tell me what we're doing with your hair today."

They walked together to the styling chair. "Same old, same old. Have you heard any more from Quint?"

"As a matter of fact, he's coming back to town and we're going out this evening."

"Oh? What are your plans?" Her mother's tone was less than enthusiastic. "You should bring him by the house. I'd like to see him again."

"No hard feelings, Mom, but running into my ex-husband the last date I had with Quint didn't exactly make for a good evening. I don't want to jinx this one. I want everything to be normal." She picked up a brush and a hair dryer and began styling her mother's short hair.

"Normal? What's your idea of normal? Dinner, dancing, gluing flies together?"

No matter how much Debbie Sue wanted to be indignant at the memory, it was still funny as hell and made her laugh.

While Debbie Sue and her mom chatted, Edwina had been busy sweeping up. "Well, no one's asked me—"

"That's right, Ed, we haven't."

Being cut off mid-sentence had never been enough to seal Edwina's lips. "No one's asked me, but I think Quint is going to expect an answer on his job offer. Since your mom's here, I think this is the perfect time to discuss it."

"Oh? You do?" Debbie Sue glared at Edwina.

"We both have a vested interest in your decision." Edwina fished a slice of Juicy Fruit from the pocket of her smock, peeled it, and folded it into her mouth.

"A vested interest?"

"We both love you and want the best for you, but *I'm* employed here and would kinda like to know if you're gonna be around."

"Ohmygosh, Ed, you're right. I'm sorry for being so selfish. It's not an easy decision to make. I guess I was thinking if I delayed it long enough it would either go away or an answer would just come to me."

"Sweetie, why is it such a hard decision?" Concern showed in her mom's eyes. "Is it not what you expected it to be?"

"On the contrary, Mom. It's more than I ever dreamed of. More than twice what I'm making now. I'd be working with horses, traveling all over the country with all expenses paid. I'd be going places and seeing things I've only read about."

"Humph. Sounds too good to be true."

There was no mistaking the skepticism in her mother's remark. "Maybe that's what scares me. It does sound too good to be true."

"Can I make a suggestion?" Edwina busied herself brushing sand and hair clippings into a dustpan. "This whole thing is a decision, not a tattoo. You don't have to commit your life to it. I could keep working in the shop. Hell, what else do I have to do? With the money you'll be making, you can pay off your debt in no time."

"But I have obligations here," Debbie Sue said.

"Like what?"

"Well, there's Mom and Rocket Man, my house . . ."

"Sweetheart, those don't sound like reasons," her mom said. "More like excuses. Rocket Man and I will get along just fine. Ed and Vic would probably keep an eye on your house. Why don't you try it for a few months? If it doesn't work out, come home. Haven't you heard the old saying, nothing ventured, nothing gained?"

Debbie Sue looked at her mother in amazed silence. She had expected a stronger debate. With a sudden rush of tears, she bent down and wrapped her arms around her mother. "Thanks, Mom, for always being there for me. You always know the perfect thing to say."

Her mom kissed her forehead. "That's because I love you."

"Christ, this is getting ridiculous," Edwina said, dabbing tears from her eyes. She walked over to the payout desk and switched off the radio. "So Virginia, what new number are you working on? I went around here for a week singing 'I Found Love on the Internet, but He's a Felon Serving Time.'"

"Believe it or not, I'm writing something serious for a change."

"You're kidding." Debbie Sue spun her mom around to face her. "I've been trying to get you to do that for years. Why the sudden change?"

"That guy I've told you about in Nashville's been after me a long time now to write a love ballad. I figure I don't have anything to lose."

Debbie Sue grinned. "Wow, Mom. Well—" she lifted her shoulders in a shrug—"nothing ventured, nothing gained."

Later at home, as Debbie Sue dressed for the

evening, she mulled over the conversation with her mother. Was Mom giving her blessing to Debbie Sue's seeing Quint? Had she given up on Debbie Sue and Buddy ever getting back together? If so, wasn't that a pretty good sign it wouldn't happen? After all, Mom did know everything that was worth knowing. It was all so confusing.

Debbie Sue took one last look at herself in the mirror while she hooked silver loops into each earlobe. Tonight she had chosen to wear her favorite outfit—a long-sleeved white satin shirt tucked into a black suede rayon broomstick skirt secured on the side with silver concho buttons. The skirt struck her a few inches above the ankle, showing off her black lace-up boots.

She topped it off with her black leather fringed waist jacket to complete the long, lean silhouette. She had always loved the way the jacket, secured by a single concho at the waist, made her waistline and hips look smaller. She had snatched it from a sale rack seven years ago and it had become a staple in her wardrobe.

Just then the doorbell rang. Quint. When she swung the door open he looked her over with a lecherous gleam in his eye. Before she could say a word, his arm circled her waist, he pulled her close and kissed her. He was an outstanding kisser who had all the time in the world to give her pleasure and she couldn't keep from kissing him back. It had been a very long time since a man had kissed her on sight, and he smelled like Boss. She had always been a sucker for a man who smelled good. The fact that he also looked good didn't subtract from the equation.

Just as suddenly as he had kissed her, he set her away.

"Wow, what was that for?" she asked.

"That's the way I like to end an evening, darlin', but with you, I thought it might make more sense to start out that way. Who knows what shape I'll be in by the time I bring you home?"

"Quint, please don't give me a hard time about Kincaid's. I really did feel bad about how things turned out, but I'd be lying if I didn't tell you that I've gotten the biggest kick out of remembering you and that pink clothespin. To be honest, I didn't think I'd ever see you again."

"I've had a laugh or two about it myself. Seems funnier looking back on it than it was at the time. But you know me, I'm an adrenaline junkie. Dating you's an adventure, sugar. Anticipating what's gonna happen next, not to mention the way you look tonight, could keep me coming back for months." He took her hand and gave her a twirl. "Pretty. Ver-ry pretty. Fringe is sexy as hell on anybody, but on you . . ."

He moved forward for another kiss, but this time Debbie Sue placed both hands on his muscular chest and moved back. "Hold on there, cowboy. We're supposed to be at Edwina and Vic's about now. They've invited us over for a home-cooked meal."

"Hmm." He planted a quick kiss on her lips anyway. "Then what?"

She slid her arms around his neck and they kissed again. "Afterward," she said as he sipped at her lips, "I thought we might check out the street dance."

"Darlin', if you keep teasing me, I'm not even gonna be in the mood to eat, much less dance."

She stepped away from his embrace, laughing. "You're right. We have plenty of time. This is homecoming weekend and Main Street will be blocked off and there's a good band. The weather's just right for snuggling, too."

"It's been a long time since I've been to an outdoor dance. I like the snuggling part."

"We'd better go. We'll be late."

The black Navigator gleamed in the driveway even in the dark. When Quint opened the passenger door, Debbie Sue stopped. Lying on the seat was a large rectangular box wrapped in gold paper tied with a rust-colored velvet bow. Her pulse quickened. Not wanting to be presumptuous, she asked with as light a voice as she could fake, "Do you want me to move that to the backseat?"

He came close behind her and placed his lips near her ear. "I'd rather you open it first."

The package was bigger than a breadbox. It had to be something to wear because she caught a glimpse of the store label on one corner of the box, an ultra exclusive Western wear store in Santa Fe. She drooled over its ads in magazines. Unless it sold socks, there was nothing she could ever afford in all its finery. She clasped her hands under her chin. "Ohmygod, it's so beautiful."

"You haven't opened it yet."

"The box . . . the box *and* the bow . . . I mean, this is such a surprise . . . It's just beautiful."

"Let's take it inside and you can get a better look."

"Let's," she said, grabbing up the package. She carried it toward her front door, weighing it as she went. Her hands trembled and she fumbled with the knob.

Once in the living room, she stood looking at the gift as if it might magically transform itself into something else.

"Well, if you're not going to—" Quint made a move to remove the bow.

"Don't you dare. I'll do it. Just let me enjoy the moment." On a deep breath she tugged the ends of the bow loose and lifted the boxtop. Nothing could have prepared her for the contents.

Tucked in sparkling gold paper was the most sumptuous jacket she had ever seen. She gasped. The fabric was smooth and black. She could see green leaves and beaded pink roses. "Ohmygod."

She lifted the garment out and held it away, viewing it. The intricate beadwork glinted in the amber light from her one living room lamp. The hand-sewn label told her it was a Manuel original. Oh, she knew the label all right. Manuel Cuevas was preferred couture for the rodeo elite and superstars. She had seen similar jackets, knew the cost had to be in the neighborhood of a thousand dollars. She gasped again.

"Let's see how it looks," Quint said. "I guessed at the size."

She lifted up her arms.

"Tell you what. Let's take off your other jacket first."

"Oh, shit. Now I'm embarrassed." Her cheeks burned as she caught herself behaving like a silly fool. She removed her treasured fringe jacket, replaced it with the designer model, then scurried to see her image in the hall mirror. The cascade of green, gold, and pink embroidery draped across the shoulders, down to the elbows and down the front beside the lapels. Her broomstick skirt and boots couldn't have been more perfect with it. For that matter, her nightshirt would have been perfect with it.

She ran her fingers over the Spanish-style embroidery, admiring the beadwork that accented it. "Quint, I can't possibly accept this. It's just too extravagant."

"You don't like it?"

"Are you crazy? This is the most gorgeous thing I've ever seen. I love it. But I can't keep it." She made no effort to remove it.

"I thought of you the minute I saw it. If you're going to be traveling with me, you've got to look the part."

The part? Part of what? Just how much was this vision going to cost her, she wondered, as she twirled in front of the mirror. She didn't want to linger on that question. Better to enjoy the look and feel of this piece of art around her shoulders. Quint was right. She couldn't accompany a big-shot rodeo stock producer wearing T-shirts and jeans. "Sounds like you're assuming I'll accept your offer."

"I'm not assuming. I'm hoping." He stepped closer and his arm circled her waist again. "Please tell me the answer's yes."

"Yep, the answer's yes." Tears burned her nose as the realization hit her just what her acceptance meant.

He turned her in his arms, and this time when he leaned down to kiss her, she didn't push him away.

On the way to Edwina and Vic's, Debbie Sue filled Quint in on the couple's relationship. Vic had rear-ended Edwina's classic Mustang at a red light four years ago. Edwina leaped from the car ready to give him a piece of her mind. Two days later, having given him that and oh so much more, she and Vic emerged from the Starlite Inn in lust and in love and had been there ever since.

"In a twisted way, that's kind of romantic," Quint said.

"It *is* romantic, Quint. They're made for each other. They're soul mates, and circumstances brought them together. They act like honeymooners."

"Don't get me wrong, darlin'. I've got nothing against honeymoons, love or lust as long as they're *not* in that order, but love that lasts forever just doesn't exist."

Debbie Sue was thinking about a reply to this when Quint interrupted her thoughts. "So I'm having supper served to me by an ex-navy SEAL? A man who's killed with his bare hands, who's strong as a bull and mean as a snake? And he cooks, too?"

Debbie Sue laughed. "Don't make fun of Vic. He's very serious about his military career."

Quint chuckled with her. "Okay. Just remind me to eat everything on my plate."

They stopped in front of Edwina's trailer, and Quint reached behind his seat and grabbed a plastic sack. He pulled out a bottle of champagne. "I brought this so we could have a toast to our new business arrangement, but I hate to go empty-handed to someone's home for dinner. How about we take it in and all four of us can share the news?"

"I've always liked men who were sure of themselves, but you take the cake. What if I'd said no?"

"I guess I would've had to use this four-hundred-dollar bottle of champagne to drown my sorrows."

"You're kidding, right? Nobody pays four hundred dollars for champagne."

"I do, darlin'. I do."

Wow. The decision Debbie Sue had made seemed to be more right with every minute. She turned toward the passenger window, looked out into the dark, and grinned.

Nineteen

 Edwina was waiting for them. She greeted them enthusiastically as she dragged them into her cozy trailer and practically grabbed Quint's hat off his head. She graciously accepted the bottle of champagne. "Oh, thank you, Quint. I'm sure this is good stuff. I noticed right off it doesn't have a screw-off top or come in a box. We'll enjoy it."

The second Debbie Sue emerged from the darkness, Edwina let out a whoop. "Somebody slap me blind. What in the hell are you wearing and where did you get it?"

Debbie Sue filled her in on the details of the surprise gift. She felt like a little girl showing her best friend the new Barbie doll Santa had left under the tree.

"Sugar, do you mind if I just put it on for a minute?" Debbie Sue removed the jacket with great care and admired it again as Edwina slipped it on.

"Vic! Vic, honey. C'mere. I want you to see something."

Vic appeared in the doorway wiping his hands on a kitchen towel. Edwina struck a pose. Vic showered her with a look of pure adoration, then took three steps across the room to Quint. "You must be Quint. Welcome to our home." The muscles in Vic's arms and shoulders rippled under his knit shirt as Quint's hand disappeared in his grip. " 'Scuse me for just a sec," Vic said then, releasing Quint's hand. "Got something in the oven."

Quint leaned close to Debbie Sue, shaking his hand to bring back the circulation. "You don't need to remind me. I *will* eat everything on my plate and love every bite of it. I don't care *what* it is."

"Hold up, hon." Edwina grabbed the bottle of champagne. "Take this with you. Quint was nice enough to bring it."

Vic accepted the bottle and moved closer to the end table lamp and read the label. He let out a low whistle. "I know for a fact you didn't run by Pinkies in Odessa and pick this up. This is an extremely fine vintage. Where'd you get it?"

Debbie Sue spoke up. "Quint, I thought you were kidding. I didn't know you were a wine connoisseur. Where *did* you get it?"

"I'm not a connoisseur. I bought it online from an auction house that deals in rare wines. I've got this hang-up. I like to own things other people want. But once I've got it, I tend to lose interest and look for the next thing. I guess the excitement of the quest is what turns me on. I was saving it for a special occasion."

Vic's gaze shifted between Debbie Sue and Quint, then landed on Edwina. "Did I miss something?"

"You got me. What's the special occasion?"

"Debbie Sue has agreed to come to work for me." Quint smiled and slid an arm around her waist.

"No shit? Well, that *does* deserve a drink. I'll get the glasses." Edwina disappeared into the kitchen.

"When does this take place?" Vic asked.

Debbie Sue was alarmed to discover she didn't have a clue how to answer Vic's question. She had been so absorbed with the issue of yes or no and the designer jacket, the date she would actually start this venture hadn't entered her mind. And now she had to wonder if *she* was the "next thing" Quint had to have and would subsequently lose interest in. She looked at him and laughed. "Looks like there's one small detail we haven't discussed yet. When did you plan on me starting?"

Quint did some mental calculations before answering. "I thought we'd get you on board by December. This is the busiest time of the year for me, and I'll need you to meet with one of my secretaries and fill out paperwork and—"

"You have more than one secretary?"

"This is a business, darlin', not a hobby. I actually have *two* secretaries and a staff." He started counting off on his fingers. "Two secretaries, a director of marketing, two bookkeepers, a couple of ranch foremen, two vets, and a handful of cowboys. You've got a lot to learn yet."

Indeed. She did have a lot to learn—about Quint's business *and* about Quint.

Edwina reentered the room with four paper cups. Vic took them from her and stacked them into one. He lifted her hand and gently kissed the top. "Sweetheart, let's use some better glasses for this occasion."

"Oh, dumb me. Of course. Be right back." Edwina made another exit. She returned with four Tupperware plastic tumblers. Vic gave her a look of pure adoration. Stroking her cheek, he said, "Mama Doll, this bottle of champagne probably cost several hundred dollars. I'll go get the good stuff."

Before he could leave, a frown puckered Edwina's brow. "Several hundred dollars. Why, Quint Matthews, do you just piss away money all the time or are you trying to impress us poor ol' country folks? I've never had anything in my mouth worth several hundred bucks in my whole life." She turned to Vic and squeezed his arm. "Uh, that is, until I met you, doll. You're worth that and then some." She planted a kiss on his cheek.

More shocking to Debbie Sue than the sexual innuendo was the pinkish hue she noticed creeping up Vic's neck and face. She wouldn't have imagined anything making Vic blush. "Edwina!" she said, laughing.

"Oh, come on, we're all adults."

Vic went to the kitchen and brought out crystal champagne flutes. Edwina took them from his hands. "Let's have a toast."

"Here, Quint, I'll let you do the honors." Vic handed over the bottle.

"You obviously appreciate good wine, Vic. I'd be happy to defer to you."

"Godalmighty, are we civilized or what? We're fixin' to have to let some pigs loose in the front yard if this keeps up. Here, let me do it." Edwina set the glasses on the table and snatched the champagne bottle from Vic.

Grasping it between her knees, she worked on the cork. Like a shot, the cork flew from the bottle and headed straight for Quint's face. With catlike quickness, he dodged the missile, staring as it hit the wall just beyond him.

"Man, you've got incredible reflexes," Vic said. "I haven't seen anyone move like that since I left special ops. What branch of the service were you in?"

Quint stuttered for a second, so Debbie Sue spoke up. "Quint wasn't in the service."

Vic's eyes leveled on Quint. "Why not?"

"He was world champion three years running," Debbie Sue blurted. "Bull riding." She had forgotten that Vic didn't understand why every red-blooded American man, woman, and child didn't serve his country.

"Oh. Well, that's too bad. The country could have used somebody like you." Vic filled each glass with the golden liquid, handed each person a flute, then sniffed the bubbling libation. When he lifted his glass, everyone followed his gesture. "Here's to new adventures and roads less traveled."

As the four glasses met and clinked, Debbie Sue felt relieved Vic hadn't pursued grilling Quint about his lack of military service. The teenage Quint, Debbie Sue remembered, probably hadn't given thirty seconds of thought to patriotic duty.

She took a demure sip and her eyes almost crossed. Oh well, she had never been much of a wine drinker, preferring cold beer any day.

Edwina took a gulp, held it momentarily, then ran to the kitchen and spit in the sink. "Good Godalmighty." She hacked and gasped. "I got vinegar in the cupboard that tastes better than that. I'm sorry, Quint, but if you really paid several hundred dollars for that, you got screwed. Or maybe I don't have very refined taste buds. Y'all can have my share."

"Don't worry about it, Ed. I don't think Debbie Sue is that crazy about it, either. Vic and I'll finish it off."

Debbie Sue left the remainder of her drink to the two men, who evidently shared different opinions from hers and Edwina's. Once the bottle had been emptied, Vic excused himself once more to the kitchen.

Quint and Debbie Sue took a seat on the sofa, sitting close with fingers interlocked. Smoothing strands of hair back from her face, he kissed her temple. "I'm happy you're with me."

Debbie Sue blushed and began to think how easily she could grow accustomed to this treatment. True enough, she had found out more about Quint and his business in the past hour than she had known before, but wasn't that what time was for?

Vic announced that dinner was served. "Hope you three are hungry. I made a big Greek salad, a great main course, and a dessert that's decadent."

Debbie Sue sniffed the air. "It smells fabulous, Vic. What's the main course?"

"Shrimp dumplings in a ginger broth. It's one of my favorite dishes, but I don't make it very often. It takes a long time to prepare. Tonight, for *you* guys, I wanted something out of the ordinary."

"Wait," Quint said. "Shrimp dumplings? Is shrimp a description of the actual dumpling or is shrimp in the dish?"

Vic gave him a bewildered look. "Shrimp *is* the dish. Is there a problem?"

"God, Vic, I feel terrible. I should've said something. I'm allergic to shellfish."

"Quint, I didn't know you had food allergies," Debbie Sue said. "Do you take medication?"

"Not usually. I'm careful about what I eat. I rarely have a problem."

Add that to the long list of information she had learned just tonight, Debbie Sue thought.

"Well, honey, you don't have to eat a lot of it," Edwina said. "Just a little bit won't hurt, right?"

"I can't even touch shrimp, Ed, literally. I'm sorry, Vic. I'm sure it's delicious, but I'd better stick to the salad. I'll make up for it on dessert. I love sweets."

"No problem. Like I said, I made a big salad. Let's eat."

The rest of the evening was pleasant. Small talk was made, stories exchanged. Debbie Sue and Edwina heaped compliments on Vic's head for his culinary talents. Vic demonstrated how to eat practically anything from grasshoppers to sticky rice with chopsticks, and Quint told what he looked for in a good competition bull.

"I sure am having a good time," Edwina said, her gaze traveling around the table. "What are y'all doing after you leave here?"

Quint put his arm around Debbie Sue's chair. "We're going to a street dance. Aren't y'all going with us?"

"Thanks, but no." Vic covered Edwina's hand with his. "I travel so much, I don't get near enough time with this woman. I'm guessing you two need to spend some time alone. And I *know* we do."

Edwina stood to clear dishes from the table and kissed Vic on the top of his bald head. "Just because there's no fuzz on top doesn't mean he's not a peach. I'll go get dessert."

"I'm afraid you haven't had enough to eat, Quint. I hope you like cheesecake," Vic said.

"The salad was plenty and I love cheesecake."

Edwina returned with the enormous dessert. A caramel-colored sauce dripped down the sides. It looked good enough to eat without the cake. It was a beautiful creation, Debbie Sue thought. Vic had really outdone himself.

"Can I have two helpings?" Quint asked.

"Honey, you have all you want," Edwina said. "You've been a real good sport tonight."

Waiting just barely long enough for everyone to receive a slice, Quint dove into his super-sized portion of the homemade cheesecake. He wolfed down three large bites, rolling his eyes and making little hums. "Thith ith wiwwy good," he said between bites.

Debbie Sue glanced at Vic, who glanced at Edwina. Edwina stared at Quint.

"Thorry I'm aking wude," Quint said, obviously enjoying his cheesecake.

Debbie Sue didn't know what to say. Vic seemed stymied as well, but Edwina said, "Hon, why are you talking like Elmer Fudd? Are you okay?"

Quint laid down his fork. "Oh thit. Whas in thith, Wic?"

"Just the usual stuff. The main ingredient in the crust and glaze is Frangelico."

"Fwangewico? Whas Fwangewico?"

"Hazelnut liqueur."

"Fug. I cannn ee nuth. Fug. I go inoo anphawac-kic thock. I nee a thot . . ."

Debbie Sue's eyes bugged as she stared at Quint. "You go into what?"

"Anaphylactic shock," Vic said, alarm register-ing in his voice. "Quint, do you carry epinephrine with you?"

"Jus a willle doze. Goo for en or enny minith. In my twug."

"I'll get it." Edwina sprang from her chair, knocking it backward to the floor, and charged to-ward the front door.

"It's going to take longer than ten or twenty minutes to get to help," Vic said. "The closest doc-tor's in Odessa. Debbie Sue, call your mom and ask her if she'll call Dr. Miller and have him meet us at his office."

Debbie Sue's brain had quit working. "But Vic, Dr. Miller's a vet."

"That's okay. He'll have epinephrine. Enough to let us get to Odessa."

Vic went to Quint and began to monitor his pulse.

"You're thaking me thoo a ved?"

Debbie Sue noticed Quint's lips had swollen and he kept pulling his hand away from Vic and scratching himself. She dashed to the phone in the kitchen.

"Hurry up, Ed," Vic yelled.

Debbie Sue's mother picked up and after hearing what happened, she agreed to call Dr. Miller.

"I found it." Edwina said, rushing back carrying a black leather zippered pouch, which she handed to Vic.

"Great. Quint, which one of these vials is the medication?" Vic displayed the contents of the case.

Quint's eyes flew wide. "Notthows. Notthows."

"Nachos?" Edwina asked. "Did he say nachos?"

"I think he's saying, 'Not those,'" Vic said. "Is that right Quint? Can you give me a hint?"

"Fuck. This is no time for charades," Edwina said. "Let's get to the pickup."

The phone chirped and Debbie Sue answered. Her mother informed her Dr. Miller was already at the clinic delivering puppies. "That was Mom," she told the group. "I said we're on our way."

"Not 'til we give him a shot," Vic said.

"What? I thought you already did."

Quint spoke up, "In tha gwuf bos. Ith willle. Wook inna gwuf bos."

Debbie Sue volunteered and dashed outside, needing to do something to overcome the panic racing around inside her. She found a small, single-dose EpiPen in the Navigator's glove box and ran back into the house. "I've got it."

Her toe stubbed on the threshold, she fell headlong through the doorway and met the floor with a painful whack. When she opened her eyes, the tiny syringe containing the single dose of medication was stuck in the linoleum of Edwina's entry floor, plunger pressed down, medication fully released into the white and gray tile pattern.

"Well, I'm just lost for words," Edwina said.

"Okay, that's that. Let's move out," Vic ordered, helping Quint to his feet.

Within a matter of minutes they were in Dr. Miller's office, where he handed Quint a minimal dose of epinephrine. Vic administered it while Edwina and Debbie Sue oohed and aahed over the litter of puppies Dr. Miller had just helped a small dachshund deliver.

"Ladies," Dr. Miller said, "I hate to throw cold water on your maternal instincts, but this dose won't last long and he needs to get on his way. Mr. Matthews, I'm sending another EpiPen with you in case you need it."

The doctor took Debbie Sue aside, speaking softly. "I'm a little uneasy about his heart rate. Granted, I'm not accustomed to humans, but I still think it's a little erratic. Be sure to mention that to the physician you see in Odessa, okay?"

"Sure. Of course."

Quint made several attempts to pay Dr. Miller, but the veterinarian wouldn't hear of it. "Nonsense, Mr. Matthews. I didn't do anything these folks here couldn't have done if they'd had the medication."

Debbie Sue gave Quint a guilty look and squeezed his arm, "You know I feel just awful about falling with your shot, don't you?"

"Cuh happen oo anyone. On't worry."

"And you know I feel bad about that dessert," Vic said. "Hell, I never thought something like this would happen."

"He understands," Debbie Sue said, mopping Quint's face with a wet towel she had picked up in Dr. Miller's delivery room.

"I'm sure there'll be something I should apologize for before the evening's over," Edwina said. "If it's all the same to you, I'll just wait 'til then."

Keeping in mind what Dr. Miller had said about Quint's heart rate, Debbie Sue asked Vic to drive. Quint crawled into the backseat without an argument and Debbie Sue followed. As they passed through town, they couldn't miss the commotion at the sheriff's office. Every light in the building was on and a dozen or more cars were parked in front. Whatever was going on couldn't be good.

They arrived at the emergency room just as Quint's shot began to wear off. After taking the rudimentary medical history, the doctor instructed the nurse to administer medication. The doctor seemed competent and in control of the situation, despite the fact that Edwina had described him as an "infant with a five o'clock shadow."

Before Debbie Sue even had the chance to mention what Dr. Miller had told her, the young doctor approached the waiting group. "I'm afraid I'm going to keep Mr. Matthews overnight, just as a precaution. His reaction to the allergens seems to be under control but I noticed something on his EKG that makes me reluctant to release him tonight. Especially since he isn't staying in the immediate vicinity." His gaze stopped on Debbie Sue, and she felt her cheeks burn red hot.

"I've given him something that'll help him sleep," the doctor went on. "There's no need for any of you to stay. I'll let you speak to him and then we'll send him to a room for the night. He's in treatment room number three."

Allowing no time for discussion, he was gone to the next patient.

"Well, my Lord, Debbie Sue," Edwina said, "what do you make of that? Has Quint ever had heart problems before?"

"I don't know. I don't know if any of this has ever happened before. This whole evening has been one scrap of new information after another. Do y'all want to go with me to talk to him?"

"Nah, you go on ahead," Vic said, taking a seat and pulling Edwina down with him. "We'll wait here."

Debbie Sue tiptoed to the curtain closing off room number three from the rest of the medical area. She wasn't sure why she felt the need to be stealthlike. Probably from her childhood when her mother shushed her in any hospital setting because of the "sick people."

She peered gingerly around the opening in the drape. "Quint? Are you okay?"

He was lying on his back, EKG leads still glued

to his chest. His head was tilted back slightly and his lips were moving.

"Quint, are you all right? Should I call the nurse?"

"I'm okay. I was just trying to figure out what it takes to stay conscious through an entire evening with you. I don't know how we ever hooked up in Vegas, I really don't. I should've shot some craps that night 'cause I was riding a lucky streak."

Debbie Sue bit her lip. There did seem to be some cosmic force keeping them apart. Their last encounter had sent her running to the unopened arms of Buddy. There was no running to Buddy this time, and circumstances had already made it apparent that option wouldn't be available in the future either. "I'm worried about your heart, Quint. Has this ever happened before?"

"I tried to tell that kid it was because I'd been drinking, but he wouldn't listen. If I take one of those epinephrine shots when I'm drinking, my heart rate goes through the ceiling. Now he's got me damn near sedated and spending the night. I should just get up and go." He threw back the covers and made an attempt to rise from the bed, but immediately fell back. "Fuck, I feel like I'm fixin' to puke."

Acting on instinct, Debbie Sue grabbed the first thing handy and shoved it under his face. Everything he'd eaten in the past few hours emptied into his silver belly Stetson that had probably cost four hundred dollars.

"Oh dear," Debbie Sue said, backing toward the drape. "I just grabbed . . . I didn't see . . . I'll call the nurse to clean that up. Maybe I should go now. I'll be back in the morning."

She made her exit, and as she walked toward Edwina and Vic they stood up. "Should we go in and say something?" Vic asked.

"Oh, I wouldn't just now. I called the nurse, and she's on her way in. He's really sleepy. I think we should just go."

The threesome returned to Salt Lick just before midnight. The homecoming festivities were breaking up. Debbie Sue woke Edwina and Vic as she pulled in front of their trailer.

"Do you need me to ride with you tomorrow morning when you pick up Quint?" Edwina offered.

"No, Ed. Thanks, but you sleep in. I'll get over there early. He's bound to have things he needs to take care of. Thanks again for the evening."

"Don't thank me. I've done less damage on a night raid," Vic said.

"Nonsense. I'll talk to y'all tomorrow."

At home, though she was exhausted, Debbie Sue went through the nightly routine of cleansing her face. She thought back on the evening and the events. As determined as she had been to have a normal evening, it hadn't gone much better than the dinner at Kincaid's.

The next morning she woke a little later than she had planned on. She didn't usually set an alarm on Sundays. She always woke at her usual time automatically. But here it was nine o'clock. She took special care with her makeup and hair. Instead of her usual jeans and T-shirt, she donned a soft red velour jogging suit. The color was a good contrast with her hair, and the fabric hugged her curves in all the right places. When she opened her front door, she was shocked to see her driveway empty. Where the hell was the Navigator?

Before she screamed in full-blown panic that a fifty-thousand-dollar automobile had disappeared from her driveway, a fluttering sound drew her attention to the mailbox mounted on the left side of her door. A note was secured with the pink plastic clothespin she remembered handing Quint to use to close his fly.

I left the hospital against medical advice. Does that make me a fugitive? I sweet-talked a nurse into giving me a ride. Tried to wake you up, but I guess you didn't hear me knocking. Got to get down the road. Call you later. Thanks for everything.

QM

Debbie Sue stamped her foot and covered her face with both hands. "Well, fuck."

Twenty

Buddy was up, packed, and out the motel room door by five-thirty A.M. He had never slept late a day in his life, yet he had set the alarm and left a wake-up call just to be sure he didn't miss his seven o'clock flight. The one-hour trip would put him in Midland around eight and in Salt Lick no later than nine-thirty. He was leaving a day earlier than he had planned. As soon as he reached home, he would start working his new leads.

Just outside the Love Field gates, he came to an IHOP. He had time to enjoy a leisurely breakfast. He was sipping coffee when he opened the complimentary newspaper and read the lead story. Several people had been shot at a local bar. A grainy picture of Luna de Neón was displayed beside the story. His heart made a little bump. He scanned the article for the name of Detective Gomez and felt relieved when he didn't find it.

Allegedly, the fight had started over a wife finding her husband with another woman. The club's only bartender tried to intervene and was shot dead, along with the cheating husband and his mistress.

Buddy finished the article a little breathless. If he had made the trip to Dallas one day later, he would have missed obtaining a valuable piece of information, perhaps the key to solving Pearl Ann's murder. Then it hit him, the only person who could identify the mysterious Mexican who had called him was now a dead man. And he had no clue who the waitress was who had helped the suspect deposit money into the phone. *Damn.*

For the hour-long flight from Dallas to Midland, Buddy felt like a caged animal. He turned the pages of a magazine for the whole hour, but didn't read a word. When the plane landed he was up and out of his seat before anyone else.

He was so anxious to get back and start working on the case, he had forgotten about his worry over Billy Don, but when he pulled within sight of the sheriff's rear entrance he knew something was wrong. Terribly wrong.

The few times they'd had occasion to make an arrest in Salt Lick, if the prisoner had a car, it usually had been parked in the rear, away from the street, to keep it from public view. Small-town talk moved faster than a racehorse, and he saw no point in creating unnecessary complications in anyone's life. Tonight the small parking area looked like a used car lot.

Buddy suppressed a groan. He would rather have walked back into Luna de Neón wearing a pink skirt than enter his own office. He circled around front and parked. He climbed out of the Tahoe and walked to the door.

Before he even turned the knob, he could hear the ruckus and above it, Billy Don's voice. "Everybody needs to just settle down. Yelling at me ain't gonna get you nowhere. And Maudeen Wiley, you should be ashamed of yourself. Do you eat with that dirty mouth?"

Buddy stepped inside. Looking beyond Billy Don, he counted seven people in the jail's two cells—two women in one and five men in the other. Besides Maudeen Wiley, he saw Brother Greene from the Calvary Baptist Church, the football team's coach, Jim Finley; and four other model citizens.

They were all talking at once. Maudeen was trying to rally a chorus of "We Shall Overcome." Buddy couldn't make out much of what they were saying, but he did pick up that they were threatening lawsuits and demanding to be released, *now*. "Deputy, do you want to tell me what's going on here?"

"Sheriff Overstreet, you're home! Man, am I glad to see you. We've had a crime wave since you left. A true crime wave."

Buddy summoned all the control he could muster. "Billy Don, open those doors and let those people go. Give them their car keys and send them home."

"But I haven't fingerprinted them yet."

Fingerprinted. Buddy rolled his eyes to the ceiling. "We know them all. We know where they live. Let's let them go on their own recognizance. I need to talk to you, and I can't even hear myself think with all this noise."

"But—"

Buddy took the cell keys from the desk drawer. "Folks, I'm sorry for the inconvenience. Please go on home now."

All the prisoners filed out with strong last words for Deputy Roberts, except Maudeen. She remained in the cell sitting on the bunk.

"Miz Wiley, do you need a ride?" Buddy asked. "Is there anything I can do for you?"

"Could I stay just a little while longer? I called the Peaceful Oasis and they're getting a vanload of residents to come down and see me in lock-up. This is the most excitement we've had in ages. I'm the only one there who still has a life. I'm kind of a celebrity."

A van full of senior citizens shuffling through his office like a band of tourists was the last thing Buddy needed. "How about if Deputy Roberts takes you back in handcuffs? He could even leave them on 'til he walks you back to your room. Would that be enough excitement for you?"

"Could he hold a gun on me?"

"No, ma'am. I can't allow him to do that."

Maudeen took a moment to mull over the offer. "Tell you what. If he'll give me a stern talking-to in front of the others, it's a deal."

"Did you hear that, Deputy? When you get Miz Wiley inside the Peaceful Oasis, tell her you're releasing her this time, but you don't want to have to come after her again."

Billy Don had an argumentative look in his eye, so Buddy added, "And when you get done there, Deputy, come back here. We need to talk."

"C'mon, Miz Wiley," Billy Don said. "I'll carry your purse for you if it's all the same to you. I don't think I could take any more blows to the head." Billy Don adjusted the handcuffs on her birdlike wrists and walked her through the door.

Buddy sat down at his desk, tamping down his annoyance. He had phone calls to make before Deputy Roberts returned. He laid his notes in front of him and retrieved his worn, crumpled list of people he had questioned about Pearl Ann's death. The first number he dialed was Harley's. After four or five rings, voice mail came on and Buddy hung up. He didn't want to talk to a machine. He had a hot lead, and he was anxious to move on it.

He keyed in Carol Jean's number. Another recorded message. He spoke quickly and with authority, asking her to call him as soon as possible and as an afterthought, he added he would like to talk to Harley, too.

It occurred to him he hadn't checked his messages at home. Perhaps the murderer had left another confession for him. He dialed his number, entered the code to retrieve messages, and heard the monotone voice announce he had six calls. *God, let one of them be the killer saying here I am, come and get me.*

This time he wasn't so lucky. He had four calls from Kathy and two hang-ups. No doubt the hang-ups were her, too. Her tone of voice changed with each communication, ranging from pleasant to pissed. He didn't want to face that issue now, but he might as well call her.

He was met with the cool demeanor he had halfway expected. She allowed him to explain where he had been and the reason for the sudden departure. Gradually her attitude mellowed.

"Goodness, Buddy," she said, responding to the news story about Luna de Neon, "if that shooting had happened just a few hours earlier, you would have been there and I wouldn't even have known where you were."

Buddy detected a catch in her throat and knew she was struggling with tears. He felt like an asshole. "Let me make it up to you, Kathy. How about tomorrow night? We'll go out to dinner someplace nice. I can be over there by seven."

"That sounds wonderful. It'll be so good to see you. I love you, Buddy."

Just then he heard Billy Don open the door to

the office. Perfect timing, as always. "Oh . . . yeah, uh . . . okay, thanks." Buddy hung up feeling more like an asshole than ever.

Buddy had always found it difficult to stay mad at anybody for very long, and his anger with the well-meaning deputy had already subsided. Billy Don sat down across the desk and went into great detail explaining that he had been stopping cars, looking for the fugitives targeted by the FBI flyer. When the citizens had resisted showing their drivers' licenses, and hadn't allowed their vehicles to be searched, Deputy Roberts had arrested them for obstruction of an ongoing investigation. He produced the flyer from his pocket and showed Buddy the faxed notice.

Buddy didn't bother pointing out the scatter fax, sent to every law enforcement agency in the United States, specified that the men were believed to be in the vicinity of Los Angeles. At this juncture, what was the point? "Tell me why you picked on Maudeen. She doesn't even drive."

"Yessir. You know, that's the meanest little woman I've ever come across. When I was putting Reverend Greene in the squad car, she came over and started cussin' and beatin' on me with her purse. I had to put her in the car just to get her off me. She's a menace, that one is."

"Billy Don, we're lucky there isn't a lawyer in Salt Lick. Every one of those people would be in his office right now. We need to do some damage control to make sure they don't call one in from Odessa or Midland tomorrow."

"But they wouldn't—"

"The flyer says, 'Be on the lookout.' I hope you didn't really search their cars."

The deputy shrank a little lower in his chair. "Uh-oh."

Buddy leaned back, let out a groan, and looked upward for guidance he knew wasn't going to be there. "Billy Don, without probable cause and a search warrant, you can't search their cars."

"No kidding? Why, I didn't know that. How do you know so much about the law, Buddy?"

Buddy looked into the face of the young man whose question rang of sincerity. He was touched by his deputy's obvious admiration, but unlike Billy Don, Buddy busted his butt to learn everything he could about being a good law officer. "I read, Billy Don. I go to school. Did you think I drive over to Odessa College two times a week just to meet pretty women?"

"Naw, I didn't think that. You've already got pretty women around you. I think Miss Kathy's real nice-lookin', and your ex, Debbie Sue, she's the best-lookin' woman I know. I saw her drive by Saturday night with that rodeo fella. She looked like a hundred bucks. I wanted to stop 'em so I'd have an excuse to get his autograph, but I was too busy. You think she'd get Quint Matthews to sign something for me?"

Buddy felt as if the floor had fallen from beneath him. *Debbie Sue had seen Quint Saturday night*? He couldn't explain why, but he thought the disastrous evening at Kincaid's in Odessa would have discouraged Quint, who was bound to be accustomed to easier prey than Debbie Sue. *Dammit, of course he's back. For him, the challenge of a woman like Debbie Sue would be a turn-on.*

"You'll have to ask her, Billy Don. I wouldn't know."

Suddenly chewing on Billy Don's ass seemed unimportant and following up on his new leads seemed less driving.

"That's a real good idea, Buddy. I just might do that. It's not every day a famous bull rider shows up in Salt Lick."

"Go on home and get some rest, Billy Don. You've had a busy weekend, and I've got to start making phone calls."

"Thanks, Buddy. That's real considerate of you. I *am* tired. There's a lot of upset to arresting people, ain't there?"

Left alone, Buddy ran his hand over his face, unable to shift his thoughts away from his ex-wife and Quint Matthews. How could Debbie Sue, or any woman, resist the world Quint Matthews could offer? Everything Buddy had demanded she give up, Quint could return. And on a silver platter. Hooking up with him, rodeo would become her life again. She would have the best horses money could buy. Financial worries would be a thing of the past . . .

So would Salt Lick. And so would he.

Christ! The irony was overwhelming. After he had stayed in Salt Lick all these years on the fool-hardy notion that someday, somehow, something would work out between them, what if she was the one who up and left?

He had to talk to her, had to tell her how his thinking had changed. Up to now, it had been easy to blame her for the flaws in their relation-ship. He'd had fixed ideas what a good marriage should be, but she had refused to give in to them. Had his demands played a part in the breakup? Had his own obstinacy been as damaging as her headstrong ways?

He thought about calling Kathy back and post-poning their dinner date, but decided against it. He suddenly didn't want to be left alone with his thoughts. Meanwhile, he began calling the seven released inmates and making nice.

I should have stayed in Dallas.

Debbie Sue sat on her living room sofa thumbing through a new issue of *Horse Illustrated*, listening to Patsy Cline sing her heart out. She couldn't re-member when she had been so relaxed.

The last few weeks had certainly given her rea-son to appreciate the tranquillity of the moment. She couldn't decide if she felt relieved because

Quint had recovered—even to the point of leaving the hospital against medical advice—or because she'd been excused from a Sunday morning round of sex she didn't have her whole heart in.

Well, she wouldn't question fate. She would just enjoy the moment. Sunday morning with nothing to do, nowhere she had to be. What a luxury.

The phone destroyed the peace and quiet. She contemplated not answering, especially when caller ID revealed a number she didn't recognize. But she caved in.

"Hello?" She didn't try to hide the annoyance in her voice.

"Hi, Debbie Sue. Did I catch you at a bad time?"

"C. J., how great to hear from you. I was just sitting here wondering what I should be doing. Talking to you is exactly what I would have picked. Where are you? I didn't recognize the number."

"I'm in Wyoming. Harley and I came up here yesterday."

"Wyoming! Good Lord, C. J., that's like a million miles away. What are you doing up there? Did y'all run off and get married?"

"Heavens, no. I wouldn't do that to you guys, or my parents. Harley had some business here and he asked me to come along. I've never been anywhere, so I just up and said yes. He's already out having breakfast with some stockholders and I'm just sitting here enjoying the view.

"We're in this gorgeous cabin right outside town. The bedroom is a loft that overlooks the downstairs, and one whole wall is glass. And there's the most beautiful scenery. I feel like a country mouse. This doesn't sound like me, does it?"

"No, but that's okay, too. What's the weather like there?"

"I thought of you the second we got off the plane. This may be the most beautiful place on earth. Mountains and trees and snow. Even the smell is incredible. You can't believe how cold it is here. Harley built me a fire this morning before he left. I didn't pack nearly enough warm clothes."

Debbie Sue thought of the temperature nearing the eighty-five-degree mark already and sighed. "How long do you plan on being there?"

"All week. I'll be back to Texas Saturday, but Harley's going to Portland."

"You're not going with him?"

"I have a job to get back to. I may be dating the boss, but I'm not taking anything for granted. It wouldn't be fair to those ladies I work with to leave them shorthanded for so long."

C. J., ever considerate of others.

They spent the rest of the conversation catching each other up on current events. Debbie Sue told about the gift from Quint, the evening at Edwina's, and the trip to the hospital. She mentioned that Vic had received another phone call from his ex-wife, and Ed was more upset than she was letting on.

"I hope things work out for Ed and Vic. I've never seen her so happy. But I don't blame her for being worried. We have no way of knowing about Vic and his ex's true feelings for each other or what they lived through and shared. Those kinds of bonds are hard to break."

"Yeah, I know."

"Just look at you and Buddy. It's been three years and he's still on your mind. Oops, I guess I'd better go. My sweetheart just walked through the door."

"You better get rid of him before Harley comes back." Debbie Sue laughed though her heart felt heavy at C. J.'s comment about Buddy.

"You're terrible," C. J. said, laughing, too. "It's so nice to be able to talk about Harley freely. When I get home, let's all get together. I love you. Tell Ed I said hi."

After hanging up, Debbie Sue sat with the phone in her hand, thinking. She hadn't told C. J. about accepting the job offer from Quint. How could she forget her biggest piece of news? Could it be she wasn't as excited as she ought to be about this new job—if that's what it was? God knew her feelings for Quint didn't rival what C. J. felt for Harley or what Debbie Sue had once felt for Buddy. Or maybe still felt for Buddy. Or whatever.

C. J. and Harley. She still couldn't get used to the idea of them as a couple. God knew C. J. deserved to be treated well and Harley, well, Harley was probably overdue for some caring, too.

* * *

By that evening Buddy had given up on reaching Harley or Carol Jean. They could be anywhere. He could reach them both at the office come Monday, so he decided to give it a rest.

Pearl Ann and her tall, handsome Mexican lover. The secret was a well-kept one. Was he married, too? It had to be an association that would seem casual to the average onlooker. The people closest to Pearl Ann should know about him, yet in the dozens of people he had talked to, no one had mentioned a person that fit the description given to him by the bartender.

Buddy had his detective work cut out for him, but this was what he had dreamed of, what he had wanted to do his whole life.

God, don't let me blow it.

Twenty-one

 Edwina lay beside Vic watching him twitch and mumble in his sleep. Though she knew a soufflé falling could cause his restlessness, she imagined him dreaming of a mission, saving lives in some exotic land. She gently traced a scar on his shoulder with her long acrylic nails, wondering when and how he had received that particular memento.

It was October 15, three weeks to the day since Brenda had first called. And she had called last night. Edwina had intercepted the message and erased it before Vic heard it. The calls from Brenda usually came once or twice a year. Yesterday's call made two in less than thirty days. Not good.

The message had been neither frantic and guilt-ridden nor an emotional plea for attention. Yesterday's voice had been warm and enticing. Brenda had relocated to San Diego. She talked of mutual friends and invited Vic to come out to the West Coast for a SEAL reunion. The invitation had *not* been extended to Vic *and* Edwina.

Edwina felt guilty for keeping the message from Vic, but as she had reminded Debbie Sue just days before—all was fair in love and war. Coming up against a pining ex-wife was something Edwina was trained for. Beating out a platoon of ex-SEALs was something else. Time for some undercover work, she thought, and slid down, under the sheets.

Over a week had passed since Debbie Sue had seen Quint, but he had called several times. Because they had much in common, they always found topics for discussion. He was so laid back he was practically liquid, which made him easy and fun to talk to. His devil-may-care nature had been what attracted her to him when she was seventeen.

He said he would be in the Salt Lick area in about a week and asked if he could come by. That was the upside to having a suitor who didn't live in town. A local boyfriend or husband saw you not only at your very best, but at your very worst. Someone from out of town, for whom you had to plan in advance, got the best you had to offer all the time—like clean breath, freshly applied makeup, and perfume. And shaved legs.

Her mom had been aghast at the expensive gift Quint had bestowed on Debbie Sue, but like her daughter, once she tried on the jacket, she had been reluctant to remove it. She had even extracted a promise that if she ever won a Country Music Association award, Debbie Sue would allow her to borrow it and wear it in Nashville.

Buddy was requestioning everyone who had associated with Pearl Ann. With her only strong lead out of contention, Debbie Sue had abandoned the mystery solving and left it to Buddy. She didn't have the time or resources to go looking for a killer. She would pay her debts the old fashioned way—by working her ass off.

Besides, her life wasn't *all* work. She had one thing to look forward to. This Thursday Quint would be in town.

It had taken over a week, but Buddy finally tracked Harley down. He ran into him at Hogg's Drive-In, of all places, and asked him if he knew the new suspect in his wife's murder.

Buddy's spirits were dashed when Harley shook his head. "I've got a lot of Mexicans on my payroll, but no one of that description. Some are handsome, but too old or too young. And none of them are tall. Did you talk to the folks at the house? They probably saw more of what went on with my wife than I did."

"I did talk to them. They either don't know or won't say."

"I know you can't see it, but there's irony in the

fact that you believe a Mexican killed Pearl Ann and that he did it out of love."

"How so?"

"She hated Mexicans. She felt they were beneath her. I don't know where she got the idea."

Buddy knew. In West Texas most Mexicans were migrant workers who had crossed the Rio Grande looking for a better life. They were employed mostly as manual laborers, and many people gave them no credit for being the hard workers the majority of them were. On the ladder of respect in Salt Lick, only Pearl Ann's family would have occupied a rung lower than a Mexican migrant worker. Yep, he could see the irony.

Quint arrived at the Styling Station on Thursday around three o'clock. The patrons giggled and feigned horror at being discovered in curlers or with wet hair by a good-looking man. Being the dutiful Southern gentleman, he complimented all and flirted outrageously. Most of the women were old enough to be his grandmother, but he didn't seem to notice. He was in his element—women swooning over him.

"Quint, you're incorrigible," Debbie Sue said. "I didn't expect you this early. You're gonna have to wait 'til I finish."

"No problem, darlin'. I'll just run up to the store and pick up some beer. Can I get you anything?"

"No, thanks. I'm fixin' hamburgers at the house tonight. Beer will be perfect."

"Homemade hamburgers? Great. I get tired of restaurant food."

"Listen," she said, catching him out of earshot of her patrons, "you're not allergic to hamburgers, are you? I mean, it's just plain ground beef and mustard—"

"Thanks for asking. Hamburgers are a safe bet for me."

When Quint left, Debbie Sue moved her last customer, Burma Johnson, from the hair dryer to her station for a comb-out.

"Was that young fellow Quint Matthews?" Burma asked.

"Yes, ma'am." Debbie enjoyed Quint's celebrity status, even though it was limited to country people and rodeo fans.

"My granddaughter gave him a ride to Salt Lick a couple of weeks ago. Ruthie. You know her, don't you?"

An alarm went off in Debbie Sue's brain. She hadn't given any thought to *which* nurses' aide Quint had "sweet-talked" into giving him a ride from Odessa. Oh, yes, she did know Ruthie Gentry, a younger version of Pearl Ann. Everyone in Salt Lick knew Ruthie, as did most of West Texas, Debbie Sue was willing to bet. "Yes, ma'am, I do."

"I'd be leery of him, hon. Ruthie didn't come home that night. She thinks it's a big secret, but her mother told me."

Fuck. Ruthie Gentry counted her conquests in notches on her bedpost. She wouldn't have let Quint Matthews get out of her grasp, oh no. She would view him as her finest trophy.

Debbie Sue had told herself she didn't mind if Quint saw other women. He had said their arrangement wasn't a commitment, and she had agreed. But damned if she was pleased to have him chase after someone on her own doorstep in her hometown. She didn't know how she would learn what happened between him and Ruthie Gentry, but she would. After all, she now had experience as a detective.

Quint returned from the store, and after doing her perfunctory end-of-the-workday duties in the salon, Debbie Sue locked up and they left in separate vehicles for her house.

She assigned the fire-starting task to Quint while she changed into comfortable clothes, all the while stewing over the fact that he might have spent the night with Ruthie.

"I missed seeing Ed today," he said when she put in an appearance on the patio.

She had changed into shorts and a T-shirt and some cute little thong flip-flops adorned with beads. "She left early." Debbie Sue adjusted the patio door, leaving it open a few inches so she could hear the phone.

"What's become of your other friend, that pretty little thing . . . can't think of her name."

"C. J.?"

"Yeah, C. J. I know some cowboys who might like to meet her."

"She wouldn't be interested. She's involved with someone. In fact, she'll most likely be getting married soon."

He chuckled. "That's a waste."

For some reason, the quip rankled her. From out of nowhere, it dawned on her she had never discussed Pearl Ann's murder with Quint. "Do you know Harley Carruthers? Seems like y'all would travel in the same circles."

"Yeah, I know Harley. We go back a ways. Is *that* who she's marrying? That's a little quick, isn't it? I thought Pearl Ann was the only one screwing around in that marriage."

"I didn't say C. J. was marrying Harley. I didn't know you knew Pearl Ann. How come you haven't mentioned her murder once in all this time?"

"I don't know. I guess I didn't think it was a big deal."

Debbie Sue couldn't believe her ears. How could he be so callous? "You didn't think the murder of a man's wife that you go back a ways with is a big deal?"

"Not really. She most likely got what she had coming. That's all."

"That's all? Quint, how could you think someone deserves to be murdered?" A thought evil enough to make her scalp shrink sliced through Debbie

Sue's head. "Unless . . . unless she did something to *you*. Did you fool around with Pearl Ann?"

"Oh, great, here we go. Yeah, I messed around with her a little. So what? It was a couple of years ago and it wasn't in this town. It only lasted a few months."

"A few months?" Debbie Sue couldn't control the strident tone of the question, but she felt proud of herself that she had tamped it down when what she *wanted* to do was clutch her head and shriek.

"Debbie Sue, cut it out. Don't tell me you didn't know what Pearl Ann was. You expect me to break down and cry 'cause she's dead? I'm sorry, I just don't feel that way."

The air around Debbie Sue's head had begun to glow red. "So she screwed around. So what? Are you any better? You didn't even take a breath making sure I knew a roll in the hay was all you wanted from me. That and a little bit of horse talk now and then on the side."

"What is this? Dammit, I—"

"And I suppose you're fixin' to tell me nothing happened between you and Ruthie Gentry?"

"Who?"

"The nurses' aide who gave you a ride to Salt Lick from Odessa hospital."

"Oh. I didn't know what her name was. What about her?"

"You met her grandmother in my shop this afternoon." Debbie Sue restrained herself from adding *asshole*. "She told me Ruthie didn't come home the night she gave you a ride."

"So?"

"So? . . . You're a chickenshit, Quint Matthews."

He stopped fiddling with the charcoal and fixed her with a hard look. "This is heading to a place we shouldn't be going, Debbie Sue."

The phone warbled, but she didn't intend to answer until she gave Mr. World Champion Bullshitter a piece of her mind. She allowed the call to go to her answering machine. Before she could launch a diatribe, her mother's voice came on. "Deb, sweetie, pick up if you're there. I'm at Dr. Miller's with Rocket Man."

Debbie Sue practically stumbled through the patio door opening and grabbed the phone before her mother could say more. "Mom! Mom, I'm here. What's wrong with Rocket Man?"

"Dr. Miller's not sure yet. Can you come? I'd feel better if you were here."

"I'll be there in a minute." Debbie Sue hung up and turned to Quint, momentarily forgetting the knock-down, drag-out fight she was primed to have. "Rocket Man's sick. Do you want to come with me to Dr. Miller's?"

"Yeah, sure. Let's go."

At the veterinarian clinic she found the doctor, her mom, and Rocket Man in one of the treatment barns in back. Dr. Miller was performing an ultrasound on the sick animal's lungs. Her mother told her she had been watching the horse closely since yesterday morning. He had a nasal discharge, difficulty breathing, and showed no interest in eating, even when she offered him a whole box of Twinkies.

"I took his temperature and it was a little over a hundred and two. I decided to load him up and bring him in."

"You should have called me, Mom. It can be dangerous taking a horse's temperature."

"Oh heavens, I've done it a thousand times. I was more worried about him than myself." Her gaze swung to Quint. "Why, my goodness, Quinton, you're all grown up."

"Yes, ma'am. Good to see you again, Mrs. Pratt."

"How're your folks?"

"Just fine. Mom's down in her back a lot and Dad's still mean and ornery." Looking around the treatment area, he let out a low whistle. "This is quite a setup, isn't it? I didn't notice it when I was here a couple of weeks ago. Salt Lick's lucky to have such a sophisticated facility."

"It helps having a rich man depending on it for his own animals. Harley Carruthers built it. I've always thought it a shame an animal has the best of everything in Salt Lick, but a sick person can't get taken care of. But then, you already know that from firsthand experience, don't you?"

Quint laughed. "Yes, ma'am, I sure do."

Debbie Sue could hear they were talking to each other, but she wasn't processing their words. Her attention was absorbed by Dr. Miller and her beautiful horse. Rocket Man must have sensed she was near because he looked at her with big eyes that showed a mixture of illness and fear. Was she near losing him? She couldn't stop the tears that welled in her throat. She moved to his side and began rubbing his neck. *Please don't leave me, Rocket Man. Please.*

A voice she would never stop knowing called from the back of the corrals, just outside the doorway leading from the barn. "Where is everybody? Dr. Miller?" Buddy stepped through the doorway. "I was driving by and saw your pickup and trailer, Virginia. What's going on?"

Debbie Sue wanted to cry out in relief. Buddy's solid stability was what she needed. Only he could understand her attachment to Rocket Man.

"Don't tell me you're in love with this animal, too," Quint said to Buddy.

Debbie Sue was stunned. She thought of grabbing the ultrasound equipment and searching for a heart in Quint's chest cavity.

Buddy shot him a murderous look, then greeted her by touching the brim of his hat. "Debbie Sue." He turned to Quint. "I didn't see your rig, Matthews. You must have parked in front. I thought Virginia might need some help, but since you're here, I'll go on."

"Please don't go," Debbie Sue said, stepping in front of him. "You know almost as much about horses as Dr. Miller. Please be here when he talks to us."

Just then the doctor moved away from his equipment. "You've got a pretty sick animal here. I'll need to do some blood work to check for further infection, but his lungs have fluid in them. He's got pneumonia for sure. His sub-mandibular lymph nodes are swollen." He motioned for Buddy, who walked over and examined Rocket Man's jaws and neck for himself.

"Umm, I see," Buddy said, while Debbie Sue clung to her mother's hand.

"I need to start him on an aggressive broad-spectrum antibiotic that'll kill strep. When the culture and sensitivity results come back, we'll make a change if we need to."

Buddy nodded and rubbed a hand down Rocket Man's neck.

Debbie Sue couldn't quell the panic darting from head to heart and back again. "But he's going to be all right, isn't he, Dr. Miller?"

The vet rested his hand on the horse's flank. "Given his age, he could have a rough go of it, but I think he'll pull through. I'll do everything possible."

Debbie Sue looked at Buddy through eyes blurred with tears. Another heartbreaking scene rushed at her—the day a doctor in Midland had told her and Buddy that their little Luke didn't have much chance of surviving. At four months premature, he was just too tiny. Buddy had been her strength. They had both prayed and fought for Luke, but lost in the end.

Forcing herself back to the present, she found Buddy watching her. Was he thinking the same thing? Was this as painful for him as it was for her?

Quint interrupted her thoughts. "I think you should put him down, Debbie Sue. He's old. He's had a good life, but what's he good for now? He's just an expensive burden."

"No." Debbie Sue shook her head fiercely.

"He's not that ill, Mr. Matthews," Dr. Miller said. "He needs about a week of medication, and if nothing else goes wrong, he should—"

Suddenly Buddy grabbed Quint by the shirt-front and slammed him against the wall with a bang. The smaller man's hat flew off and landed beneath Rocket Man. The horse promptly stepped on it.

"You self-centered sonofabitch. Don't you know how much he means to her? What it would do to her if she lost him?" Buddy shoved his face menacingly close to Quint's. "Do you even care?"

Debbie Sue grabbed Buddy's arm, at the end of which was a cocked fist. "Buddy, stop!"

"Buddy," Debbie Sue's mom cried, her eyes tearing. "Son, you're the sheriff."

Debbie Sue saw her ex-husband shaking with uncharacteristic rage, but he released Quint's shirt and stepped back.

Quint bent down, picked up his hat, and began

reshaping the crown where Rocket Man had stepped on it. He glared up at Buddy. "Stay away from me, you goddamn loser. I *am* thinking of Debbie Sue. She deserves a better life than staying in this shithole town, in that shithole *beauty* shop, baby-sitting a worn-out horse. And waiting for *you* to decide what you want to be when you grow up. *Texas Ranger*?" He huffed. "You wouldn't make a wart on a Texas Ranger's ass."

Suddenly a fist made contact with Quint's chin and he slid down the treatment room wall. Debbie Sue looked up at Buddy, momentarily too stunned to speak. She finally found her voice. "Oh my God. Did I knock him out?"

Without a word Buddy pulled her to him and kissed her as in the old days, when they had been so much in love kissing was all they could think about. A thrill rushed through her. Home. Finally, after the tears she had shed, after the bleak years without him, she was home. She arched to get closer. If she pressed against him hard enough, she would be enveloped by him and wouldn't have to live without him any longer.

Eventually he set her away. "Debbie Sue—"

"Oh, Buddy, I—"

"Buddy? Sweetheart? Are you back here? Bud—ohmygod, what did I step in? . . . Ooohh, yuuuck!" Kathy Bozo came around the corner of the building holding one shoe away from her body and tiptoeing on her bare foot.

Buddy peeled Debbie Sue's arms away and

walked over to Rocket Man. Debbie Sue stared at him dumbfounded, then at Kathy. Had Kathy been here all this time?

"Is everything all right, Buddy? I got cold and you took the keys." Kathy's attention swerved to Quint who was struggling to his feet. Her eyes popped wide. "Is he all right?"

"He's fine," Buddy said, a hint of a tremor in his voice. "You can't hurt a damn bull rider." He dug into his pocket and came up with keys, which he handed to her. "Go on back to the pickup, Kathy. I'll be there in a minute. We've got a sick horse on our hands. I need to finish my talk with Dr. Miller."

"Oh, too bad. Whose horse is it? . . . Oh, Debbie Sue. I didn't see you over there. Buddy, will you be much longer?"

He put a hand on her shoulder and turned her. "Start the engine and let the cab get warm."

Kathy placed both hands on his arm, raised to her tiptoes, and kissed his cheek. Then with a faint little smile, she walked out of the treatment barn.

Debbie Sue flew at Buddy. "You bastard! You call Quint self-centered? And whose best interest did you have in mind when you practically broke my arm shoving me aside so your fiancée wouldn't see you kissing me?"

Buddy's hands opened. "Debbie Sue, I forgot she was even—"

"You forgot? That's supposed to make me feel better? You forgot? Just get out of here, Buddy. *I'll* take care of my horse. Just like I take care of myself."

Quint, now on his feet, brushed straw from his clothing, ran a hand through his blond hair. He glared at Buddy. "That was a lucky punch. You hit like a girl." He clapped his hat on his head. The crown, irreparably crushed, stood taller on one side. "Debbie Sue, let's go. We can talk about this later."

"No. We don't have anything to talk about. All of a sudden I don't like you very much."

"Why? Because I said something you don't want to hear?"

"No. Because you don't care about animals. You don't respect the dead and you don't respect the women you've slept with. And I wouldn't like myself if I kept seeing you or if I went to work for you. As we say in this shithole of a town, don't let the door hit you in the—"

"You're turning me down?" Quint gaped at her. "You can't be serious—"

"Quint, if you don't leave, I swear I'll hit you again."

Quint's gaze shifted between her and Buddy. His jaw muscles worked a few seconds, then he stomped out.

Buddy spoke up. "You did the right thing—"

"You get out, too. I have to take care of Rocket Man."

Buddy hesitated, his hands resting on his belt. "Deb—"

"Go! Now. Your fiancée's waiting, remember?"

His eyes seemed to be pleading, but his mouth

remained closed. Finally he turned and walked out of the barn and left her alone with her beloved horse. It had always been that way, really—just her, her mom, and Rocket Man. No one else.

Before she could tear her hair and wail, her mom and Dr. Miller returned. She hadn't even noticed when they left.

She forced herself to listen as the doctor explained Rocket Man's treatment plan. She thanked him and said she'd be back tomorrow morning. "Mom, can you give me a ride home?"

"Of course. Have you eaten?"

"Please, Mom. I just want to go home. I don't want to make any stops along the way."

As soon as she was in the confines of the little house she had once shared with Buddy, she lost it. Her tears came in great waves, grief mixed with anger. She might never stop crying.

For the next week, each morning, noon, and evening, Debbie Sue drove to the veterinary clinic and checked on Rocket Man. She didn't let herself think about the bill for his stay in the state-of-the-art clinic. Dr. Miller was enthusiastic about his improvement and planned on sending him home by the weekend. Rocket Man seemed to be enjoying all the attention.

Edwina came by and brought an afghan for his hindquarters. "It would be a lot less trouble if you had a dog for a pet." She combed and braided his mane because, she said, "it's important to keep looking *good* when you're feeling *bad*."

Dr. Miller allowed Vic to bring an unfrosted, special Asian ingredient carrot cake to the patient. He was especially interested in the recipe because the horse seemed to have rallied after eating the homemade concoction.

She knew Buddy had stopped by because she could smell peppermint on Rocket Man's breath.

Life moved on.

Twenty-two

 Debbie Sue's days returned to the humdrum of pre–Pearl Ann's death. Busy days, money worries. Quiet evenings at home, money worries. Boring.

Rocket Man had been released from the veterinary clinic and, as she had feared, the bill for his treatment left her breathless, even with the employee discount Dr. Miller had given her mom. The upside was that the horse was now as frisky as a colt. Mom had installed him in the barn near the house to keep close watch on him for a few more days.

The gossip about Pearl Ann's death had worn thin. Nothing new had come from the sheriff's office, so Debbie Sue assumed her customers were tired of talking about the same stuff over and over. Since she had given up on collecting the reward, her interest had waned, too.

The atmosphere in the salon was upbeat. Unfortunately, Debbie Sue's attitude wasn't. Her life had sunk into the pits. In the past ten days she'd had to come to terms with the fact that she wouldn't be taking an exciting job offer from Quint, her financial problems were *not* going away, and Buddy hadn't even tried to contact her after the sudden passion they had shared when Rocket Man came down sick.

She was still astonished he would do something so out of character as kiss her when he had Kathy waiting for him outside. She was giving up men. They were too complicated and took too much of the mental energy she should be devoting to saving her ass from bankruptcy.

In a place where no entertainment existed except school sports, citizens had to improvise, so Vic announced a backyard barbecue for the coming weekend. The weather forecast for Saturday was perfect. It was what kept many people enduring the hardships of life in West Texas. While northern neighbors shoveled snow and shivered in frigid temperatures, West Texans basked in seventy-degree days and comfortable low-fifties evenings. A trade-off for the blistering summer heat was only fair.

Debbie Sue couldn't psych herself up for a party. On Saturday she added the last touches to her final cut and curl for the day and made her departure for her mom's house, intending to give her mother a break from caring for Rocket Man. Her mother met her with a firm admonition for even suggesting she would forgo Vic's backyard picnic to stay near the recuperating horse.

"You're only young once," her mother said. "Rocket Man had so much company at the vet's he needs a rest. Go and have fun."

And Debbie Sue, being the dutiful daughter, decided to do just that. She drove home and changed into what she called her high water pants, which other people called capris, banded her hair into a ponytail, and slid her feet into a pair of sandals. She grabbed her contribution to the feast—plastic cups, plastic silverware, paper plates and paper napkins—and she was off. Oh sure, most people put thought and time into preparing what they donated to a big feed. Big deal. If diners didn't have utensils and had to eat with their hands, all the delicious food in the world wouldn't be enjoyable.

Harley was out of town, so she swung by and picked up C. J. In the backyard behind Vic and Edwina's trailer, strands of tiny white lights hung on every protrusion and the smell of smoldering mesquite wood permeated the air.

Meat hadn't even touched the grill and already Debbie Sue's mouth watered. Edwina had gone overboard by making potato salad with her own hands and cooking a pot of pinto beans chock full of tomatoes, chili powder, and jalapeño peppers. A case of cold Budweiser was iced down in a cooler. C. J. had baked a Black Forest cake eight inches tall. Debbie Sue wasn't fond of a beer, barbecue, and chocolate cake combo, but she was game to try anything once, a fact that had often brought regrettable consequences.

Vic was in fine form, wearing a T-shirt with a navy SEAL insignia and a motto that read, "The Only Easy Day Was Yesterday." Edwina told them the saying was the SEALs' motto. Debbie Sue tried to apply it to her own life, but she couldn't because yesterday hadn't been any easier than today.

They piled their plates with more than they could eat and settled down to enjoy.

"Guess where Vic's going next weekend," Edwina said. "I think we should all go with him."

"Okay, I give up. Where?"

"Terlingua."

Terlingua. The world championship chili cook-off. The last good hell-raisin' party left that teenagers hadn't taken over. Of course, hundreds of people competing in a barbecuing and chili-cooking contest probably wouldn't appeal to most kids. "He's cooking in the chili contest?"

"No, but he likes to go. He meets up with some of his friends from the navy. I've never gone with him, but if y'all went, I would. Wouldn't that be a hoot?"

"I've never been, either," C. J. said. "I've lived here all my life and I've never been to Terlingua. Isn't that odd?"

"Not really," Debbie Sue answered. "I've never been, either."

"Well, that settles it." Edwina slapped the tabletop with her palm. "We're going."

"When is it?"

"This coming weekend. We'd have to get there Thursday to get a decent camping spot. They're expecting fifteen thousand people this year."

"Ed, I can't afford to close the shop for three days."

"You said yourself, last month was your biggest ever. You need to take some time off. Celebrate a little. This may be the last chance we girls get to go off together and have fun. This time next year C. J. will be married to Harley and you'll probably be back with Buddy."

Debbie Sue sent Edwina a dark look. "I wish I hadn't told you about him kissing me. That does *not* mean we're getting back together. In fact, that kiss may have been the last straw for any chance between us. I haven't heard a word from him since."

C. J.'s eyes rounded. "What? What have y'all not told me?"

Debbie Sue filled her in on the events with Rocket Man, Quint, and Buddy.

"I agree with Edwina, Debbie Sue. You have to get away. If I say I'll go, will you come, too?"

"Whoa, now," Vic said. "My camper only sleeps two."

"Then we'll stay at a motel," C. J. said.

"Won't work. The hotels and motels have been booked for months, maybe even years. I can try to get a larger camper. I'd really love it if y'all came.

I've been wanting Ed to come with me, but she'd get bored when I get with my buddies. Reliving war stories isn't something most women enjoy."

"I know what we could do. I could ask Harley if we can borrow his Winnebago. It's just sitting in one of the barns out at his house."

"How big is it?"

"I don't know. It's bigger than a Greyhound."

"That figures," Vic said.

Edwina followed up. "Well, of course it does, Poodle."

"Ooohh, say you'll go, Debbie Sue," C. J. begged. "It won't feel right without you there."

"You'd better come with us," Edwina chimed in. "We'll make your life miserable with all the funny stories we come back with. You'll always regret not going."

Debbie Sue sighed. "The last thing I need is more to regret. Okay, I'll go."

Later, as she drove C. J. home, her blond friend asked, "Debbie Sue, did you hear about the new lead Buddy has for Pearl Ann's murderer? Harley's real encouraged."

"New lead? No, tell me."

C. J. told about the mystery phone call Buddy had received and his subsequent trip to Dallas. "He's asking everyone close to Pearl Ann if she ever had anything to do with a tall, handsome Mexican man. Buddy said he's supposed to be about thirty-five, well dressed and professional-looking. I told him I didn't know anyone of that description that Pearl Ann might have been with. Hasn't he talked to you about it?"

"No." The new clue struck a familiar chord in Debbie Sue's memory. Her brain strained to make the connection until it came to her. "C.J., do you remember Harley's party when Pearl Ann got so mad because you were dancing with the cook from San Angelo?"

C.J. shrugged and smiled. "Yes, I remember. That's when Harley and I first got acquainted."

"The cook, he was tall and good-looking."

"But he was Italian."

"C.J., he was as Mexican as he could be. His name was a common Spanish name. I can't remember it, but he was well dressed and had a great haircut." The memory grew in Debbie Sue's mind. Pearl Ann could have had only one reason to get so mad over C.J. dancing with the cook. "Oh, shit. Now I know why Pearl Ann lost her cool."

C.J. looked at her, round-eyed. "Really? Why?"

Debbie Sue barreled toward the sheriff's office. She intended only to share the new clue with Buddy, she told herself. She saw no light, hadn't expected to, really.

It was just as well he wasn't there, she thought, creeping home. In a way, she was grateful. If she had seen a light, she might have barged in and made a total fool of herself. Again.

She didn't dare drive by his apartment.

She felt hollow inside and couldn't shake it. As she drove, she made a mental list of how she would fill the hours between now and Monday. She would do constructive tasks she had put off doing, preoccupied as she had been with solving Pearl Ann's murder, followed so closely by Rocket Man's illness.

At home, after putting on a mellow Willie Nelson CD, she stripped off her clothes and stretched out in a warm bath, reading up on pneumonia in horses, knowledge to have in case Rocket Man suffered a relapse.

When the water grew too cool, she climbed out of the tub, dried with a big fluffy towel, and slathered her whole body with scented cream.

Last, she slapped a mudpack on her face and finished the horse pneumonia article while she waited for the mud to dry. Once the mudpack was removed, unable to think of anything else to do to her face and body, she pulled on her oversized nightshirt and brushed her hair a few hundred strokes. She almost didn't hear the faint chime of her ancient doorbell.

Anxiety stabbed her chest. *Mom? Rocket Man?* She shoved her arms into her robe and made her way through the dark house to the front, switched on the porch light, and yanked open the door.

And stood there paralyzed.

"Buddy," she said, deadpan. Instinctively she tugged her robe more tightly about herself.

He stood there, too, grave-faced, hanging on to the brim of his hat. "I thought . . . I'd come by."

"Oh . . ." She blanked out for a full ten seconds. "Well, yes. What's—what's up?" Her voice sounded as if it had climbed an octave. Before she knew it, she had backed up and he had come into the house.

And the next thing she knew she was in his arms.

The tension she had carried inside for three years broke like a great wave and engulfed her and she sobbed against his wide chest. Then he was kissing her, bracketing her face between his large hands as his lips moved over her face, murmuring her name and sipping away her tears. And she was kissing him back, her arms tightly wrapped around his waist.

It seemed perfectly natural and normal to untie her robe, slip her arms out of it, and let it drop to the floor. Her nightshirt followed and she stood before him naked but for her lacy panties.

He set her away and his eyes moved over her. "Oh, God, Debbie Sue. You're so beautiful. I've never forgotten—"

"Don't disappoint me," she whispered, tears close to spilling over.

He pulled her into his arms and kissed her again, his hands touching her everywhere. "I don't have anything," he murmured against her lips.

"I don't care," she sobbed. And she didn't because she knew without a splinter of doubt she was *meant* to be with Buddy. She was *meant* to have his children.

"If you don't, neither do I." He lifted her in his arms and carried her to the bed they had shared the five years of their marriage.

She let him peel away her panties, then he let her help *him* undress. After all, he had on far more clothing than she, and hadn't she always been his helper in all things? Once he was naked, she worshipped him with her hands and mouth, reveling in his soft, deep groans. When he could endure no more, he pulled her up, his mouth finding hers.

There in their wedding bed, the bed she had shared with no man save him, she opened her heart and body and took in his hot, hard flesh. The thing she feared she had forgotten became a profound revival. As he paused above her, breath ragged and desperate, their gazes locked. She could feel his trembling, or was it hers?

"I love you," he murmured. "I've never stopped."

"I love you, too," she whimpered and thought she might rise and float away on a cloud of sheer joy.

Sunlight poured in on them. Debbie Sue awoke and without opening her eyes, snuggled against Buddy's big, muscular body. They had made love all night. And talked. And made love.

He pulled her even closer. "Did we make a baby last night?"

"I don't think so. Did you want to?"

"If that's what's meant to be. Would you be afraid?"

She hesitated, not having thought of being pregnant again. "Maybe. But I'd be more afraid of never trying again."

"You are gonna marry me, aren't you?"

She fought back tears of bliss. "Do we have to adopt Kathy?"

"I figured out the lie she told you. That night when Rocket Man was sick and you said *fiancée*, I finally figured it out. Don't worry. She's not a problem. I settled it."

She squirmed closer to his warm, naked skin. How had she lived without him for three long years? "Oh, Buddy, I'm gonna be so good. I'm gonna learn to cook. I'm gonna do laundry. I wanted to tell you months ago, but—"

"Shh. You're plenty good, just like you are."

"No, I'm not. I'm loud and I cuss and I'm hardheaded."

"I know. And I love all of it."

"Oh, Buddy. I've loved you for so many years, you're part of me, like my arm or my leg. I told myself if you ever came back, I'd be a good wife."

"You were always a good wife, Flash. It was me. I should have been more understanding. I know what losing little Luke did to me, but I didn't think about what it did to you. I should have helped you more. I was just so disappointed in everything, in myself. I lost faith in *us*."

"No, you were right about everything, Buddy. It was me. I know it was me."

He chuckled, a deep, rich male chuckle that surrounded her with warmth and love. "I guess if we're busy blaming ourselves, we won't be blaming each other."

They played in the shower, then dressed, and between the two of them, scrounged together a breakfast from the near-empty cupboards. "I heard about your trip to Dallas," she told him over coffee after they had eaten.

"Little bit of a water haul. Can't find the tall, handsome Mexican."

"Remember last year at Harley's party, when C. J. and Pearl Ann got in a fight?"

"I heard about it. I wasn't there."

"It was a tall, handsome Mexican they were fighting over. Pearl Ann brought him in from San Angelo to cook the Mexican food they served."

"I questioned Carol Jean. Why didn't she tell me?"

Debbie Sue smiled. "She thought he was Italian."

"From San Angelo? Cooking Mexican food?"

"What can I say?" Debbie Sue lifted a shoulder. "You know C. J."

Buddy reached across the table and picked up her hand, placed a kiss on the back, then held it close to his heart. "I thank you, Flash. But I thought your plan was to solve the case yourself. Get the reward. Pay off your debts. Get out of Salt Lick."

"Seems my plans don't work out for one reason or another."

"Yeah." He leaned forward and kissed her. "But you can always make new ones."

She smiled and straightened his mustache. "Yeah, I can, can't I?" This time she leaned forward and kissed him. "Besides, Harley and C. J. can't go on with their lives until this is behind them and I—I was just thinking that . . . I mean, I was hoping the information might help you, too."

He smiled, not a grin but a slow upturn of his lips that brightened the space around them. If she were any happier, her chest would explode.

Twenty-three

 Buddy didn't leave until Monday
morning. As soon as Debbie Sue had bid him
good-bye, she picked up the phone and called Edwina, told her she would be late and why. Her
good friend broke into tears and laughter and
yelled the news of the reconciliation to Vic.

On the way to the salon, Debbie Sue shoved
an old Buck Owens CD into her player and sang
along.

By the time Buddy returned to his little apartment
and readied for work, he arrived at his office late.
His first task was to talk to Harley Carruthers. He
soon learned Harley was in Louisiana. After a
half-dozen phone calls, Buddy reached him and
asked him if he recalled a Mexican cook from last
year's homecoming party.

"Only that Pearl Ann threw a hissy fit until I

agreed to hire him," Harley said. "Why are you asking?"

"The cook was tall, dark, and handsome. Mexican."

Harley was silent for a few seconds. "Oh, man, I can't believe it."

"Do you remember his name?"

A few more seconds of silence. "Jesus, I don't, Buddy. Too long ago and I probably didn't pay that much attention in the first place."

"Do you remember how he was paid that evening? Do you have a record of some kind?"

"Pearl Ann said she paid him in cash. All I remember is being pissed off. I never pay anybody cash for anything. But Buddy, that was a year ago. Carrying on with someone for that long wasn't her pattern."

"Did your kitchen help assist him?"

"Gloria did. She was mad that that guy took control of her kitchen."

"I want to go out to your place and talk to Gloria again."

"I think she went to Juarez over the weekend to check on her mother. Won't be back until Wednesday morning. I don't have any way of reaching her, either."

Shit. *Wednesday. He had to stay focused 'til Wednesday.*

He did his chores, looked over the two domestic complaints that had come in, read the dispatches that came in by fax, then set out to interview the local complainants. Until Pearl Ann's murder, drunken disturbances and domestic abuse were the closest thing to crime he encountered.

Later in the day he stopped by the Styling Station. He dragged Debbie Sue outside and told her again how much he loved her, how much he appreciated her help. He added that he was going to San Angelo after he talked to Gloria on Wednesday and would see her when he returned.

"Oh hell! I won't be here," she said, as if the information stunned her as much as him. "I promised Vic and Ed and C. J. I'd go to Terlingua with them early Thursday morning."

Though that piece of news stung a little, he bit his tongue. He had made a promise he would be more open and understanding about what she wanted to do. One of the problems in their marriage had been his attempting to corral her free spirit. "The chili cook-off? You'll never get a room on short notice. Y'all planning on roughing it?"

"Not hardly. C. J. asked Harley to borrow his mansion on wheels. You don't think Edwina would go anywhere she can't plug in her curling iron, do you?"

Damn, damn, damn. He hated thinking of Debbie Sue off partying with ten thousand strangers, but anything he said would come across as mistrust and criticism. "Guess you'll be gone three days, then?"

She must have read his mind because she slid her arms around his middle and kissed him. "I'll

behave, Buddy. I promise I won't be out partying
behind the horse trailers. I wouldn't even go, but I
promised them."

"Hey, I'm not making any demands," he said. "I
said I'd change. And I'm trying to."

"I know," she said and kissed him again. "Me,
too. I'm cooking something for supper tonight."

"Yeah?"

"Burma Johnson gave me a Mexican casserole
recipe. I figured I'd start with something simple.
Brave enough to try it?"

"You know damn well I am."

Wednesday morning Buddy was at the Carruthers
ranch early. Gloria was uneasy finding the sheriff
waiting for her. "I am legal," she told him.

Buddy assured her he wasn't making an illegal
immigrant sweep and explained the reason for his
visit. She indeed remembered the Mexican cook.
"*Bastardo*," she said and spit onto the ground. He
had ordered her around in her own *cocina*. His
name was Martinez and he worked in a fancy
white man's *restaurante* in San Angelo. She apologized for knowing so little, but Buddy assured her
the information was very, very helpful.

Buddy drove back into town and informed Billy
Don he had to go out of town again, possibly for a
day or two. Billy Don, eager to redeem himself, assured Buddy he would make him proud. He
wouldn't bother anyone. He would only help. If

he became tempted to do otherwise, he would lock himself in the jail.

Sometimes Buddy wondered if Billy Don's family tree was a shrub, but he was so primed for the four-hour drive to San Angelo, he didn't question what the deputy called *helping*.

He arrived in San Angelo shortly after three P.M., thankful the city of San Angelo wasn't like the sprawling Dallas/Fort Worth Metroplex. He reminded himself that a "fancy white man's *restaurante*" was a subjective description that could cover everything from Taco Bell to the country clubs.

By late in the evening he had talked to a dozen cooks and managers, none of whom knew of anyone fitting the description of Pearl Ann's alleged killer. Still, he was so close he could taste it. He checked into a room for the night.

Early Thursday morning Vic, Edwina, Debbie Sue, and C. J. piled into Vic's crew cab pickup and motored to the Carruthers ranch where they picked up Harley's Ultimate Freedom Winnebago. Harley'd had it gassed up and cleaned to perfection just for them. Every surface outside and in shone like a new diamond and it smelled like lemons. When Vic saw it, he let out a low whistle.

Everyone but Vic had overpacked. The only real need in Terlingua, he told them, was a change of underwear.

Edwina had brought clothes for every conceivable occasion and two overnight bags of makeup. She had packed a different pair of shoes for each outfit and an economy-sized bottle of bubble bath.

Debbie looked at the array in awe. "Lanolin-laced, lavender-scented bubble bath? You know, Ed, from what I've heard, most people at Terlingua have to squat behind bushes to pee."

"*Most people* aren't going to be driving up in a three-hundred-thousand-dollar motor home, either."

Edwina told how she had loved calling Earlene and casually asking if her son Curtis could look up this particular Winnebago for her on the Internet. She used the excuse she wanted to plan on what she would need in the way of toiletries. Earlene had choked on her iced tea when Edwina told her it had a split bath with a garden tub. Some things in life are just too sweet not to experience once, she said.

As Vic pulled the luxury motor home onto the highway and pointed it southwest, Edwina sat beside him talking nonstop about what they would do if this vehicle were theirs—the places they would go, the things they would see. Debbie Sue and C.J. explored the interior like children in fairyland. They opened drawers, peered into closets. "Have you stopped to realize," Debbie Sue asked C.J., "that this will be yours someday?"

"Oh, I don't mind. I can put up with anything as long as I have Harley's love."

Debbie Sue gave C. J. a flat look, thinking of her gentleness and the years of laughs her innocent, blond dumbness had fostered. "All I can say, C. J., is Harley Carruthers doesn't have any idea what a lucky man he is."

Her mind shifted to Buddy and she missed him. She hoped he was safe. They hadn't even reached the county line yet and she was already eager to return home and hear how he had fared in San Angelo. For the first time ever, she wished she had a cell phone.

She would just have to force herself to endure what was probably her last party as a single woman. The cook-off had been held for over forty years and was world-famous. People came to it from everywhere. The majority came to party in the spectacular, but ethereal beauty of the Texas Big Bend country. Surely she could find something to enjoy.

Edwina was disappointed to see that their home on wheels was not the only luxury motor home present. Her dreams of being the Queen of Terlingua were dashed. Vic told her not to worry because he was anointing her the Princess of Commandos.

While Vic set up camp, Debbie Sue, Edwina, and C. J. searched for a calendar of events and found one posted nearby. There was no shortage of reasons to party, and from what Vic had told them on the way down, each campsite hosted its own shindig every night. There was opportunity to sign up for every conceivable contest. Clearly an excellent chili recipe wasn't the only thing that was prizeworthy.

Debbie Sue had fun just watching the assortment of people. Doctor, lawyer, rich man, thief. The childhood rhyme played in her head. The roughest bunch was a group of bikers she had seen parked a short distance from their campsite. No doubt they were entered in the "Group Most Likely to Cut Your Throat in Your Sleep" contest. She wished Vic had chosen a different spot to park and wondered if it was too late to mention it to him.

"*Hooyaah!*" The bellow bounced off the mountainous landscape.

Looking around for the source, Debbie Sue saw Vic standing atop the motor home calling out. A chorus of "Hooyaah" echoed from the group of bikers. *Well, great.*

They returned to the motor home to find Vic handing out bottles of cold beer to the bikers. Introductions and salutations were exchanged and Debbie Sue learned the bikers were all retired navy SEALs. She had seen somebody on TV say a U.S. navy SEAL was the deadliest man on earth, and after seeing a flock of them, she believed it.

Edwina announced she had signed up herself, Debbie Sue, and C.J. for the "Margarita Most Likely to Get You Naked" contest to be held the next day.

"I think this calls for a rehearsal," Vic announced and dragged out bottles of tequila.

Debbie Sue had to admit she was having a good time, as was everyone else. Vic was right, the war stories never ended and seemed to get more graphic in detail as time and tequila passed. She longed for Buddy's company, but knowing she would be back in his arms in a few days made the ache bearable.

By late afternoon she, along with C.J. and several others in the group who wanted to still be conscious by the evening's end, stopped drinking and made the trek to look at the natural hot water springs and watch the magnificent sunset.

Strolling back to their campsite, as Debbie Sue and C.J. talked about what they hoped Vic had prepared for supper, Debbie Sue stopped dead in her tracks.

C.J. turned around and faced her. "Ohmygosh, Debbie Sue. You look like you just saw a ghost."

By late Thursday afternoon Buddy felt the hard fist of failure punching at his brain and pride. He had been in and out of every eating joint in San Angelo and knew nothing new except that he might never eat in a restaurant again. How could he be so close and not produce at least another lead if not the suspect?

He had read that detective work, *real* detective work was slow and methodical. He now knew from firsthand experience that was true. Murphy's Law dictated that the last restaurant on his list would be paydirt. Fingers crossed in hope, he walked inside and asked for the manager. An older woman approached him with a friendly smile.

"My name is Sheriff James Russell Overstreet," he told her. "I'm from Salt Lick. I'd like to talk to someone who works here or did work here. His last name is Martinez. He's tall—"

"He's not here tonight. You'll have to come back Monday."

Forcing calm, Buddy reminded himself that Martinez was a common Hispanic name and this didn't necessarily mean he had found his suspect.

"Could you please give me *your* description of Mr. Martinez?" Tall was an unusual description for a Mexican. "I want to be sure I've got the right person."

"Oh, he's the old cliché. Tall, dark, and handsome."

Buddy's pulse quickened "But when you say tall, how tall do you mean?" When he heard tall, he thought of his own six feet and two inches, but other people might have a different perception.

"Tall as you. Is a jealous husband gunning for him? I keep telling Alex somebody'll catch up with him someday."

Deep breaths. Stay calm. "I need to talk to him before Monday. Do you know where I might reach him?"

"Sure. He's in Terlingua. He judges in the chili cook-off every year."

Fireworks shot off in Buddy's head. Terlingua was probably a seven-hour drive from San Angelo. If he left now he could be there by midnight. He thanked the woman and dashed to his vehicle. *Alex Martinez.* He knew where Alex Martinez would be for the next forty-eight hours.

He only hoped it wasn't anywhere near Edwina, Carol Jean, and Debbie Sue.

Twenty-four

 "Shit, shit, shit," Debbie Sue said, her heartbeat kicking up.

"What," C. J. asked, "what is it?"

"That cab-over motor home we just walked past. The one with the Texas flag painted across the front. See the guy sitting on the steps drinking a beer?"

C. J. nodded, her blond curls bouncing.

"That's the cook from San Angelo, the one you were dancing with when Pearl Ann picked a fight with you."

"We only saw him the one time, Debbie Sue. How can you be sure?"

"I don't know. I just am. When I saw him, my blood turned to ice. C. J., I think he could be the one who killed Pearl Ann."

C. J.'s big blue eyes blinked. "Wow. Does he know you? Did he look at you?"

"No, he was talking to some other people. Besides, he wouldn't recognize *me*."

"Let's walk past again. This time, *I'll* look."

"Okay, but don't stare. Just look."

The two friends turned and walked toward the camper, strolling as if they hadn't a care in the world. Just as Debbie Sue was about to nudge C. J., the crazy little blond left her side and boldly walked up to the group sitting in a circle.

Yikes, C. J.!

"I was just noticing your Texas flag," C. J. said in her best Scarlett O'Hara drawl. "You've got it wrong. The red goes on top of the white."

The group looked in the direction of C. J.'s pointing finger and broke into laughter.

The Mexican man stood and walked closer to her, staggering just a bit. Oh, he was good-looking all right, a taller version of Antonio Banderas.

"You must not be a Texan," he said to C. J., flashing her a perfect smile, one that was bound to have won him invitations into many bedrooms.

"I am, but I must not be a very good one." She laughed. "I guess I'm wrong. It's supposed to be just like you have it, white on top of red, huh?"

"Have we met before?" He glanced at Debbie Sue for the first time, then turned his attention back to C. J.

"No, I'm sure we haven't." She batted her lashes at him. "I'd remember meeting *you*."

"You and your friend will join us, yes?"

"I'm sorry. We can't just now. But *I* could come back . . . later."

"Ah. Later is perfect. Bring your swimsuit. We'll go down to the springs."

She shrugged, feigning embarrassment. "Okay."

"You are too beautiful to be shy." He lifted her hand. "I'll be waiting."

C. J. returned to where Debbie Sue watched and listened, then turned back, giggled, and wiggled her fingers at him in a wave.

Debbie Sue waited until they had walked a safe distance from the campsite before landing on her. "Are you nuts? What in the hell do you think you're doing?"

"Flirting. That's all I was doing. Flirting."

"Oh, flirting. How about making a date with a killer? Did you forget that part?"

"We don't know he's a killer. Just because he looks familiar doesn't mean he's the one."

"Why are you cheating on Harley? We're in his motor home, for crying out loud."

"I'm not cheating on Harley. I'll just spend a little time with this guy and see if he's the one at the party. I'll find out his name, then I'll tell Buddy."

"We could have sat down with him just now and found out both those things."

"But while I'm at the springs with him, you could search his trailer for proof."

"What? Are you crazy? Proof of what?"

"His involvement, silly."

Debbie Sue's brain churned. C.J. was right. How would Buddy prove this stranger had anything to do with Pearl Ann's death without a tangible piece of evidence? A drunken phone call didn't prove anything. A dance interrupted by the victim didn't exactly spell out a motive for murder.

Motherofgod. She wished Buddy were here.

Just before sundown, she and C.J. eased away from the party Vic had organized, consisting of retired navy SEALs, Arizona rockhounds, and retired Canadian railroad employees who had come south to escape winter. Everyone was having such a good time, no one would even miss the two women.

The plan was a simple one. C.J. and the Mexican man would go to the springs together, leaving Debbie Sue to search his trailer. Afterward Debbie Sue would go down to the springs and tell C.J. she needed help back to their motor home because she was feeling ill. C.J. would leave the man's company and that would be that. *Piece of cake.*

As the two women approached the trailer, they could see the man in front. He was sitting in a chair, and a woman was behind him rubbing his shoulders. She leaned over and whispered in his ear as they walked up. When he saw them, he flung the woman's hands away and stood up. The woman tossed her head and walked off.

"Ladies, I thought you'd forgotten me. I didn't expect to see you both."

"I hope you don't mind," C.J. said. "She's had

an awful lot to drink, and I thought the walk would do her good."

In fact, Debbie Sue had drunk only one beer since spotting the tall Mexican man. She would act tipsy, but she had never been more alert. The only thing disturbing her was the suspect appeared to have stopped drinking also. He was certainly more sober-appearing at any rate.

"Are we going swimming?" Debbie Sue asked. "We've got our suits on."

"Not really swimming." He leaned toward Debbie Sue. "We're going to sit in a big ol' hot tub."

"Uh-oh." Debbie Sue wedged her forearm between herself and the stranger. "If we're gonna sit in water, I gotta pee first. Can I borrow your bathroom? You've got a bathroom in there, don't you?"

"Sure, I have a bathroom. We will wait for you." He helped Debbie Sue up the steps into his RV.

"Nah. Y'all go on without me. I may just go back and go to sleep early. Really, y'all go on."

C. J. tugged on his hand. "She'll be fine."

Debbie Sue could see the temptation of spending time alone with C. J. in the hot tub was too much for the ladies' man. He instructed her to be sure to close his door when she left.

Debbie Sue waited until they walked out of sight. Her heart beat a tattoo as she began her search. She wasn't sure what to look for—old letters or photos, maybe. Something along those lines. She supposed finding a confession would be too much to expect.

In the quiet dimness of the compact motor home, she opened and closed drawers, looked under linens, and went through receipts. She fanned the pages of books, hoping something would fall out. She found several pieces of paper and held them with shaking hands to the light—a Texas map, a proof-of-insurance card—coming through the small windows. She saw the name Alex Martinez several times. Aha! His name.

Completing a thorough search of the back, she moved upfront to the cab. Under the driver's seat, she felt the coolness of a tin box. She pulled it out, carried it into better light in the tiny bathroom and lifted the lid.

Inside she found Alex Martinez's name taped inside the lid, two CDs, and a stained handkerchief folded in half. When she lifted the handkerchief, two articles fell from the folds to the floor. Debbie Sue bent over to scoop them up and stopped, feeling as if she had been stabbed with an icicle. Looking up at her from a photo was the smiling, still beautiful face of Pearl Ann Carruthers. Debbie Sue's heart began to beat so hard, she had to pause and take deep breaths to calm herself.

Lying beside the photo was a gold bracelet that appeared to be broken. A charm in the shape of the state of Texas was attached to its links.

Debbie Sue felt as if she were trapped in the eye of a hurricane. Everything seemed to be whirling and moving around her, yet she was in a silent vacuum. With trembling fingers she picked up the two items and turned sideways for better light. She swallowed a scream when she realized the stain on the handkerchief was dried blood, the same blood, no doubt, that still showed on the gold bracelet and charm. *Ohmygod. Pearl Ann's blood.*

She nearly gagged as nausea swept over her. Tears sprang to her eyes. She hadn't seen Pearl Ann's corpse in the Cadillac, but she had heard tales in the salon. Billy Don's wife had given them a graphic description. Pearl Ann had been shot once in the forehead, almost between her eyebrows. The nickel-sized hole had left her face bruised and discolored, not to mention the marks left by gunpowder. The once-beautiful woman had been almost unrecognizable.

Along with grief and terror, rage began to rise within Debbie Sue. She wanted to put her hands around Alex Martinez's throat and choke the life from him. For sure, she wanted to see the murdering sonofabitch arrested and prosecuted, then poisoned, stabbed, and shot.

She carefully put the photo, the handkerchief, and the charm bracelet back into the small box, then slipped the box into the pocket of her jacket and looked around, preparing to leave the motor home.

Footsteps crunched on the gravel outside and the motor home door opened. "We were worried about you, *senorita*."

She turned toward the sound and found herself staring into the barrel of a gun. And it was in the hand of Alex Martinez, the expression in his Antonio Banderas eyes as grim as death.

"Where—where's C.J.? What have you done with her?"

"Ah, yes, C.J. That is her name? She is back at the springs. I am glad I decided to come back for some wine. You found what you were looking for, yes?"

Debbie Sue faked bravado. "I don't know what you're talking about. I was borrowing the john." Trying to ignore the gun, she made an effort to walk past Alex.

He grabbed her arm and stopped her, pulled her back. "Don't test me, senorita. I *will* shoot you." He released her arm and made a beckoning motion with his fingers. "Give me the box."

Fuck. Fuck. Fuck. With a shaking hand, she took the tin box from her pocket and handed it to him.

"You did not find *this* in the bathroom," he said.

She swallowed hard, but the tight knot in her throat and stomach wouldn't go away.

"Who are you?" he asked. "And how did you find me?"

"The sheriff in Salt Lick's onto you. He's got your description. When I heard it, I knew it was you."

"You and that smart sheriff make quite a couple, don't you?"

She began to sniffle. "Yes."

Gripping her arm again, Alex forced her to the RV door and outside. He pressed the muzzle of the gun into her ribs and pushed her along. "We are going for a walk."

"If you're thinking of killing me, you'll never get away with it. They'll come looking for me. Buddy Overstreet will hunt you down like a dog."

"See that stream of water? That's Mexico on the other side. I will be there before your body gets cold. With *mi familia*. I will be vapor. And you know what you gringos always say—we all look alike."

"Buddy'll still look for you. He won't care *where* you are."

"That may be true, but I get several hours' lead time, he will never find me."

They continued walking. Somehow Debbie Sue's brain continued to function at warp speed. He was forcing her away from the throngs of campers, and to her relief she saw that the campsites stretched out a long way in front of them. To her relief they faced a long walk.

"What did Pearl Ann ever do to you? Please tell me why you killed her."

"I didn't mean to. We were going to live in Fort Worth. She laughed when I told her I had made the plans. She called me a wetback. Told me she was going alone. When I tried to talk to her, she pulled a gun out of her purse and told me to vamoose. I wrestled it from her, but it went off and—"

Like I believe that. "Yeah, right. She was shot in the head. Between the eyes, I think they said." It came to Debbie Sue it was dumb to confront him. Better to go along with him. "But look, I believe what you say. I know how Pearl Ann was. If it was an accident, you can plead that. You could even plead self-defense if she pulled the gun . . . But if you kill me, it's murder."

"Senorita, you think a Mexican that kills the wife of Harley Carruthers will not get the needle? No one will believe me."

"You're wrong. Listen to me. In the trial they'll bring out every little piece of Pearl Ann's life for public view. And believe you me, she had *quite* a life to view. The men she slept with—"

"Shut up. Don't say another word about Pearl Ann. I loved her. I still love her."

Debbie Sue realized they had walked well beyond the campers. The only available light was provided by stars. Alex pushed her a distance ahead. Debbie Sue turned and faced him. Why, she didn't know, because she really didn't relish seeing a bullet headed straight at her. She just knew she had to keep talking. "But wait, Alex. What about the bracelet? Why did you keep the bracelet?" She slowly inched to the right as she talked.

"It was a gift because I loved her. I couldn't give her gold and big diamonds. All I had was my love.

The Texas charm had a little diamond where Fort Worth would be. She threw it in my face."

Alex was following her movement, talking the entire time. He didn't seem to notice that their positions had changed by a full half circle. "Alex, you should let a jury hear your story. It's only fair."

"You should learn to mind your own business. You're a beautiful lady. I am sorry." He raised the gun level with her chest.

Debbie Sue now had the campsites behind her. She remembered seeing on the Discovery channel that someone's chances of hitting a mobile target were significantly lower than hitting an immobile one.

So. She became mobile.

She dashed into the pitch darkness as fast as her legs would carry her. Toward the camp lights. Toward help. Toward safety. She ducked and dodged rocks and brush, zigged, then zagged, then zigged again.

Thirty seconds into her sprint she was blinded by a beam of light coming toward her. She shielded her eyes. Could Alex have gotten in front of her? Should she run from the light? *Shit! Decisions, always decisions.*

Suddenly the light was upon her. An arm grabbed her. She hit the ground with a loud *oomph.* A deep voice ordered her to stay down as a body covered hers. She knew that voice. *Buddy?*

"Stop or I'll shoot!" the voice attached to the flashlight ordered.

Alex Martinez dropped his gun and threw his arms in the air. Seconds later, he practically clung to Buddy as a dozen or more retired navy SEALs and hammer-wielding rockhounds surrounded him.

An hour later, with the killer locked away in the Alpine jail and SEALs and rockhounds high-fiving and toasting one another with tequila shooters, Buddy explained to Debbie Sue how he had come to Terlingua in search of Alex Martinez. He had been talking to Vic and Edwina when Carol Jean had come running into the campsite in a state of panic. C. J. told him she had seen a big Mexican take Debbie Sue into the desert at gunpoint, and Buddy had wasted no time.

He questioned campers around Martinez's trailer and followed the direction they pointed out as the last place they saw him walking with a striking young woman. Finding her had been pure luck—or an answered prayer.

Debbie Sue sniffled. "Oh, Buddy."

He pulled her into his embrace, his strong arms wrapped around her, and she finally felt safe.

"I think we need to leave these two alone," Edwina said, grinning. "Buddy may need to interrogate her."

By then Buddy was kissing her, and by the time he stopped they were alone. "I'm glad I already asked you to marry me again. Otherwise you might think I'm after your money."

"I don't have any money," she said in a tiny voice.

"Well, fifty thousand dollars may not be much money to you but it's a heck of a lot to me."

"What do you mean?"

"You deserve the reward. You figured out who murdered Pearl Ann and risked your life confronting the killer. I'm sure Harley will agree."

"But you—"

"Shh." He kissed her again.

Epilogue

A year to the day since the trip to Terlingua had passed. She and Buddy had wasted no time renewing their vows. The nuptials had taken place at her mom's house with Edwina and C.J. serving as bridesmaids and Harley and Rocket Man standing up for Buddy.

She and Buddy had lived for a short time in Austin while he completed DPS training, and afterward he had been assigned to the Midland-Odessa area as a state trooper. His dream of being a Texas Ranger would be a reality soon.

They again lived in the home they had shared throughout their first marriage.

Edwina ran the Styling Station these days. She had taken it on while Debbie Sue and Buddy lived in Austin, and that arrangement hadn't been reversed. Vic hadn't made the trip to California. He spoke to Brenda on the phone and told her she should stop calling him because he had met the most wonderful woman in the world and intended to marry her. Edwina had been eavesdropping and cried for half an hour before Vic could make her understand that *she* was the wonderful woman. Harley had given them the use of the motor home for their honeymoon, and they had toured Vic's beloved U.S.A. for three months.

Billy Don had run for sheriff unopposed and been elected in a landslide victory. Currently Vic was teaching him self-defense. No more idle time for roping the fire hydrant in front of the sheriff's office.

C. J. and Harley had made an announcement of their engagement and a no-expense-spared, cowboy wedding was planned for Christmas.

Alex Martinez pleaded not guilty to the charge of murder. A plea bargain reduced the charge to second degree, and he was given twenty years. He would be eligible for parole in half that time because of no prior history of criminal activity.

Things hadn't worked out too badly for him. He had become a minor celebrity. Throughout the hearings, throngs of woman packed the courthouse to get a glimpse of the handsome man who had killed the woman he loved in an act of passion. He had dozens of marriage proposals, and it was rumored that Benjamin Bratt would be portraying him in a CBS movie version of the story.

The doorbell rang and Edwina and Vic came in carrying platters of food. Tonight was the American Country Music awards. Virginia Pratt was one of the nominees for Song of the Year. The serious ballad she had been talked into writing, sung by Alan Jackson, had been an overnight hit. "Sorry, You Both Deserve Better" was still riding high on the country music charts. Now Virginia was one of the most sought-after composers in Nashville.

"Hurry up, Buddy," Debbie Sue called out. "They're showing the people arriving. You're fixin' to miss Mom." Virginia's escort to the awards ceremony was none other than the vet, Dr. Miller, her employer of years and her secret lover.

Vic and Ed settled into the loveseat. Buddy brought in a large glass of Pepsi and handed it to her before he sat down. All eyes were glued to the TV set.

To everyone's astonishment, emerging from the backseat of one of the black stretch limousines was Quint Matthews.

"Great day in the morning," Edwina exclaimed.

Buddy picked up the remote and made a gesture as if to switch channels.

"Don't you dare," Debbie Sue said. "I want to see who's the unlucky woman he's with."

Quint reached back into the limo, and a gloved hand took his. A ravishing redhead made an exit, giving the crowd a million-dollar smile.

"Wow," Buddy said, "wonder where he found *her*."

"I've seen that woman somewhere," Vic said.

Debbie Sue moved closer to the television. "I don't believe it! . . . Ed, look!"

"My God! Is that Eugene/Janine?"

"I think it is."

Edwina threw her head back and hooted. "Looks like Quint finally got lucky."